T0131569

DUSK

An Epic Journey

Christine Hallfeldt

Balboa Press books may be ordered through booksellers or by contacting:

Balboa Press
A Division of Hay House
1663 Liberty Drive
Bloomington, IN 47403
www.balboapress.com.au
1 (877) 407-4847

Print information available on the last page.

ISBN: 978-1-5043-1080-2 (sc)
ISBN: 978-1-5043-1079-6 (e)

Balboa Press rev. date: 10/25/2017

DEDICATION

To George Lucas, who first set my sights on the stars…

From the farthest reaches of the universe to the inner recesses of the mind, each unto its own is an epic journey—Unknown Archives

The Parliament itself was a terrible structure of harsh lines and bulky shapes. Sean had shut the door on his beloved hovercar with a snap. It was a beauty when he purchased it and it was a beauty now, though others would have seen it as trash.

When Sean purchased the hovercar he distinctly recalled the rather pretty saleswoman, and what he said to her on the day. "You know, it's the mileage that counts right?"

The saleswoman at the time had looked resigned and almost offended. But when Sean flashed his credits at her and his genial smile, she melted like butter and happily handed over the car and her number.

Seeing the great Parliament itself, like a snake head over the horizon, Sean hit his great dirty boots down onto the arid soils of the desert. Australia was capital of the world yes but it was also a desolate wasteland converted into a civilization with great difficulty.

Sean looked up at the blazing sun overhead but his rustic sunglasses blocked out most of the harsh rays. The sun was thought a cruel bitch but it was also what made Australia what she was today, including pockets of paradises called Free-lands.

Humankind was doomed to burn from day one the cloth was cut. All humans shared an inherit need for violence. And though in the 29th century still that archaic trait tore a divide between all. It created a movement for the Free-lands, for a recovered Earth.

As Sean made his way in his grungy military pants and basic black tee, he tried to think with a positive attitude. But no matter how he angled it retiring his title, his position as fighter pilot still tasted bitter as hell. The only reason to do this was because there was no cause left to fight for, no reason to shed blood or to put himself on the line. This way at least he could repay his aunt Mayes who sheltered him and brought him into her house as one of her own.

To think on retirement at this age was less than a positive thought. He did, however, relish on the thought of not working for a bunch of stuffed suits. "Well, best get this bitch over and done with," said Sean. He made the longish walk toward an ascent of stairs to a short building guarded by laser beam bars: The Parliaments Registry and Admissions Office. Just as ugly as the Parliament itself, thought Sean.

"Sean Mathewson Caleb." The automated AI looked as sterile as her voice did. "Serial Number 72988 C. You are hereby requesting deactivation of services to the Parliament, and resigning your command as Sergeant of platoon Blue Dogs. You will no longer be employ as a space fighter and your privileges to the New Fleet will now desist. If correct please confirm with retinal scan."

A small device appeared in front of Sean. He placed his eye to the laser presented for detection. He waited till a loud beep had sounded. "Your retinal scan has been verified. Your NFI card is now rendered inert. Your severance pay of two million credits will be deposited immediately in accordance to the years you have served. Thank you for using Station B; I am Vicky your AI assistant. Have a pleasant day."

Sean walked out and down the steps as the laser beam bars dropped for him. He then placed his inert NFI card in the flat of his back pocket, a feeling of weight gained rather then lifted. He should have felt pleased or happy not this pressing downness like he had. He never figured himself for the ordinary life and had the uncomfortableness of imagining himself as a farmer; a pick-axing, mud-boot coated farmer with a beer gut and no ambitions. Sean's hovercar blazed down the track. And left the Parliament Capital behind trailing a tail of dust.

When logic doesn't make sense anymore, will one turn to nonsense to better understand the unravelling madness?—Unknown Archives

Within the great surrounding barricades of the wall was the shining jewel itself the Parliament. The Heads inside the large walls gathered in a circular room at the east wing. The main chamber itself was grand as it was functional. A sense of the rich era rang through its great halls. The chamber was a mock of the eighteenth century royalty with large stone slabs for walls.

The infrastructure, however, was fashioned entirely of 29th century technology including comprehensive security systems and monitors. The great Head himself Harold was dressed in a dress-robe and on each of his fingers bulky jewel- encrusted rings. His great bellowing sleeves swung side to side as he made his plodding way toward the main chamber.

Harold sat upon the middle throne that was the grandest and largest of all, whilst the other Heads Bradshaw and Carlton, took their places on either side of his throne in smaller less substantial ones. They looked like perched gargoyles, each as ominous and eerie- looking as statues of stone.

"The rift has returned," Harold announced. His voice caused a mild echo in the room like a treble upon a harp. Harold nodded for the other Heads to speak their minds.

Bradshaw stroking his minimal beard, a-hemmed before parting his lips. "After all these years?"

Harold stroked his longer beard in turn, amused. "Yes, yes, Bradshaw. The thing unfortunately is back. And I intend for it to be gone. But first we must discuss how ... as a group."

Carlton remained silent among the three, and for good reason though it were not out of fear of talking. In fact Carlton seemed stiffer and less animated then the other two Heads. It was because he was a automaton; an artificial puppet to keep the people thinking they had an advocate for their concerns. Carlton, however, only voiced what he was programmed to voice.

"For whatever reasons Bradshaw, it has returned," said Harold. "Now, I see two things happening here. One: we detonate another nuke inside the rift and hope for the best. Or two: we send in a Fleet to find out what threats we may yet encounter in the future."

"An exploration mission?" Bradshaw asked astounded. "And why this sudden idea? You as Head have only ever wanted to "safeguard" the Earth; to protect it from would- be enemies? Wouldn't this mission ensure outside attacks if we left Earth?"

Harold smiled like a gloating toad. "Yes, yes. Of course Bradshaw, Earth as always comes first. I have put in place defences to ensure that Earth will not be touched."

"What defences? And shouldn't we inform the public?" Bradshaw said.

"Ah, yes, yes, my friend. In due time. In due time. Carlton will handle that side of things. But until then all must be hush hush. We mustn't cause panic amongst people who are rallying fast to these Revolutionists. These trouble-makers must not be given a reason to expedite matters. We tell them nothing and Earth will continue a blissful uninterrupted life."

"Harold, really? More lies?" Said Bradshaw. He couldn't have protested more. "Don't you think hiding the truth has only caused us far worse mayhem than peace? We should tell the public the truth."

Like an uncle ushering in his nephew for a well deserved talk, Harold leaned over and took Bradshaw by the shoulders gruffly. It made Bradshaw feel slightly uncomfortable. "Bradshaw, yes yes, we have never really seen eye to eye have we? Aliens are not our way forward; has the past not instructed you of that? Humans would panic. They would rebel or become extremists. WE need to handle this from the inside. I think you an asset, an extension of my arm you could say. I value your opinion just as I value your dutifulness," announced Harold.

Bradshaw later stood at an open window bay looking defeated beyond compare. He was staring out at the lands that was completely dry and characterless. What had this great race come too? Force and violence as always, he thought. Bradshaw gave an almighty roar at the top of his lungs so that the birds nearby flew off in alarm.

Bradshaw had been nominated by Harold as Commander of the Sword of Light. Harold's idea of a purifying crusade. For Harold did see Bradshaw as his extending arm, and so he was chosen to bring about the word. And to destroy those who would defy human rule.

Down below the window was a whole courtyard of experimental ships like the Sword of Light that spanned for kilometres, glittering in the sun like many jewels.

The militia that governed the lands around the Parliament were stationed at designated points around the perimeter. They functioned to both protect the Heads inside and to protect the walls from any outside threats. These military guards were dubbed the Watchdogs.

"Hey! Darcy!" called out a beefy middle aged man called Rick. Rick threw an incoming drinking can and hit the guy called Darcy in the head so that the contents splashed all over his face. Looking pissed, Darcy muttered under his breath. He took no notice of them while he fiddled with something under his jacket that wasn't his rifle.

Rick went over to Darcy and slapped him across the back. "You know Rookie, we old dogs have been here long time. We teach you how to take out those feckin Revolutionist scum. One placed grenade, like fish in a barrel. Boom!"

Before anyone could react Rick's arm was bent back cracking from the force. As his men came to pry Darcy off, Darcy took out an object he been fiddling with and held it aloft. He shouted: "For Free-lands, for freedom. Long live the Revolutionists!!"

The detonation blast ripped through the men like thrust-about leaves, leaving nothing but a smoky crater and an entrance for an attack.

And even unto the end we will always see them for who they are: our family, our soul mates—Unknown Archives

Mayes trundled to the door of her private room in her floppy slippers. Days seemed to become shorter. She remembered herself in the hay-days when she was a loyal Revolutionist, in fact, the leading Revolutionist. They never "won" perse but their efforts did fuel the fires for what the Revolutionists were today.

Though marked as an enemy against the Parliament, the Revolutionist Mayes previously worked for the Parliament as New Fleet On-field Medic Nurse. She saw to many grotesque injured men and witnessed gruesome death and gore beyond what anyone should tolerate.

At age sixty-five she retired from poor health but the battle between Revolutionist and the Parliament raged on without her. Having no choice other than to make a deal with the devil for her own slice of heaven she was able to purchase her own Free-land.

"I do not need the crutch of a doctors' petulant advice! I'm a nurse, I can diagnose myself!..." she said to a Dr Chan whose long face appeared before her own.

Mayes threw the Plax in her hand (a slim paper-thin device used for all methods of communication) against the desk causing it to fizzle and crack. Conceited man, she thought.

There was a sudden knock at the door. Mayes's raspy cough could be heard as she made her way toward it. The creakiness of the wire door opening sent bugs scurrying in flight. The porch light went on and settled a halo upon the official- looking man, who was by no accounts an angel.

"Well well...Never thought you'd grace my porch again," said Mayes, while shooing away the bugs that longed to come in, pondering whether to let the biggest one of them all in.

Robert was a private last time she saw him, no more than a bottom feeder. She now saw the gleaming extra star on the left side of his hat.

"May I come in?" he asked like a schoolboy with his dear grandma.

Mayes knew she shouldn't. All encounters with Robert since that dreadful day in The Legal Court had caused nothing but heartache. She also believed in second chances, or at least hearing out what this two-faced man had to say.

Robert felt odd coming into her living room. Last time he was here it was different, he was different. He oddly perched himself on the edge of a couch, clearing his throat as he did. "Mayes, I know I haven't been the perfect nephew like some... But I have to say I am so sorry you got caught in our little feud."

Robert always half-combed his hair to the exact line. He ironed his uniform until it was starchy still. And here was the imposter with his intentions clear as day even with her impaired vision.

Having had enough "basting" from her beloved nephew, Mayes interrupted Robert asking: "Tea?"

"S-sure." Robert had almost bit his tongue having been interrupted like that.

Mayes returned with two cups and sat them upon the table rather shakily. "Two sugars, if I remember correctly." She did her best to flash him a sweet smile.

"I am not here on a personal call, Mayes." Robert took off his hat out of curtesy.

Enough "basting", eh? thought Mayes, as she watched Robert place down his untouched tea. Now, Mayes may have been old but she was by no means senile. An old crone could be just as sharp as the young man with a habit for falsehoods.

"I am here to inform you that Sean Caleb is to produce himself to court upon the judges request. The charges laid on him have come to term and we would like to re-examine what really happened that night."

"The case was acquitted. Who did you have to talk too to get this case re-exhumed, huh?" Said Mayes rather astounded.

Robert fidgeted where he sat. "No. I am afraid, aunt, that the judges believe there was more to it than a mere accident."

No doubt, thought Mayes. All these years Robert lay blame upon Sean like he were the judge and jury. This was just an excuse to sink in the dagger.

"You know nephew, your antics will never seize to amaze me. You come here into my house throwing about demands like your some high and mighty with a star on your head. Sean has been more family to me than you ever will be. Now get out! Out now."

Mayes began to cough violently. Robert, seeing he had outworn his welcome, hastily made to leave. Before leaving, however, Robert held his hand on the door handle only cocking his head to the one side. "For what it is worth, aunt, I am, really sorry. But Sean needs to answer for what he did...For Cheyenne sake."

Mayes stopped her coughing abruptly. Her eyes were iced over coldly and almost dead-like. Her voice came out harsh as a rattle snake. "Cheyenne was his sister!" Mayes's wheezing voice croaked.

"And my girlfriend!" Robert cried.

He threw back the door rather roughly, causing the hinges to groan and snap. Robert looked back, and saw Mayes taking a few steps back in fear. He recomposed himself as best he could, and breathed through his nostrils calmly. “Sean lost a sister, you, a niece. But does anyone recognise that I lost the love of my life?”

Mayes silently fumed and brought a wrist- napkin to her lips, spitting. “Goodbye Robert,” she said, facing away.

Robert placed his hat on his head arranging it till it sat perfectly.

She cast her eyes down overcome by the rolling-boil of emotions. Robert sped off in his hovercar showing his equally vehement anger.

Good riddance to trash, thought Mayes. She took away her napkin to see fair-sized droplets of blood soaking through the fabric. Mayes seeing Sean coming over the horizon pocketed her napkin quickly, trying to fake a smile.

Sean’s hovercar came in just as Robert sped off beside him. “What the hell was that all about?” said Sean, snapping the hovercar door shut and whipping off his sunnies. Mayes came out looking like she had been in a catastrophic battle. “I’ll kill him!” Said Sean realising what that mongrel cousin had done. Sean spun on his heel, ready to pursue Robert but Mayes stopped him before he could.

“Let cooler heads prevail tonight,” said Mayes. “Nothing more you can do. Just, please, get me in would you? It’s rather chilly now.”

Mayes inched up her shawl, as Sean rubbed her upper sore back. The coughing fits were getting worse, thought Sean. But as she refused to seek medical advice, Sean did what he could to comfort her.

Mayes always welcomed the loving hand of her nephew Sean. It would be dark soon and the mass of mosquitoes would descend as the cocktail colours of dusk began fading into darkness.

What we cannot explain we counter with the most homely of human stories – religion – Unknown Archives

Sean had a turbulent night tossing and turning; his head buzzing. The heat didn't help either as the quilt stuck to his skin. He felt incredibly uncomfortable.

Around his boxed-shaped room lay mountains and mountains of dirty laundry. The walls around him were bare and peeling paint. On numerous occasions his aunt Mayes suggested her doing it up for him, but Sean refused and always replied with: "I care not for personalization, Mayes, it is just a room."

Sean's thoughts swirled around in his mind. He thought on the future, of the court hearing and affairs of family. That hookworm cousin, he thought. Finally, he'd had enough of looking at the walls that peeled away on him like his sanity. He threw off his sheets, quickly dressed, dove into his boots, and went straight to his hovercar.

The cool night air was refreshing as Sean sped on in his hovercar. He couldn't have felt better as the wind lashed over his face and tore away at his turbulent thoughts. The stars above him still held their sway and their call was like that of a Siren. Years as a space fighter would not quash down easily for a man like Sean.

Sean cruising along pumped the song "Firestarter by Prodigy" through the speakers. He rocked his head back and forth rhythmically. He stopped, however, when a large star caught his attention. He stared at it concentratively when it began hurdling towards him like a fast comet. There was no time to swerve.

Sean held a hand to his mouth as he attempted to breathe through the dust that had formed around him. Darkness enveloped him lessened only by the partial headlights of his beloved hovercar now smashed. He got out difficultly and beheld the mayhem of whatever he had hit.

Sean tore at his hair when he saw the state the hovercar was in, but then, in the haze of the light his attention was called away to an arm sticking out of the rubble like a weird daisy. He gave her hand a light squeeze but it was limp. He spoke as loud as he could. "You feel my hand. I am here. Don't worry. I'll getcha out. You feel my hand."

While Sean devised of ways of getting her out, he also thought on how completely weird all of this was. He took back his hand and came away with blood, red blood. Whoever was underneath was bleeding, therefore felt pain and probably dying.

Time against Sean he heaved with all his might. He was straining and lifting each layer of twisted metal like they were heavy cover stones. Finally the layers disappeared to reveal the most beautiful but peculiar woman he had ever seen in his entire life.

Sean's bewildered eyes drew immediately to the large, magnificent white wings splayed on either side of her. And then to her demure face as he caressed it delicately with his hand. He moved aside her luscious hair and traced along her elvin ears only to come into contact with more blood. He followed it to a serious head wound. Time was definitely not on his side. Sean scooped her up as best he could and carefully draped each of her wings over like enclosing her in folds of her own blanket.

Mayes's raspy voice rang in his ears: "Dear Sean, remember the good old book when lacking understanding. To the verse 91:11 "For he will order his angels to protect you wherever you go." Was this his protectorate? An angel? An alien? A woman?

The 'lady' he held in his arms was taller. Sean imagined her to be about 7-8 foot. Sean, exhausted, slumped down onto the porch floor of his aunts.

"Oh, my!" exclaimed Mayes, having come to the door and seeing Sean down on the ground with a great being laid beside him.

"What the hell, Mayes!?" Sean angrily looked up to his aunt Mayes towering over him. Sean acted like he had been thoroughly assaulted.

"Sorry for slapping you," said Mayes. "But you have a concussion, Sean. And I need your help getting her inside."

The being was laid inside upon the couch. "I will examine this head injury. In the bathroom there is my old nurses med kit. And the Iodine as well, would you?"

Sean rubbed his face, staggering around like he were heavily medicated, heading toward the cabinet in the bathroom. He thought it odd that his aunt Mayes was taking this on so well, too well, he thought suspiciously. Sean, Iodine in hand, paused before the corner as he heard Mayes talking to herself, "Celestial Being perhaps? But they are so shy and hardly seen; thought exiled. The odds!"

Sean returned with the Iodine and the med kit in hand and a burning question in need of answering. "What is a Celestial Being?"

"She is... an alien, simply put Sean." Taking the bottle of Iodine from Sean's grip, Mayes averted Sean's accusatory glare. She feared to peer into Sean's face and face judgement. "I will fix her head wound first. And then, yes, I will explain everything. Promise. Ok? Just let me work, Sean. For this woman's sake."

Sean hurried to the bathroom and closed it shut rather loudly. He ran his hands through his dishevelled hair shaking. The blood from his undoubted concussion dribbled down the sides of his face. No matter how much he was trying to rationalise the situation in his meagre mind he always returned to a fuzzy blank.

In the bathroom, Sean's breathing became more laboured. He saw the bottle of booze hidden in the crack of the open cabinet as his knee jutted it open. A concussion and booze didn't combine well but Sean didn't care for sensibility at this time. His hand shook as he moved it towards the bottle. He could feel the rise of the demon inside. It told him: drink. It told him to lose himself...

And so he did; the bottle was unscrewed and the lid tinkered into the sink bowl.

The most wondrous of things can often be the most unexplainable
– Unknown Archives

The disassembled pod glistened like wet paint. Parts were strewn across the impacted area that formed a gargantuan crater. Authorities were on it faster than a fly on shit, as stern official-looking men jumped out of their unmarked black vans.

Yellow tape was being placed all around the impacted area dubbed "Ground Zero". A woman of roughly sixty years of age, wearing black rimmed spectacles with ruby red stilettos, and a crisp white scientist coat, approached the men in black confidently.

"Who are you?" one cautioned as she simply moseyed on past him.

She removed her glasses and then brandished her ID tag at the man while she continued to move on forward. "Special Xenobiologist Dr Stella McCartney Rain. Secret department. I have all jurisdiction here. This is a matter for the Parliament sub-sector. You are dismissed."

The man in black looked absolutely gobsmacked. He couldn't believe the cheek of this old prune who came marching in like some high-ranking official without any respect for him or his men. He took out his gun and swiftly pointed it at Stella. All intent displayed clearly upon his disgruntled face. Stella who was now walking all over the scene, bended over and prodded at parts and pieces with her pen. She made as if the armed man in black had not pulled out a weapon. The man in black may as well have pointed a water gun.

"Listen, lady, I have never heard of a Xenobiologist. And what's more we are employed by the Parliament, so whatever sector you're from you're going to need to show us more than a little badge with your pretty face on it."

Stella continued to crouch down inspecting the debris not once glancing up to the man with the gun. "Very well... Stanton. Jules. If you please..."

With a single command, out of the dark bushes emerged two very muscly men with large semi-automatic guns, along with several geared up GI-Joe style soldiers; all of them heavily armed.

The man in black swiftly holstered his gun. With a waving gesture of his hand his itching men resigned to standing down. "Whatever lady. But we will be speaking to the Head about this... in person."

"Please do." Her demeanour was cold to the point of crisp.

Mayes opened her book across the coffee table. A book she hadn't turned to in a long time. The bible. She turned to the passages referring to angels. The bible was actually a viable source of information if you bypassed all the fabrications.

People had begun to turn to religion—more so than any point in history. There were those who believed in angels, heaven, and hell, even the presence of God, angels. People speculated the existence of angels for an age but no proof was ever unearthed. Was it possible that they really did exist? That they were actually aliens so closely sculpted to heavenly likeness it was indistinguishable between myth and reality?

Later in the kitchen, Sean and Mayes were discussing the events that had led to a Celestial Being recovering on the couch in the living room. "Mayes. You are going to have to explain this to me and from the beginning. Not in fractured parts that make no sense."

Sean quickly glanced around the corner and saw the ladies long elongated white wings, now sprawled apart like some majestic eagle.

Mayes sat down upon a stool, and taking in substantial breaths began, indeed, from the beginning. Sean remained standing against the wall to hear this great tale of woe, while resigning himself to a aching headache.

"There are four star systems in the galaxy Kale," said Mayes. "The star system Angelic, a populated system with the Nebula Truth and its infamous station Alpha. The star system Satanic, far removed from the inner core with the Nebula Faith and its rundown station Omega. The star system Le-chuisa with Nebula Hope and its station Delta. And star system Dark Horse with what remains of its station Beta in Nebula Honour. It rumoured to be both haunted and abandoned.

"Dark Matter Entities—or Sprites, as they are better known—were considered worse than the dreaded Raiders who ravaged our race years ago.

The Parliament had in their possession a device given to them by an unknown person. This device indeed eradicated the Raiders from our planet and those in orbit but it also had some unsavoury after-effects on humans."

"What are these Sprites anyway?"

"They consume body mass leaving sacs of flesh behind. They are non-corporeal malevolent beings that believe all corporeal life, all matter in the universe, is insurmountable to their own existence. They believe that their ethereal plain is a paradise and that our own is an impurity upon theirs. More than half of the universe is dark matter, did you know that?"

"Had no clue," Sean said, again with hard sarcasm followed by a suppressed groan from his thumping hang-over.

"We would be over-run. The entire universe eviscerated by these, these ghosts birthed from the dark."

"Do they possess too, like demons?"

"Don't make light of it, Sean. And yes, actually, they do possess. And it isn't pretty like in the horrors. You bleed through the pores before being totally devoured from the inside out. But just giving enough time for you to do their bidding like a sick meat puppet, whilst your being internally eradiated of course."

"The Parliament... The lies...Not alone in the universe..." Sean muttered this more to himself than Mayes, before directing it straight at her.

Mayes noted the redness in his eyes.

"You knew the truth, the real truth all this time and you said nothing!"

"Of course I wanted to tell you. But this is the Parliament we are talking about, Sean. They have every ball in every court. That beings landing has probably already been discovered. The men in black will be at our doors... soon, unless..."

"Unless what, Mayes? We protect her. Hey? I protect her with fuck little I have?"

"Sean, you have to help her." Mayes's hand went to touch Sean's face delicately but he threw his arms at her like she were poison to the skin.

"You are her shield, Sean. She was sent here for you."

"Not this. Not now. Surely not when you have proof, had proof for years that intelligent life exists out there and yet still hold on to your faith, the idea of God?" said Sean.

"Can I not believe in both?" remarked Mayes.

Sean felt so enraged. "No! Because it isn't possible. She isn't an angel, and an alien! There isn't a universe with alien beings other than humans, and a BIG guy in the sky who created us in his image. Okay?! I don't believe in it. I never will!"

Now the time had come thought Mayes.

"Sean, that side-effect I talked about was total global amnesia. No one knows the truth because it was erased from their minds."

"Then why do you remember? Mmm?"

Mayes hung her head like she were defeated. "Sean." Mayes brought Seans' hands together in her own, almost as if in prayer. "Your father gave me something. A letter to give to you. He also gave me a warning of what the Parliament were going to do, and so I made sure I was well away when the device went off."

Mayes moved her hand to a drawer under the countertop. She withdrew an envelope from it, the letter she was talking about. The envelope was dusty from the years of lying there.

Overcome with unsure feelings, Sean grabbed the envelope in Mayes's hand while gripping onto hers. He let go of her hand though, reluctantly, and then looked to the envelope scrunched in his own hand, not sure when, or if too open it.

The stars, ever present with their inner glow, sing their unheard songs in the amplest of lights: knowledge—Unknown Archives

"Parliament HQ. We are receiving you on a secured line. Please state clearance code."

"I need to speak to the Head."

"Please verify."

"Skeleton Station B-1."

"Clearance code."

"This is important."

"Clearance code."

There was rummaging coming from the signal. And what sounded like the unfolding of a crumpled piece of paper.

"Sandman."

"Your clearance code has been verified. What is your query?"

"I wish to talk to the Head. It is urgent."

"I am sorry. Mr Columbus is a busy man. All inquiries must be passed onto HQ and we will pass it on accordingly."

There was the sound of a disgruntled sigh.

"Fine. Then you can tell him that we have had unidentified phenomena popped up on our screens, and that -"

"HQ is aware of this information as you informed us before."

"Yes I know I did but there is more to it. No more than two hours ago an object streaked out of it. The Pulse Ropes had no effect. There was some sort of a glitch in the system. The Pulse Ropes are now off- line. I repeat the Pulse Ropes are off- line. I am the only working communique in the vicinity, due to the static the frayed ropes are causing. Please relay this message with the greatest of urgency."

"Thank you for your update. We will endeavour to process your intel as quickly as possible. I am K-1 your HQ delegator. Remember, your opinion matters. Thank you for contacting Parliament HQ. Good day..."

The line went dead. Bloody Automatons, cursed the Skeleton Master, while facing his other screen and returning to his game of SWTOR - an online game he had managed to get from a seller of relics. Two-hundred credits later, and a little bartering, and he was now the owner of one of the most played universes in history.

Mayes returned quickly with a tea in hand. She went and checked the woman's airways and at her bandaged head wound. "She is lucky. The debris just missed. Had it embedded a few centimetres more it would have pierced into her brain. She is very lucky."

"She certainly is. But what I don't get, right? She is an alien, yer? Why was she in that death pod? I saw the debris as I lifted them off. They were not constructs of a vessel, they were walls of a tomb. She was being transported."

"Sean, this is all very new territory for me as well as you. Have you read the letter yet?"

"What? The one from my dead father who abandoned us? No, I haven't, Mayes."

Mayes felt so upset. She knew Sean had a reason, very good reason to feel the way he did. But he didn't know the whole truth. And part of it lay in that letter.

"Just bare with me, Sean, and please read the letter. You might find what you seek, you may even find closure."

Sean sighed heavily, and made to stand when the Celestial Being stirred in her sleep. Sean paused like a cat stuck in a car light. He watched her in concerned concentration. Sean's face was almost nose to nose to the Celestial Beings, as she began to sweat and become distressed in her sleep.

Then the being let out a hollering scream that made Sean fall back onto his arse. The Celestial Being, awake for the first time since her arrival, became erratic; her eyes darting hither and tither, not sure of her surroundings or her whereabouts. She felt her head and the strange sensation of something on it: the bandage.

"Wh-who are you people? Where-where am I?"

Mayes explained to the shockingness on Sean's face English was a well versed language in the galaxy of Kale.

"Darling, darling. Look at me. That's it. Look here. My name is Mayes Caleb. This is Sean Mathewson Caleb, your rescuer. And you are in the Sol System on planetary system Earth, Milky Way galaxy."

"You, you are...human?"

"Yes. Human. And you are a Celestial Being, yes?"

"Y-yes. I am, uh. My name is Celeste."

Sean was gobsmacked. He imagined what her voice might sound like but to now hear it, was amazing. Her voice was velvety and smooth. It was soft and small, but not mousey. He likened her voice to that of, yes, an angel.

Sean made to advance at Celeste. She moved back in retaliation. He put his hands up in defeat. "Easy. Easy. I am placing my hand like this. This is called a hand-shake. It is a hand gesture we humans make when we meet someone, usually for the first time, as symbol of our good intention."

Celeste looked Sean up and down like he was some dumb human. She then reached her hand over and embraced his hand unsurely.

Sean felt the silky skin of Celeste and he almost groaned with pleasure. He made, however, every effort to right himself discreetly. "Nice to meet you, Celeste." He sounded like a stupid robot. That was electrifying, the thought of her skin on his.

"How did I come to be here?" Celeste said, while her eyes continued to dart around the room. Celeste particularly concentrated her gaze upon Sean and his peculiar mannerisms.

Mayes and Sean exchanged looks on the Celestial Being's lacking knowledge of coming to be on Earth. Sean's theory was becoming more and more viable. "Well, we were hoping you could tell us that, dear," answered Mayes.

Sean occupied with all manner of thoughts, was perturbed when he noticed a slit in her neck. Like something embedded inside he thought. He went over to touch there when she turned around snappishly. He held his breath for a moment awaiting for another outburst, but instead she held his hand there moving it over the slitted area.

Sean let Celeste guide his hand like he were reading brail.

"This is why. I am tagged. I guess the easiest explanation I can give you is tracking device. I escaped a hunter but then I was captured, tagged, and bound for the Slave-Trade Markets on Station Alpha. This, this really shouldn't be happening. The pod was designated with a programmed destination. How it malfunctioned and lost its trajectory is a complete mystery to me."

Sean realized a very dangerous thought. "Tracking device? Does that mean this hunter could track you...to...here?"

Celeste could see that that thought troubled Sean. She focused on her bony knees before answering him. "It is a possibility, yes. But given my whereabouts I doubt it. The Milky Way you call it, is not a galaxy we know. So it is possible he won't know where to look.

I remember running fast. I heard his footsteps as they approached closer and closer. I heard the release of the Net Disperser. I turned around to be ensnared by the net, entangling me like a web. I was still half conscious when he dumped me into that pod and then, then coldness. A deep freeze as I was put to sleep. I dreamt. But then those dreams turned to nightmares as I imagined myself hurtling through space, imagined that hunters sharp claw-like hands on me, imaged my life as the end of that journey as I would be put in binders and taken to the markets. But you, you saved me."

Sean saw what was happening here. He had seen it ALL to many times while in command of many young soldiers during the Non-Existent Wars.

Sean grabbed his aunt by the elbow and edged her into the kitchen. "We will be right back," said Sean. He noted the forlorn gaze in Celeste's eyes. He tried hard to ignore it.

"What are you doing, Sean?" she whispered to him.

They were in the kitchen. "She has PTSD. I should know. I have seen my share of it; under my command."

"So have I, dear," said Mayes. "I will tend to her; make her a cuppa."

"I doubt that will do it, Mayes. But, but it can't hurt."

What is life...? A never ending cycle, a constant circle towards demise. In the end a pointless death as embracing and pathetic as meaningless life - Unknown Archives

An old lady, a human, carried the tell-tale signs of Blue-vein Virus. She gave out a raspy cough as she proceeded forward along the winding lines on Station Alpha. "Nothing but cattle we are," she droned to no one in particular. Her coughing increasing.

A woman in her mid- twenties walked beside her who did not say anything. The young lady Cleo proceeded to not talk to the old prune, not out of rudeness but out of her inability to do so. The girl was mute. Cleo's dirtied face was only highlighted by her dulled eyes, like large dark pans. She seemed to be only an empty pretty shell.

Eventually, the woman who persisted to drone on chatted the off ear another sorry sod, a person shuffling forwards beside her. All humans here were stampeded into the ground. They had no hope and no desire to live and yet could not kill themselves due to a failsafe encoded into their genome; curtesy of their alien masters. They were oppressed and depressed and there was nothing anyone of them could do about it.

Cleo had long matted blonde hair hiding most of her slender face. She hardly visited the luxuries of a shower, nor felt the freshness of water. She had a slight gap in her teeth and was half starved. Most slaves only received the barest of food staples, which meant only so few nutrients, enough to keep their eyes open but not enough to be brimming with vitality.

The line moved up slightly. The women here, were on their way to getting inoculated. It was part of their conditioning. Man-made chemicals pumped into them to stop or terminate pregnancies and keep them agreeable docile slaves.

Nobody had ever heard Cleo talk. Some talked of her tongue being ripped out or simply that she was an attention seeker. No one really knew the actual reason for her being mute; the truth they chose to cultivate was to make a sensible explanation for something they knew nothing at all about.

The lights of the slave-trade market beamed overhead. But they were not symbols of hope or fun, it was a light of death, an omen. The brighter the life the harder the oppression. As Cleo rubbed her left arm from a wound sustained by the Conditioning she bumped into the locals.

Full of colour and vibrancy, the locals were a complete contradiction to herself – a dull and lifeless thing. A tall Boric prostitute stared down Cleo, this meek human girl, sizing her up like she were a tenderloin. Her eyes were steely and yet her touch seemed soft and warm. "How much for you pretty darlin?"

The tall Boric prostitute smiled as she twirled Cleo's dull hair strands around her finger. A guard assisting herding the humans along like cattle, shoved a prod into Cleo's ribs. "Back in line. No free samples. Not until your bought and paid for at the auctions."

The Claspher slaver snared at the Boric prostitute who simply hissed back. Green-skinned with large clawed hands and pointy buffalo horns, these slavers were just as vile as their hunter counterparts. Any person who saw them would take two instinctive steps back.

When we leave reality, do we ascend through the clouds into the unknown or deep into the abyss below?—Unknown Archives

Sean awoke to the feeling of wetness. When he stood up he held onto the rim of the sink to prevent himself from slipping over. His foot moved forward slightly like he were an old man, knocking the empty bottle of booze across the tiles. Forty-five percent of that alcohol had sent him into a nice abyss but the recall to reality was by far the worst.

In his dark slumber he dreamt of many things, things he wished he didn't. He had had his head nestled against Celeste's soft breasts. He moved his hand subtly towards hers. Then he looked up to see her a dark maw about to engorge on him. And then awoke with a thud on the bathroom floor saturated from his nightmare.

He staggered into the living room to find Celeste now curled up at the end of the sofa. Sean crept in quietly and placed a blanket over Celeste, stumbling slightly from his hangover. Celeste shifted uneasily, a sheen of sweat forming now on her brow. Night-terrors, thought Sean.

Sean took out the letter in his pocket and sat by Celeste, ready to read it to her. He didn't know why he wanted her to hear it, or if she would. He only knew that he had an unexplainable compulsion to read the letter out-loud to someone other than himself. He unfolded the letter and began, focusing on the words to prevent them from doubling.

"Dearest son, I know by now that you probably don't even remember me or to some extent hate me, but as your father I must let you know why I left you, why I am gone. The wars were ruthless and displayed an uglier side to humanity that at the end of the day left me bitter. My dear sister will look out for you both, I know it. I have more to say though, one day your world is going to be blown apart by the truth, a truth that only a few remember. Son, the reason for the wars was not because of money or struggle for power. It was domination of the galaxy. See we were once seeded by many alien races and ventured to and fro to other galaxies via rifts. In fact I had a ship called Thorn and now as my last ditch

effort to make it up to you, I leave him in your possession. Let it be my legacy to you, son. Here attached to the letter is the access card to one of the Skeleton Station's *- your aunt will know which one. It's been untouched for years and inside will be your treasure, your vessel to explore what we have been denied by the parliament. I leave you son with one word of caution: Beware the human race, we flicker from face to face but our true nature in the end will never falter. I love you son and please forgive me...for everything."*

Sean put down the letter, breathing hard and thinking on thoughts too strong to describe. His father would do this. He would torment him from the grave. The bastard, Sean thought. He then scrunched the letter up and dropped himself onto the floor.

He succumb to his flood of emotion and to his knees, head down, sobbing uncontrollably.

Celeste watched as Sean became lost to his emotion. It was strong and unrestricted. Her hand came on top of his. Her skin upon his. Sean watched her soft hand like in a trance. She was so kind, her touch felt like it.

"It is a world of eternal light. We have Dusk forever. The clouds are touched with golden rays and the clouds are a soft pink."

Celeste was deviating Sean's mind from his feelings by describing a pretty picture. Sean had no protests to Celeste's melodious voice washing over him, like the calming flow of water over his damaged soul.

"The Nest Forests are filled with abundant wildlife and surround the Empyrean with an ensnaring root system upon towering pinnacles. I, however, would love to explore your world."

Mayes tapped her lightly on her shoulder. "Unfortunately it wouldn't be possible, dear." Celeste stammered shocked by Mayes's sudden appearance.

Sean righted himself suddenly better and took up the access card that had clattered to the floor. "The parliament," he simply said.

"Correct, Sean. Look what we have done to ourselves. We are no good, Celeste. We destroy anything we come in contact with. I am not so hard on my race that I would say we are all bad—there are the few exceptions. But darling, we are not the most civilised species. Sure we act like it. But all of that is just a front. We are as brutal and primitive as before. Take away all our technology and that is all you are left with."

Celeste became forlorn. The sadness in her weighed heavy on Mayes.

Sean took his card and put it in his back pocket. He took up the scrunched letter and pocketed that too.

The next morning came harsher than Sean liked. He sat up suddenly in bed, his lamp shining brightly in his eyes. He went to knock it off its stand when a brisk knock sent him diving for his shorts. But in no time his door swung open; Sean had failed to reach his shorts in time clinging onto a handful of sheet to his nether regions.

A mere slither of sheet concealed him as he was standing there butt-naked. The tall, fair beauty stood before him in the doorway and aroused certain appendages. Celeste halted with her tray of what looked like breakfast.

Sean could tell she was abashed as she was looking away so Sean could finally find his shorts.

"I apologise. The human anatomy is not what I envisioned," said Celeste.

Sean watched her standing there so timidly, so he gestured her over to the bed. There were no other chairs or sofas to sit on.

Sean smiled with a smile that turned into a giggle. "You envision us humans much?" Said Sean.

Celeste was now laughing lightly like soft singsong of birds.

"It was clumsy of me," said Celeste.

She laid the tray on his bed and made to stand. Sean saw that it was scrambled eggs with a glass of orange juice. As Sean took a sip of the orange juice she said, "I made it from the oranges you have outside."

Sean narrowed his eyes down to the glass and saw the small pips swimming in it. He placed the glass down and discreetly spat them in the dying potted plant next to him.

Sean ventured to try the scrambled eggs, though his faith was slightly shaken. "I made it myself," she began, as Sean took a spoonful and the sound of crunching egg shell contacted with his teeth.

Sean smiled awkwardly. Celeste looked away, obviously pleased with herself and he took the time to spit that out also into the pot plant. "Thank you, sweetie. It was a... valiant effort."

Celeste stood up and stretched her wings. And she gave them a quiver. Sean made to move as they stretched across him. "Such a wondrous thing, these magnificent wings."

Celeste looked at them sceptically like she hadn't noticed them before. "Yes, I suppose they are." She half smiled. "So what are we doing today?" she said.

Sean hazily reached for his shirt and began dressing properly now that breakfast was out of the way. "Whatever you want." Sean felt the blush of his own cheeks mirrored upon hers.

We are but small pieces in a puzzle that is forever being solved—Unknown Archives

The alarms sounded not long before Harold could have a chance to turn in. He jumped out of his bed and nearly out of his skin. Harold hastily got dressed and hurried to where Bradshaw and Carlton were first on the scene. Harold strolled over to Bradshaw and Carlton who both parted to allow him through.

The large circle of felled men charred to the bone sent chills to everyone. But Harold had a different reaction. "Shit, shit, shit! Do we know who he was? Do we know how he got passed our security? Do we know anything, people!?"

Harold turning a lovely colour of purple began pacing up and down. How could this happen? He had all protection and security measures in place. That was what these Watch Dogs were for? What kind of watching did they achieve? Sweet fuck all, thought Harold.

They parted for an unofficial woman who presented herself before the Head himself. Skinny, with long wiry hair placed in a bun, and stylishly placed glasses she held herself with regal confidence. It was Dr Stella McCartney Rain.

The men in black turned up skidding their van to a halt. The guy came out flustered. He saw Stella right away and wasn't shy to point her out. "Sir, sir, this is the woman! This woman has interrupted in Parliament affairs and contaminated the scene at Ground Zero."

Harold held his hand up for the mans immediate silence. "This woman works for me, Alfie. I'd hope for you to hold your tongue to make sure you still do."

The man in black faded into the back like a whipped dog.

Harold brought his lips to her proffered hand and kissed it affectionately. "Welcome, my Stella. Have you seen this? I have every corner watched and this is the kind of security I end up with....."

"Well, its no wonder, Harold, with the men in your employ."

Stella's red pumps were sinking into the mud. Stella simply walked with no care for them dirtying and knowing her way around the grounds, led the way.

"The situation has escaladed. I am no doubt in the need of hearing you request, your pleading request for my help and assets?" Said Stella.

Bradshaw could not believe that this meek woman had such power over the most powerful man in the world. Old flame, perhaps, he thought.

Human suppression was widely used in the galaxy Kale. Any human was either enslaved, or devoid of any humanity. When the Thirty-Five arrived into the alien galaxy the human stragglers had no choice but to bow down to alien supremacy.

The four popular systems were regarded as the central systems. And as such were policed fiercely. The Space Cops of the Interstellar Division Corp were the finest in the regime, but occasionally bad seeds would surface.

Sergeant Space Cop ST-10C was assigned to the Satanic System on surveillance. Of course they had names like any person but to prevent internal bonding they were given identification numbers instead. It maintained a plutonic working relationship with their peers. But it also made them feel less than human.

These humans were created, not born. Artificially constructed for the protection duty of the galaxy. There was a certain irony in there somewhere, or perhaps a cruel joke to real humans and synths.

The maker of the Space Cops no one knew. The synths were to never be used, left in their creation pods for years on end until an epidemic erupted in the galaxy and the inhabitants were forced to wake up these peace enforcers.

Onboard her scout ship SC, Admiral ST-10C watched as the space particles drifted by excruciatingly slow. Everyone knew this mission was bogus. She knew it of course. But as mere cop and not commanding officer she had little say in the matter. Go where ordered

Kill whoever. And do not ask questions. They were the three abiding codes to live by. A refusal would resort in decommission. And everyone knew what that meant. A one permanent stop back to the pods, kept on chill for years, for a possibility of reactivation via cerebral wipe. No Space Cop took the chance. So all obeyed orders. All except for ST-10C. She had a tendency for asking questions she ought not too. So they put her in a position like this, watching the thrilling spectacles of space dust till her drool would drop onto the console; someplace where no action would be sought, no possibility for trouble could arise.

How wrong they would turn out to be...

The night was colder than usual, so Mayes had the log fire burning. Sean was seated across from Celeste who looked at his red steak quizzically.

The table they all sat around was made from an old red gum felled many years ago before they were deemed endangered and put under protection.

It had intricate knots and dark swirls engrained into its surface.

Sean took a slice of the red bloody meat to his lips and began chewing. Unfortunately about 5 minutes into eating, Sean felt the distinct burning sensation of eyes on him. He looked up and saw the incredulous look Celeste was casting, like lasers.

At long last, he could no longer take the torture. "What?"

Celeste daintily held her salad upon the tip of her fork. "You eat bloodied meat with such, er… vigour. Is that supposed to bleed?" she asked.

"Only way to have it," he said taking another bite and chewing quite exuberantly.

"Blood…we do not consume it. It is considered taboo on our world, indeed on most worlds that have suffered by the hands of those blood-drinkers Raiders."

"Raiders?" Sean uncomfortably swallowed hearing the insidious nature of that term. He helped himself to a good glass of beer to force down the large bits of remaining half-chewed meat lodged in his throat.

If indeed there were such things as angels then why would there not be the direct opposite? And Raiders...? They sounded demonic. And the more Celeste talked of them the more Sean really wished she hadn't.

By the end of dinner Sean's fantastic steak was left cold on his dinner plate.

And then we looked unto the heavens and everything made sense; we are but specs in this wide universe—Unknown Archives

The time has come, thought Sean. They had to make the move tonight. Celeste was not safe on Earth, if ever she was. Sean took the access card in his hand and played with it moving it in between his fingers.

Mayes came in quietly. She could not be heard like a rabbit on the soft layers of snow. "Sean, I think this is a good idea. You need to help her. She is -"

"I know," he said rather snappishly. He breathed in recomposing himself. "I know the responsibility on me, Mayes. I just thought that I was done. I thought that my fighting days were over."

Mayes smiled and placed her hand on his shoulder comfortingly. "Did you really want it to be, nephew. I appreciate the money. And it will go towards this house and the maintenance of this free-lands. But you wanted something to fight for a long time. The retirement was simply because Earth had run out of things to fight for. Now you have a chance. I'd take it."

Harold watched Stella walk away as she did all these years. She was something else, like an element of nature. He knew better than to cross her. Stella usually got what she wanted, and if you crossed her she made sure you paid for it.

"You have looked better, Harold." Stella smiled as she walked away blowing him a kiss.

Only Stella could get away with something candid like that. Harold simply looked away rather abashed. He a-hemmed and ordered the staring men to continue with their investigation.

Stella went into an awaiting black chopper. The grass bent down from the gusty force. Stella walked in her red heels onto the ladder and stepped aboard, helped up by a soldier.

"Henderson."

"Ma'am. I believe we will be arriving at base one in forty minutes. Have you acquired what we needed from ground zero?"

"Yes Henderson, we have." Stella took out of her pocket a single feather with enough DNA to run a spectral analysis.

Celeste looked out at the forlorn window, the droplets of rain mirroring her own sadness. She knew what she had to do. She realised now that she had to make one of the most difficult voyages yet: a voyage back home.

Sean was geared to the T. He looked at Celeste and at his aunt who just walked in. "Celeste. Are you ready to go home?"

Celeste gave a shaky smile. "Yes but there is something you must know about what you'll encounter in the Kale Galaxy. The Raiders are like tumours upon worlds. We have fought them for many years. You must understand their ferocity and not underestimate them at any given time."

Sean took his gun out that he had hidden away. He never thought it would be brought out and polished ever again. "I think I can handle a few bloodsuckers."

Celeste smiled at his obvious ignorance, but also at his valour to do what it took to get her back home in one piece. Her man in armour, she thought secretly.

Sean went up to Mayes who looked away saddened. He took her chin by his finger directing her gaze to his. "I am sorry Mayes for acting the way I did. You been nothing but a mother to me." He hugged her long and hard.

Mayes pulled away teary. She whispered in his ear. "Go see the Tracker. His an old friend. He has transport to take you off world." She turned to Celeste smiling broadly. "And you my dear. I believe we will be meeting again some day." Ginger the cat came strolling in and rubbed up against Mayes's leg affectionately. Mayes grabbed her. "Don't worry. Ginger here will look out for me." Ginger the cat gave a weak meow.

The past is the past, what matters is the present; to foresee a future is just as futile as looking back – Unknown Archives

A Raider wore a fabric interwoven into their skin called a Weave that helped keep their cells regenerated—a eternal youth suit.

When landing on planets they would come in Detachment Palaces, a segment of their ships that would land on planets to unleash hordes of their kind.

The Corr Weavers were known for their speciality at creating the cloth by using discarded Sendicar seed husks to make the fine silk thread. The husks were dispensed by the Krelians.

Regenerative Pods were not initially created by the Raiders but stolen from another race to retain youth indefinitely. The Raiders weren't shy to say they were scabs and pried the technology willingly from the ancient aliens' cold dead hands without a moments hesitation.

Raiders were parasitic anomalies, a plague upon this galaxy; unnatural. And somewhere in some unregistered station was The Maker, an old man responsible for it all. He was the talk among stations as far as the twinkling stars went. Why had he made these creatures? Why unleash them on a seemingly innocent galaxy? Where was his station?

The Maker, like most men had passion. But his passion lay in the fineries of DNA. His brilliant mind gave him the ability to play God using saved DNA from extinct species across the cosmos, the most successful being a race called the Vernom. They were vampiristic aliens who once thrived in the Kale galaxy until the Sprites arrived. The Sprites were wiped out by a cascade called the Wave of Redemption.

Raiders were wounded but not gone.

However, Omend Krelian Clan leader Shakik wasn't afraid of them. Indeed he wasn't afraid of anything

The risks of travelling the Voids without certain adaptations to ships could lead to starvation, madness or worse. Shakik, however, cared only for the success of the mission.

The Krelians were space gypsies; nomads constantly on the move. A Krelian had yellow eyes with slit black pupils and their skin was tanned and almost leathery looking. There had never been talk of Krelians consorting with other races. They tended to stay with their own.

There were thousands of clans. Krelians were good at one thing and one thing only: reproduction. That was why most of them were viewed as pests, something to be exterminated. They were fighting for existence; their right to live.

Led by Shakik, the clan Omend had no choice but to follow him—even into the abyss, the Voids. Violating law Shakik imprisoned an illegal pilot, a Vernom; the very last of her kind in fact.

Inside his ship, the female pilot twisted against her binders (electrical cuffs that delivered jolts of pain). She fought harder.

She lashed out, hissing, fangs and sharp teeth baring and a thin trail of saliva hanging from her mouth. Vernom were pale green-skinned creatures; pallid, sharp- toothed with protruding fangs and dark eyes as well as a hairless, almost emaciated body. Her sunken face looked haunting.

She forced against the immense pain to better reach her captor's face. "I will not go there, no matter the pressure you put on me. There's nothing but darkness and death!" she hissed.

Shakik smirked, moving his hand ever so slightly so she flinched. "Oh Cardvia, I know more than anyone what your intentions are. I know that you will comply, otherwise..." Shikak pulled away in a threatening manner that made her recoil, but he instead withdrew a pack of red substance: blood from his right pocket; blood that wracked her body with longing hunger, "...you will be in more than physical pain."

She knew the mental torture he could perform on her only too well; Shikak had certain resources at his disposal that most Krelians would never have considered. This would have skimmed over their minds like a pebble over water, but for a devious creature like Shakik, it came as easily as breathing.

The pilot doors sealed shut, the loud cries of Cardvia falling behind. Shakik had no shred of compassion. He was power hungry, more than the primal hunger of the Vernom. This was far more sinister because it was a choice, a voluntary act to do evil. It seemed strange though: a creature as dark as any nightmares and yet it was the Krelian gypsy with a handful of Reapers and the face of the devil.

Krelian ships were used as disassembling houses. Their trade usually found them on farming planets. They were roughly put together, some having sustained well enough not to have breaches but equally shoddy enough as paddle pop sticks and glue; that was the rough estimation of their craftsmanship.

The Krelian gypsies' livelihood consisted of shipping many kinds of grain across the galaxy. They didn't make a large profit but it was enough.

Sendicar grain was amongst the more popular grains used for trade, grown on planets that weren't usually populated but rich in another source—worlds used for farming. Sendicar grain was a beautiful smooth seed harvested, used for the making of brewed Haldo and encapsulated by a fine husk; the tough husk was discarded but the Corr used them for the making of the fine fabric to make the Weave used by an evil so profound it almost demoted the fine beauty the grain represented.

Meanwhile, on board Shakik's vessel, the Vernom alien fast becoming delirious without her daily intake of blood started seeing phantoms in dark corners. She thrived on sentient blood—no animal substitutes—but she could have settled for anything at the moment.

She never knew torture before this; Shakik was hell-bent on making her suffer because of what she was. Yet he had blurred the black and white lines and entered an obscurity far removed from the ordinary grey area.

Cardvia was actually a placid and timid creature in nature, her subtle nicety often ignored because of her demonic appearance. Just because she craved the blood of sentient beings didn't mean she was a savage.

The Maker knew the qualities her species held and obtained DNA samples of her dead brethren and used it to create these Raiders who tainted the intigrity of her kind. It disgusted her to no end to know that she was somehow linked to these monstrosities, even to some extent their mother. And her captor wanted her to remember that every second.

Going through withdrawals, Cardvia could feel the sleeping beast of bloodlust awaken within her. She had until now kept it under submission. She would be ravenous soon if she wasn't given a blood bag and Shakik would have more than a little trouble on his hands; they would be soaked with his and his crew's blood and all fault would lie with him.

We are far less significant that we actually think – Unknown Archives

Sean held the access card in his hand. It was strange that this little thing could unlock something so incredible. He wanted to fly more than anything else. He thought that he wanted retirement, he thought he wanted out, but deep down Sean wanted to shed himself of responsibility and chase danger like he used to.

The Skeleton Station was out of commission and therefore had no master; it was designated a ghost station. Because the Parliament was so indebted to the late Mitchell Caleb, they kept it off limits under his orders.

Sean wished more than anything that he didn't feel the splinters of hate working into his heart. He should have felt gratitude towards his father. But still, even this, didn't make up for it, for any of it. He had the coordinates of the station.. It was located somewhere behind the moon Titan.

"Where are we going?" asked Celeste as she ducked and weaved as Sean did from bush to bush. They stayed on hidden paths.

"We are going to see a friend. It's okay. Trust me."

They walked under the cover of darkness, making their way to see old Mikey.

"So, who is this tracker?" she said.

"Oh, you'll like him. Him and my dad were old war buddies. Mikey is old fashioned. He can help."

Celeste's eyes darted all over the place, checking that they weren't being followed. She kept skittering to the side every time she heard an unknown sound in the darkness. After all that time at Sean's aunt's, she had grown accustomed to staying concealed. Now she was out in the open, she felt vulnerable.

She inched ever closer to Sean. He didn't grumble. At one point Sean thought he heard her purr. Sean caught her distress and placed a casual arm around her shoulders, savouring the time of their closeness. "Don't worry, I won't let anything happen to you."

Mikey looked like a shady character thought Celeste, as they came to the shack that was, by all means, a hovel. The sound of a gun being cocked alerted Sean to move quickly. Celeste stepped back and hid behind a bush. A shot was fired into the sky and Sean held the gun aloft. Catching Sean's face in the light of the fire, Mikey smiled apologetically. "Sorry 'bout that." Sean knew he was not Mikey if he did not try to take your head off in the first few minutes of meeting you.

Mikey was an old Aboriginal tracker. He had that slur that most Aborigines had when they spoke. Celeste slowly came out of the bush.

Sean introduced Celeste to a very stunned Mikey, who must have scanned her up and down at least three times. "She is just like the paintings depict." Mikey was astounded by the likeness.

Celeste's nose wiggled. She could smell something nice. And before long she was downing the fish that was piping hot over the coals. It did not bother her one bit. "Please help yourself," said Mikey.

"She's cold." Sean laughed it off hoping Mikey would too, which he did. That was the thing about Mikey. He was a down-to-earth man and hopefully a gracious one too.

"Take a seat, mate."

Sean went to the log offered, the one harbouring fungi.

"So," Mikey said, sliding under his shotgun.

Both of them side glanced Celeste, who was downing the fish at exceptional speed. "I, um…I am here to ask a favour," said Sean, trying hard to shield his eyes from the distraction of Celeste downing the fish whole, tail and head.

"Well, I thought as much. What can I do for ya, mate?"

"Well, I need to get off-planet."

"You need a shuttle?"

"Maybe the spare you keep in that hill of yours?"

Celeste had now finished, shuffling forward ever so slightly near the warmth of the fire. She was so used to her world of warmth, she was easily susceptible to cold. Plus, she didn't like the cold anyways. She gave a shiver recalling the deep freeze.

"I know, I wouldn't normally ask but since you owed my father..."

"You thought I'd be indebted to help? You don't need to hold that one over me, son. Of course I will.... You know I always regarded you as family? It's just a shame that you came to see me only to say goodbye."

The cave drawings of the dreaming portrayed weren't lying about the foretelling about the Celestial Beings. The ancestral encounters were real. He brought out beers. "Well son, you can certainly have the ship. Where you headed? If you're trying to get her home, I don't think you'll get far in that ship," he said. He gave Sean a cold one. Sean then grasped the beer from Celeste, her lips about to land on the rim. "I don't think so."

Sean waved about his card.

"He still pulls out the good old surprises. Okay, matey. I'll let you have her, but for a price," added Mikey with a swig.

"What's that? My boots?"

"Yeah, matey, and your word that whatever you're doing up there once you hit dirt again you report back to me. I may be out of the game but I am still a mighty curious story hunter."

Sean smiled and they all headed toward the mysterious hill. Following the trail up the hills, they came to a cavernous cave. As they ascended the wonky path, it was clear this construct wasn't of natural devising.

"Ships blew that lid clean off back in the day, you know. I had a house for her before it even needed one." His laughter was like treacle, smooth and sweet. And there was the shuttle, a little rusty and rundown but intact and hopefully flyable. "Will it suffice?" said Mikey.

"It's a fix-er-upper, but I think it is doable."

Over the next few hours, Celeste was entertained by Mikey's culture; he told her all about the paintings and their beliefs while Sean worked on the shuttle.

Mikey was then left behind in the desert, waving up at the shuttle that ascended into the sky. "I'll see you soon, matey, you and yer girlfriend." And he had the last swig of his beer.

The truth often comes in driblets and before we know it we have molded one large lie
—Unknown Archives

There was a species with a peculiar scaled head that looked like a cross between a large pinecone and an armadillo. They were known as the Boric race. A female Boric called Selisca had a scaly head, as was typical; the scales would lift when agitated or aroused, revealing beautiful salmon pink tissue underneath. Most females were considered exotic merchandise to slavers and the like.

Selisca had been taken from her home planet Sadie by a most unscrupulous character. Boris: the most ruthless Claspher hunter.

Stern, a Celestial Being Seraph, took residence with the Boric in a confining cage, ready for transport. He tried his best not to make her too uncomfortable with his puffed, feathery chest. "What is your name?" he finally said, trudging up the courage.

Selisca was a fine beauty, but he didn't want to make her feel awkward.

She did her best to conceal her tears of fear. "I am Selisca. I am not supposed to be here. I don't understand why they took me," she said, looking into the warrior's beautiful blue eyes and finding solace there.

The turbulence of a shipment being unloaded rocked Stern and caused him to wrap his arms around the obviously petrified girl. She hesitated at first and then just sank into his hard chest in between timed sobs, surrendering to his warmth.

The cold hearted hunters prowling outside made her get as near to this stranger as she could, practically climbing over him. The hunters carried prods in their hands. Stern held her tighter as though no one would dare challenge him. "New tasties," mumbled one hunter, leering ever nearer with a mouth full of foul teeth.

Selisca whimpered.

"It's okay. They are only teasing. I won't let anything bad happen to you."

They took her scratching and screaming and Stern was left with a bludgeoned head from trying to stop them. Stern awoke later alone in his cage, signs of her struggle evident. He snapped to the bars and yelled for her. "Selisca! Selisca!" but only the burly men's laughter echoed back.

Finally, the noise drew some hunters. "What, ferret?" one leered.

"The woman I was with, where is she?"

The hunter grinned and didn't answer.

"Hey!" But it was useless; the hunter was already walking away.

Shuffling in his chains, Stern was coming from the auctions when he happened upon something most horrible. It was Selisca, displayed right in the open for everyone to see, curled up in a pool of her own blood, though it hardly made a scene to anyone. They absently passed by as if she were nothing. She had been killed somewhere else and taken to the promenade to be viewed by the public. It was a Claspher tactic. They did it to assert their dominance, to show what happened to those who resisted. Stern had managed to slip out of his binders and made a dash for her. He touched her pallid face, almost too scared to feel the contact. She was a distant voice, no longer the warm wind.

Stern felt the irritation at the back of his head where they had punched the Tagging Chip into the base of his skull; his new master would be on his trail soon. He held onto her limp body. The warmth would soon disappear through his fingers and into the cold floor. Frustration and anger engrossed him. He had got to her too late and failed as a warrior.

Stern touched her face once again—confirmation. It felt odd. He had formed a relationship with this alien yet he had only spent a total of 2 days with her, the times spent more or less in silence. He would not have traded one second of it.

He almost had to steady himself to the stillness, like he had been spinning for too long and only now came to a standstill. "Oh, Selisca...How I wish I could have been there for you," he said through hysterical sobs. "I let you go when I should have held on tighter."

Her beautiful scales had now closed fully; she was involuntarily curled like the beautiful armadillos that once occupied Earth.

He cradled her in his arms, knowing the tramp of their boots would soon be heard from behind him. He held her closer to his chest, hoping his beating heart might resurrect her, but he had to face facts, cold and harsh as they were. She was dead. They killed her.

Stern started when he was shoved in the back by the barrel of a pistol. "Hey!" The voice was gruff.

He had hoped the same fate would not address him as he turned to see a pistol positioned in his face. He slowly laid Selisca's beaten body on the cold floor, reluctantly and almost forcibly moving away like his feet were cemented to that spot.

A bald man stood before him. He was human with a few modifications. "Dangerous business, boy—escaping your master."

"You are not my master," he seethed with gritted teeth.

Maverick stowed his pistol, convinced that Stern wouldn't run again. "Someone you knew?"

Stern remained silent.

"Sorry, kid."

"I know that you aren't. I don't care for your condolences. What are you but another pariah," he said tersely and held his hands out to be binder cuffed. He knew he was testing his limits, but after losing Selisca his own safety seemed trivial.

The tides of the universe wash in and wash out and take everything with it
– Unknown Archives

Station Alpha was the most used station in the galaxy—so much so it was falling to bits. The vilest Hunter lived there: Boris. He was infamous for his brutality and feared by those under his charge; he was a notorious murderer and rapist.

Finally, Boris came up to his door, a clear dent evident from his last rant, and swiped the panel with his hand. "Welcome back, Boris," the AI said coolly.

Boris entered the door making a low thud as it closed behind him. He rounded his desk, the middle splayed with red blood where he had gutted that slut who refused to pleasure him. To his right was his wall of horrors with all manner of faces staring back. They were mounted and stuffed, predominately Celestial Beings, their emotional faces captured to the minutest detail and their wings carved from their bodies and displayed separately.

Picking up a bottle of Haldo, the liquid sloshing around, he poured himself a tumbler. He went and sat in his chair and placed his feet on the desk. Boris avoided the politics; he got others to do that for him. He was a brute, a hunter and he never conveyed to being anything less. He loved the thrills of life. Sex, drink, the hunt, and snuffing people's lights out. But politics? Nah, that was a bore he would not touch.

He was enjoying his drink when he paused. Something wasn't right. Then a shadow came over him, his Haldo balanced elegantly in one hand. He had hoped to see Cleo standing there, his human slave, but he was rudely misled. He stood there rigidly and the glass slipped from his grasp, smashing to bits on the floor. "Kressangah?" he said dryly.

Kressangah Tran. He thought he would never see her again, and yet there she was like she owned the place.

"You just stay here, lumbering around like an old fossil soon to crumble into dust," she said derisively, leaning to one side on the wall, arms folded and half cast in shadow. She was still as radiant as ever. He had to gnaw the stupid thought away with a sharp prick of his teeth. He had a weakness for beautiful women and Kressangah, well, she definitely was that but she also had a brain, unfortunately. He had never been able to dominate her, though he had tried.

"I see your handy work," she referred nonchalantly to the rug of an unnatural colour, soaked in blood.

Boris's face remained placid. He half smiled to better shatter the lingering vibe. "Would you expect anything else?" he replied candidly, going to pour another tumbler. "Besides, it's not of your concern."

"Selisca was my business."

He drew near and while holding his drink choked her with his other free hand in what seemed a shaved second. "A Tarok assassin," he said, exerting no effort in strangling her. "I had hoped you would have learned by now. I don't go down easy." He then hit her hard against the wall and let go as she turned blue. "They thought if they sent a pretty one, I might be inclined to show compassion?" he said through gritted teeth, smelling her. When he felt anger it was like a brewing storm, and he liked the destruction that came with it, how he gorged on it.

She coughed and spluttered, trying to get her breath back while scrambling to her feet.

"They forget to calculate into their plans our past history, or is that what they were betting on?"

"They?" she squeezed out hoarsely, continuing to rub her throat.

"The Order! The pains in my arse that sent you here!"

Kressangah rubbed her throat gingerly, coughing and wheezing. "I volunteered. Selisca was a dear friend. You don't even like Borics. Why did you go to Sadie? Why did you have to stray the path?"

"Honey," he leant in, taking a deliberate slurp of his Haldo, "I strayed a long time ago. You should not have come."

"Careful, Boris. You sound awfully close to someone who cares about what happens to me," she ventured. "I thought I told you to stop sticking your fingers into other people's business or ever coming as far as Planet Sadie."

A smirk played on Boris' face. He loved to taunt, especially with this one. "No, Kressangah, I don't care what happens to you. And where I conduct my affairs is up to me, not some old flame who was half decent in the sack." His voice was distant and cold now. Something was about to happen, static in the air. "And I don't care for others either as you can see," he said, placing his tumbler to his lips and downing it all.

Depriving him of the opportunity to pin her down again, Kressangah started to pace, watching his outstretching arms. "Selisca was a friend of mine. You have little understanding of what is to come from your meddling and your stupid habits."

The two prowled after each other like Degas Wolves in heat. At least that was what they always had—heat, fire. But fire destroys until all that is left is a blackened corpse.

"You couldn't get your way, am I right?"

"You do not know what it is to be a true hunter. I am not some cheap assembly line, I am an entity. What's it feel like to be a poor substitute? The Order is outdated and just because the war still rages doesn't mean you can inflict your moral toxicity towards me. You will fall just as the Order will. Take your high-minded philosophy and tea and friggin die!"

In that moment, Boris was overcome by insurmountable rage and threw the glass at her in one misdirected throw, embedding the glass in his hand, but feeling no pain. She dodged and shards of glass flew everywhere, cutting her slightly. She kneed him hard in the genitals and brought him down like a sinking ship. She didn't waste time and ran out the door for her life. She knew what would have happened if she stayed. She would have been the next Selisca. As she stormed out, a figure stood there in the half light. Cleo waited half draped in cloth as commanded by Boris, who kneeled down and bled rapidly.

"This isn't finished! Not by a long shot!" he yelled after her trembling wake, glass embedded in his palm and nursing his gonads. "Bitch."

Kressangah knew she had stopped Boris finishing what he was about to do—a short and brutal rape leaving her for dead. He hadn't changed, not one bit. Kressangah was hopeful if not belligerently so. That was her problem.

Kressangah whooshed past a half-naked slave girl. Cleo continued to stand there in the flickering hallway not quite sure whether to come in or not.

Left in the halo of the light floating in and ripping cuts on his hand with welts on his knuckles Boris smiled up at Cleo. It was a smile that usually followed by some form of indecencies.

"Not a moment too soon," he breathed.

Boris always placed violence and sex together. For Boris, there was no indistinction between the two. They were one and the same.

Cleo was briskly taken inside by Boris who took a half-filled bottle of Haldo and roughly poured it over his cuts.

Little was known about Boris's past. No one ever had the goal to actually ask him about it. When he was born he killed his mother in childbirth. Then when he was nine he killed his father in a so-called hunting accident but still, suspicions were raised. Boris could still taste the metallic tinge of blood in his mouth. He hungered for the kill after that, like a drug. Family meant nothing to him and love was a foreign concept.

He was tired of letting his stupid flashes of potential get the better of him. He chiselled himself from stone so that he wouldn't have to worry about developing cracks. And now a visit from Kressangah agitated him beyond compare but he didn't know why?

Kressangah meant nothing to Boris; she was a notch on a very long belt. He hated being doused in potential to be "better". He felt like having a shower in blood to dilute the idea. He was one for filth—he liked to frolic in it, slather himself in the mess. Power and money and violence and sex. It was always about power and money, and sex…nothing else equated. He didn't care for relationships. In fact, he never had one. He was a user, a killer, an abuser.

Then when we see the evil inside do we run and hide, or do we embrace it and become the thing we're scared of? Do we become even worse?—Unknown Archives

On the promenade of Station Alpha, a young alien boy holding hands with his mother glanced over at a young Celestial Being girl destined for slavery. She was holding her hand out desperately begging for food, her skin and usually sheened feathers coated in filth.

"Can I have one, please? I'll clean her and everything," he pleaded to his mother, who was desperate to leave and tugged her boy along.

"Help me," pleaded the young girl. The mother ran with her son in her arms for fear of contamination.

The mother hissed insults to the girl, as the boys eyes never left the gorgeous but tortured eyes of the little girl he hoped to one day marry, flickering his snake tongue to better absorb her scent.

Stern was in the lobby inside a dingy ship in much disrepair, a bloodied knife to the side. He reached to the back of his neck and tried to extract the chip but its tendrils drove deep. Maverick had been watching quietly at the door's archway. "You know you will only make it harder on yourself. There are worse things in the universe than little old me," he said tapping his very own dagger.

Stern reached over to the dagger and trembled, unsure what to do. "Do you even know what you have done?" he finally said after the inane silence.

Maverick lit another smoke, unfazed by Stern's distress. "Why? Should I?" Maverick intended to mock him, to demean him, but continued also to listen.

Stern stood still like comatose. "You took me from my home; you separated me from my family. You—"

Maverick held up a hand that made Stern stop dead silent. "Son, before you say it, I had nothing to do with your girlfriend dying. Yes, I remember her. A fine specimen, but I had no part in her death. You could even say I saved you from a similar fate."

"How convenient for you." He left the knife on the table and went to fix his minor self-surgery that achieved nothing.

Stern knew he was stretching the limits with his master but he was a warrior, he flew in and out the clouds defying hunters all his life. He was unlucky the one time and now he was another's bitch. He wouldn't submit to this butcher just because he was sold to him. He belonged to no one.

Maverick's past was murky if not obscured. Not one of his crewman knew of his back story. Where was he from? He usually smoked his herbs and paid no mind to any of them.

No one even knew what his main objective was—if he even had one or if he was simply plodding through the universe like the rest of them, uncertain days, uncertain future.

Jathmoora was a sorceress. She and Hariot were aboard a city-ship called Mystic. The sorceress dabbled in the Choc-ra (a mystical energy said to exist inside subspace interwoven in the undercurrent of spacetime).

With her one other crewman, Hariot; an unclassified species who loved the study of alien plant life, mainly cultivating them for medicinal purposes.

Planet Sadie was a swamp world, a huge bog. As Jathmoora discovered stepping right into a knee-deep mud puddle. Hariot pushed past her with his jars ready for specimen collection. And forced her a few inches deeper.

"Look at this, Jath! All this plant life thriving in such pristine conditions!"

Jathmoora thought not so much, considering the minuscule bugs flying around her ear and the humidity sticking her clothes to her.

"Lovely. Honestly. Why don't we go to places more like this? I know. 'Cause it's a shithole! Hariot, get your samples and let's make this snappy. I don't want to stay here any longer than needed," she said, heading back to the ship dragging her soppy hemline behind her.

The natives—Boric-kay (humanoid species with dreadlock hair and quills together)—were situated in the northern regions in their straw mud huts.

The city-ship Mystic was parked in an isolated part of the planet. Any unwanted attention would warrant investigation and that would be followed by inane questions that Jathmoora had no desire to answer.

People didn't believe in the existence of the Choc-ra or its power. However, there were a spattering of individuals throughout the universe that were heavy dabblers. And like Jathmoora practised it on a daily basis to the point of addiction. Then there were the less devoted like Maud.

He was a touchy subject for Jath. He would spend most of his days meditating rather than using the Choc-ra.

Jathmoora was in love once, yes, but her devotion to the practice of the Choc-ra shattered her relationship. She believed in the Choc-ra wholeheartedly. She believed in it so much that she drove a lot of people away.

When she tried to explain to Maud that she was not an addict and simply a devoted servant, he told her he couldn't stand by and watch her rip her mind apart. He explained it was something far too powerful for one individual to use.

That was the last time she ever saw his gentle face.

The day Jathmoora found Hariot, barely clothed, underfed, and badly beaten, she knew she had to help him. No one wanted the orphan alien because he was a mixed breed, just like her.

People like Hariot and Jathmoora who looked really alien, really unusual were met with scepticism, distrust and often violence. The humans who occupied some of the galaxies were not all slaves; some had eluded it, even escaped it all together and they had a severe distrust of anything remotely alien. Which was strange considering the galaxy was filled with them. No one knew the reason for the human's hatred of aliens, only that they had brought the disdain with them during the Great Move. And that disdain turned around to bite them in the arse as the large portion of them were shunted into slavery.

In the rules of life there is a balance between good and evil, right and wrong—only when we favor one over the other does chaos unfold—Unknown Archives

Sean placed his hand in his pocket and caught the card nestled against the innards. The slow hiss of the doors preceded the rush of a sour air.

The Station must have been at least fifty years old; the dilapidated walls were rusting around the bolts. Sean dreaded for a second that they might suffer a breach; skeleton stations were known for that.

"C'mon, stick close. Who knows what's been harbouring in here over the years," Sean said, referring to the Neglar Bats often found on Skeleton Stations abandoned by their demised Station Masters.

Sean shone his torch into the station's dark tomb; cobwebs from Chaka spiders spread everywhere. Chaka Spiders were rumoured to be of the same species as the Bats only mutated and not fussed to make a meal of their inferior cousins.

Sean made sure to grab Celeste. He wanted her close by, an excuse he thought to grab her hand. He relished any chance to touch her delicate skin.

Their steps were soft, cushioned by the dust collected over the years. They went down some winding corridors at first, then their torches highlighted certain cargo. Yet nothing was as noticeable as a giant space ship.

Celeste was trembling slightly obviously not acclimatising to the cold; Sean could feel it through his hand. He guessed she wasn't used to cold considering her planet stayed a constant 30 Degrees Celsius.

He tugged her in closer to him. "Don't worry, the Chaka spiders are easily frightened and the Bats usually devour them anyway. Where is that ship?" Sean paused, his torch glinting something ahead.

“What is it?” she inquired, coming to an abrupt halt so that she ended up bumping into Sean.

Sean gave a slight moan.

He brought his torch down back over the last section he passed and there it was—a vision in its own right: his father’s ship.

Celeste moved towards it, hand outstretched. “It’s an Altran Class Ship,” she said in awe while touching the metal like it was silk.

“And a grand vessel,” added Sean, bringing himself closer. He could feel the old threads of his pilot days unravel within him. He hadn’t felt the thrill of flight in the longest time. Putting this ship up in space was all he could think of.

Suddenly there was a clawing sound coming from behind them in the swath of darkness. Both jumped to whirl around, facing only a brick of solid darkness as the torch flickered, beginning to die.

“Neglar bats nesting. Don’t worry,” added Sean reassuringly, though he kept a wary eye.

At that moment as Sean’s back was turned something large lunged at Celeste bringing her down and flinging Sean and his torch to the side.

Celeste fought against a jumble of clawing nails and sticky mucus, her wings fluttering. A direct hit could break a bone but with the darkness and panic rising, to coordinate was an impossible task.

“They will know! They will know!” whispered the creature that looked like death itself. It seemed to want to get somewhere: to the back of Celeste’s neck.

Sean wasted no time and tried to pry the creature off of Celeste but the thing was solid rock; scratching and relentless.

Before long the creature whipped Celeste’s head around, yanking hard a clump of hair and cut into Celeste’s neck with its razor nails in a quick motion.

The creature also lapped the blood while it was at it. The creature then pulled out something from the wound she created. At the same moment, Sean copped an elbow in the face as he went to fully shove it off. Blood spurted from his ruptured nose.

The creature smashed the object with the base of Sean’s wayward torch.

“Now they will never know, not come, not come now,” it said, backing away like it was frightened all of a sudden.

Dazed but still conscious, Sean grabbed the torch. He brought it up to Celeste, who was a jumbled mess of blood and tears. He eased her up. “What was that thing?” he said to himself as Celeste was incoherent.

Sean took Celeste up into his arms. Sean armed with a failing torch wandered aimlessly in the dark. He held onto Celeste and felt his way across the ship.

The torch flickered and then when it came back on Sean saw the starved skeletal creature with sunken eyes in front of him, advancing, its mucus sack abandoned to the side. It was one of them.

“Raider!” screamed Celeste.

The torch flickered again. Sean backed up, trying to shield Celeste while fumbling behind him to find some way to activate the ships door. The creature leered with dark, haunting eyes. Her mouth was open, fangs popped down. She advanced slowly. "I want to leave but bloodlust calls. You help me," it said like they would willingly open a vein.

Finally, there was a slight click and Sean pushed Celeste inside in one swift move. And he just made it in himself as the creature darted for him, grabbing for his feet.

Sean kicked hard and heard the thud of the creature breaking her nose. Her wailing screams could be heard and he almost felt sorry for it. Almost.

Soon it stopped and the darkness in the ship was suddenly illuminated by the lights up above and the degree of Celeste's injury could be seen.

It took a while to navigate the labyrinth corridors of the ship. Celeste winced as Sean held the gauze against her bleeding neck. So far they had found what appeared to be the med bay. She was still tearing after the horrible assault but working hard to compose herself.

Despite her injury, Celeste wrapped her hands around Sean and lost herself in his manliness. "I'm sorry Sean. I've brought you into a nightmare."

"Shh babe."

The two stood there holding each other, the sounds of the ship around them whining and creaking in an unknown language, the bulkheads watching, the atmosphere almost breathing. This ship was alive.

And then the wise know that they have found the key, but what does it unlock and what will it hold?—Unknown Archives

Sean had his hands in the cold condensation of the viscous fluid. Riding up its way into his nails Sean couldn't help but form looks of disgust on his face. Celeste, on the other hand, had a wide smirk planted on hers.

"Stop moving around. Just hold them there. The ship needs to integrate your DNA into its form."

"Why couldn't we have a ship like Jim Kirks?"

"Hmm?"

"Nothing. How long do I have to do this?"

"Until the ship is satisfied with its new pilot. Its a type of bonding if you will. Try to enjoy it?"

"Sure. No problem. Easy for you to say. You haven't got your hands elbow deep in snot buckets."

Celeste, amused, smiled.

"I'd stop smirking, missy." Sean whipped one hand out and wrapped his gloopy hand round her waist.

Celeste dove his hand back into the slots. "Don't break the contact. It will only prolong the procedure."

"At least I got you good and proper."

After a good hour of integration, Sean watched Celeste sit next to him in the chair two sizes too big for her, but watched on as it started to reshape to her perfect form.

Sean turned to her before doing anything else. She looked troubled. "What is it?" he said.

"I just remember, that's all. I remember the Elders talk about it. There was wide spread war. Most planets were out of defences. And as though a call from The Old Timer these mysterious vessels appeared. No one knows where from or how. They were just there. So people began using them."

"Huh. Whats the Old Timer?"

"Well, when I was taken I was in the midsts of embarking on The Rite of Undula. For the longest time, the Elders forbid anyone taking on this rite because it meant leaving our beloved paradise. I, however, have never been a caged bird.

I always wanted to try it. To explore space and stars without the hindrance of staying home. And to discover the oldest star in the universe was a dream beyond dreams. I don't want to just exist, I want answers. I want an experience of the most profound level.

Though experiencing the brute of the hunters, I understand fully the Elders having a good reason for protecting us, but you cannot hope to contain which is not meant to be contained. Eventually, it will break free. Our race revere the stars, see them almost as gods. I myself have always felt the tug of the stars. I was on my way to find a pilot and begin the Rite when a hunter found me. I still don't know what happened. The pod shouldn't have malfunctioned, but it did and fortunate that it did. A true gift from the Old Timer."

"So the Old Timer is said to be the oldest star in the universe—the first in creation, hey? That's pretty cool. I too have a fascination with the stars. Just something about them."

"That is what the Rite of Undula leads too; that is its destination. Now move the ship with your mind, try to feel the ship with the connection you have established."

Sean couldn't figure how he did it; he just thought it and it kind of happened. The bay doors yawned opened and the fresh glow of the stars greeted them. "How could I have forsaken this? You ready, darling?"

"More than I'll ever be. Take me home."

Travelling through the rift was instantaneous but seemed to take an eternity before they finally exited. Sean wiped away beads of cold sweat.

He was sure the ropes must have been fried on his way out. Parliament would be having a field day with that one. Even sitting he could still feel the shakiness from the experience. He looked to Celeste, who was serene as a statue and totally undisturbed. Meanwhile, he was still trying to catch his breath and quell his trembling.

Sean suddenly doubled over like he was in pain. Celeste snapped to his side instantly. "You okay?"

Sean's dog tags banged against his chest as he squinted up at her. 'It's okay. Strange sensation. A tunnel of voices just exploded in my mind. I—"

Celeste felt his head with her delicate hands, pushing back his ruffled hair as though examining him for a sickness. "That would be Thorn. He is reaching to you. The transition to my galaxy must have triggered his presence. You need this, Sean. I will leave you because it needs to just be you two.

He would see me as an intruder. The language you speak is secret. That is the bond between pilot and ship." And before Sean's outstretched hand could catch her fingers, she was gone.

Sean could feel the threads in his mind netting and begin furthering as he found his neural pathways firing and re-growing into other vestiges he never knew existed. He seemed to have developed a bond with the ship and it was like being connected to some super intelligence, a great power.

Feelings of euphoria washed over him. Celeste was right. He needed this; he needed it like he never thought he would need something. It was a primaeval call calling him. There was more than language here; there were memories.

Sean felt a pang of irony. By leaving him this legacy, Sean felt that the gap between him and his father's absence slightly shorten. Sean couldn't believe that this was his alone and that his father made it all happen. Funny, he had to be dead to do something right for a change.

Sean leant back feeling rather like a cowboy when his hand brushed against something stashed alongside the chair. He dove his hand down and grasped a package, not neatly wrapped he did note.

Once unwrapped, he held in his lap a gun, but no ordinary gun; this was something else entirely. Sean's eyes lit up like he had just opened the best Christmas present ever.

"Father, you couldn't have. You-you didn't!" It was a Decanter, one of the rarest guns made in humanity's history and one of the shortest lived. In fact, to his knowledge, the entire line was said to be destroyed, burned out of existence. But somehow his father had saved this from the scrap heap and now it was his. As he brought it up to his eye, a note fell onto his lap.

"Sean.... for the battle" And that was all the note read. Sean wasn't sure what it meant but either way, he was eternally grateful. He gave his piece of mastery a kiss, feeling like he was on a high.

"Celeste, are there others like Thorn?" asked Sean as Celeste re-entered and was informed of Sean's discovery.

"Of course, but they tend to stay hidden." Celeste spun in her chair, examining the gun like it were a weird complex device.

"What do you mean?" Sean took the gun away from her; her lack of handling perturbed him.

"It's only when the first pilots tried to take control that people began to realise these weren't ordinary ships. Terrible…backbleed."

"What is blackbleed?"

"Trust me, you don't want to know. But for the most part, these creatures were peaceful. They didn't pose any harm so we kept them, unsure of where they came from or why. We didn't really ask any questions. We needed all the allies we could get, what with the war and all."

Sean's interest piqued. "The Generation War, right?" Aunt Mayes had explained on the subject but only lightly.

"Right. The war between the Taroks and the Gaul that spilt out on to every other race. Backbleed tended to happen to pilots who did nothing but stay with their ship. It became a co-dependence. In the end, the flood of memories and sensations felt by the ship bled onto the pilot and being too much for the brain to handle cause backbleed. It's like being insane."

"And you let me bond with this ship knowing that danger?"

For the first time, Sean looked at Celeste with anger. Why had she allowed him this great thing if there was a risk he could end up raving mad?

"You won't. You're different. The others were weak-minded. You aren't."

"Well as much as I admire your faith in my strength of mind. I would have preferred to have known about backbleed before now."

Sean left Celeste alone. Celeste tried to grab at him but he ignored her.

What harder truth is there than one's lack of ability to keep up the lie?
—Unknown Archives

On Jelec, a beautiful world of grass fields and pristine lakes, the Corr race experienced the loss of their leader the Sultan Sesnar. This death was not addressed with grief but rather elation that a domineering tyrant had finally bit the dust.

Under the rule of Sultan Sesnar only hardship prevailed. Many of the people felt his wrath, but no one more than his own blood. Now that he was gone, some manner of order descended among the people. This is also allowed any staggering for power to fall into the cracks opening up in the ranks.

The Corr race were strange in appearance with their overly large almond eyes and felt tip nose. Corr children were designated one of four Prosper Tattoos when born.

Prosper Tattoos were a way of classing each of the person's prosperity, which to them was a way of cultivating their life and ambition. Given to them at birth Corr were branded with the tattoo by Acid Quill Tip their cord said to still be springy.

Some say the pain to be great but babies thankfully never remember the procedure. Once they are branded they bare all the virtues and gifts that went along with being either Sharp of Mind, Kind of Heart, Caring of Soul, or Tranquil of Thought.

The flower was so gentle, so unflinching. Lolalia hoped to mimic its flawless nature. Face and flower looked toward the Siren Moons drawn to the celestial glow emitted.

Designated the Siren Moons the unusual satellites of the planet were notorious for luring ships in and devastating them upon their rocks, creating a debris ring around the moons.

Lolalia knew only too well the sting of the Muskar flowers that dangled so close to her face. "Come, sister!" one called Nadia shouted out. "You have been out there for ages."

"Be there in a minute," she called out.

Lolalia continued to lean on top of the sill, gazing up at the moons; the Muskar flowers touching her skin yet not producing their usual sting. “One day, I will find you, Mother.”

Many mysteries surrounded the function of the Siren Moons, their allure and their power, but it was undeniably there and no one dared to question it.

Lolalia headed inside the palace and closed the windows. Her four other sisters were only half of her blood. She was full blood and yet she always felt out of place with them, and in fact at the palace.

She felt it a sort of jealousy, that they shunned her for being so beautiful and so pure.

They knew the truth see: she was more than just pure of blood. But pure of heart and full of kindness for she was designated Prosper Tattoo—Kind of Heart. It made her very desirable amongst the males and fierce competition to any other female.

Over the years she had grown accustomed to her sisters’ resentment and consistent bullying, but that didn’t mean it hurt any less each assault. Dinner was eaten in silence as usual when… “Still gazing at those moons, sis?” said Val, the oldest and perhaps snarkiest of them all. “Like some loon on the streets.”

Lolalia delicately placed her fork and knife down to better reply to her sister. “They are beautiful, aren’t they?”

There was a smattering of laughter before Val talked again with increased animosity. “How can one love anything so freakish?”

“I am not a freak!” Lolalia said it under her breath but all the sisters could hear her.

Val was on her feet before Lolalia could return to her now cold meal. “Yes you are. I meant the moons. But now that you say it you are a freak. A freak of nature.”

The one called Nadia went to grab Val by the elbow but she wrenched it free. “No, Nadia. Let her speak. We all would love to hear what dear sister has to say.”

Now in the spotlight, Lolalia slowly rose to her feet rather shakily. She looked around and then caught a picture of her mum—her staring with those loving eyes—and she found an ember of courage. “Val, Nadia, Crescent, Macey. You are sisters to me yet you do not treat me as a sister. All I have ever wanted was to belong, but you deny me what I desire.”

“And what’s that?” said Val, the storm of rage swirling in her eyes as sarcasm bit away at her remark. She had always had a temper.

“Love. Acceptance. Family.” There were only sincerity and genuine longing in her voice.

Donning the Prosper Tattoo Kind of Heart, Lolalia was indeed gifted with great kindness but also cursed with turbulent emotions of empathy and compassion, which wasn’t always a good thing.

The sisters erupted in laughter and left the table. Lolalia stood there, head down and feeling broken.

The late Sultan Sesnar, in fact, had many people conspire to kill him. It wasn’t really a surprise that one day an attempt on his life would become successful. One should always have the respect of his people, not their hatred.

The Sultan had many twisted secrets within his family. He loved his granddaughters overly for a grandfather. The Sultan's perversity and gross adherence to life's pleasures made him the dead man he was today. He had become so engrossed in life's luxuries that he neglected to see the vipers forming around him.

Over the course of several months, the Sultan ate his soup, unaware of the toxins dumped into his bowl until the day of his death. His granddaughters had had enough of his un-grandfatherly ways and lurid touches. Lolalia had no idea that her sisters had conspired and carried out the death of their grandfather. Would she feel sad for the man who had robbed her of her childhood—of her mother?

In the Pits, located on a transportation asteroid in a dingy cell, Lavinia Crotch slowly knitted her umpteenth weaved rope using the bits of fabric she gathered over the years.

She had tossed back and forth thoughts on how to use the rope: to escape the cell or to escape her nightmares indefinitely. But the latter was never considered because she knew that was the cheater's way out. She needed to live, to be there for her daughter, to find her. Or her daughter find her. She was coming. She could feel it like a sixth sense overcoming her fears.

As always the Pits remained a dark and wet hell. The smell of mould lingered with the scent of death. She had been incarcerated for well over nineteen years now.

She should have been oppressed by now, have no fleeting hopes of possible escape but still, she fought. She still weaved her rope that she prayed would pry the bars apart. She still had hope, tattered as it was. And yet in the Pits, such woes were not considered, as most were trapped within the nightmares of their own poisoned minds.

Lavinia glanced up sharply as she heard the scuffling of feet. A guard stood there gloating through her bars, tinkering with a prod in his hands. She hid her rope just as he started jingling the keys. "Come now, 427, you know that we have to search. It comes with no satisfaction. Well, maybe a little. You know the procedure 427," he said, referring to her number rather than her name—a demeaning tact—and pushed her flat against the wall. No one here had an identity. They weren't people. They were just numbers; a long line of prisoners who had no rights, no form of individuality. It broke some and took the lives of others.

The guards that entered the cell each carried a prod—deadly electrical sticks that with enough pliancy could render a person unconscious or even cause severe burns. The guards were human, but the vilest humans imaginable; the crud of the shit bucket. They had surpassed slavery but in exchange had lost anything close to humanity. For them, the extra coin in their pockets and possession of the most notorious prison complex in the universe was reward enough.

The prod was painful but at least not as painful as the binders that actually singed the hairs underneath. Lavinia felt so disgusted propping herself against the wall, but if she did not comply matters would be worse.

Lavinia allowed them to upturn her bed mattress; she allowed them to disrobe her and search every crevice. They luckily bypassed the tile and hidden compartment she visualised in her mind's eye.

Lavinia hid her sigh with a quickly placed hand. The guard threw her around. "Now you have two choices: one, you pleasure each of us, or you receive nice jolts from our prods like last time," he snarled, his face so close to hers she wanted to flinch or puke from the putrid smell.

She tried hard not to cry out but tears streamed down her face anyway. "I asked you a question!" said the guard and backhanded her so hard that she was thrown to the floor with a satisfying crack. She was sure she broke her wrist. Lack of nutrition and proper food meant all muscle and bone were less than optimal.

"Over here," suddenly implied his counterpart before the hulking man could turn over a whimpering Lavinia. He had found the loosened stone. Lavinia felt the ground drop from underneath her. They had discovered it: the entirety of her labour. "Looks like our rat here has been sneaking in some prohibited goods."

The humans that ran the Pits chose a life of indiscretions and a filthy existence. Some speculated that they were, in fact, devoid of humanity, that it had been burned out of them through years of gluttony and greed and become something else entirely.

They held onto that attitude of superiority because if they truly saw themselves for what they really were, they would see nothing but cowards.

Lavinia knew now that she was in a worse situation than five minutes ago. The prods sparked dangerously close. She held onto what hope she had and onto the sheet over the upturned mattress, managing only a strangled sob.

Lavinia was numb to their attacks. It was only a body. She didn't care for the physical; she knew that what was important was left untouched and kept hidden. She was Caring of Soul and as such knew that she had the power in the end; she had the power to not succumb to them. Stay strong inside however the soul tendered to shake.

Lavinia heard the clang of the door. She returned to her shabby upturned bed and wrapped herself in the sheet. In this hole of hell and torture, she was still content; she was still holding onto something. Her daughter.

She cast her mind back to her little face wrapped in a blanket moments before unceremoniously being ripped out of her arms by her own father. She knew she was out there, and she knew she would find her because the Old Timer demanded it. And because if she didn't believe that she truly would be better off dead and cast a wary glare at her failed accomplishments.

"Bless the Old Timer. Give me the strength to hold on. She will come. Please, with the aid of the moons, bring her to me." She didn't cry, she didn't do anything but wait for the onslaught of the next session of hallucinogen gases.

What is it about life that makes us run? Is it the size? Is it the journey that we must take or is it the end we fear; the fact that one day we will all cease to exist, or is it possible that there is a beyond to the end, that we continue never-ending and this is but the next step?—Unknown Archives

The men in black had come at night. Mayes had no choice but to let them take her in her sleepwear. She was taken to the Parliament, hooded like she would really have forgotten where the seat of evil lived.

The man came in like a slithering snake. "You must have faith. Belief. You must be a woman of great courage too if you are here in between the teeth of the lions and the claws of the dragons."

Mayes tried hard to hide her nervousness but her shaking legs and tapping fingers gave her away. The man sat down, deliberately scraping the chair backwards slowly. He folded his fingers on top of the table and stared at her with a stupid grin.

"Here to whittle me to nothing then?" Mayes looked away and continued to drum her fingers on the table and bite her bottom lip.

"You know who I am?" He said his representation somehow local news.

"I know you. Zias Zechariah Davis." She couldn't hide the conceit in her voice "A man my nephew was kind enough to warn me about."

Zias feigned interest. "How is Sean?"

Mayes did not answer, knowing she was probably giving away too much already. She neatly tucked away her hands. "Hardly a boy anymore."

Zias and Sean had a history. They fought in the war together till a falling out one day. Zias ended up somewhere for a long time and hoped nothing more than to exact his revenge upon the one man who deserved it. "Your nephew…? Quite the adventurer, I hear. Is he around?"

Mayes knew he was hinting at something. He didn't have to clarify further. She straightened all of a sudden, trying to look innocent but failing entirely. "No. And I don't think he will be making the trial."

"Oh, that is a pity. But I think we have bigger things to fry, don't you think?" What was he getting at? He was a stout man with a balding hairline. He stood and began pacing up and down. Always on edge. "You know, I tried to let things lie with Sean but, you know, he has always been stubborn."

"You never would let it go. You could never accept that he was doin his duty. That you got caught and paid the price for it. It always drove you crazy."

Zias slammed his hands down, making Mayes jump in her seat. "Oh, I don't think I am the one in the wrong here. I have made ends meet. And for Sean, wherever he is he can't run for long."

Mayes became tight-lipped.

Suddenly Zias was summoned away and when he returned his demeanour was different. "We see no reason to keep you here. You are free to go."

Mayes went to leave and heard the voice of Zias behind her. "But remember, we have endless resources at our disposal. If he is out there, we will find him and even a trial will seem like cake after what we put him through."

The winding paths of the mind are as mysterious as the roads through the stars
– Unknown Archives

Eric, a.k.a. The Maker, knew about recombinant DNA, molecular cloning, and gene splicing the minute cells of life, but he knew not how to live; he knew nothing of living. His entire existence was dedicated to creating abominations, a patchwork family to make up for the one he lost.

For the longest time, he worked to the bone. His work was his life. You could say he worked his life away. He was old, already sprouting white hair, yet he was focused and brilliant to the point of evil. But he knew not his wrongness. He knew not that he was bad. He was in that sense delusional.

He was nothing special. He was only an ordinary human. Through isolation, he became detached and did things most certainly inhuman in the pursuit of greatness. But how can one see the wrongness when sheltered from prying eyes?

He had a friend, one singular friend that he himself created—his counterpart Charlie, an AI construct who was his only companion save for his degrading mind. Though he was a genius he was also quite mad, for both usually occur side by side. "So, Charlie my friend, what stories do you have for me today?"

Charlie harrumphed knowing what his master was asking and what he would answer with. It was the same question day after day, part of some sort of dementia he thought.

"Well, my master, I have the story of your wife and children. Do you wish to hear it?" He asked in modesty, fully knowing the answer.

"I don't think I have heard that one. Please do."

Every day Charlie had to rewrite what really happened to his wife and children as the reality was too ghastly for his frail mind to comprehend. And every day Eric believed that they were okay, that they were safe somewhere in the universe and that he wasn't the devil of the story that irrevocably ended their lives.

His sanity broke now he would never stop. He would keep at it, creating, splicing and integrating DNA because that's all he saw, day- in day- out in his mind.

He had a vision but it was poisoned from the moment of conception. He believed he was a tinkerer of life, making his toys like soldiers. Everyone was made of DNA; it was the source of everything that we saw and felt and he saw through many of its guises, right down to its single-celled potential.

Surrounded by his vials and tubes, Eric worked at a fast pace. He was a brilliant scientist but he knew not how to keep himself from straddling the edge of insanity. It was like a disease eating away at his mind day by day.

He needed them; he needed a family because he had forsaken his own. Somewhere inside Eric knew; he had that gaping hole that told him something was terribly wrong.

Eric sustained his youth through the means of a Regenerative Pod he had acquired through unconventional methods. That's why he had not died of old age yet, but it held onto him like an irritant cloak. The effects unfortunately without the aid of a Weave were not enough to protect him from ageing completely. Eventually, even he would succumb to death, but a good few hundred years more than a mere mortal.

The large canisters that held the maturing bodies of semi-formed Raiders surrounded him in his dingy lab. They were like a horrid freak show display, yet it did not deter him in the slightest. They seemed to smile at him, call him, and thank him for giving them life.

He had overturned about 10 million manufactured Raiders and unleashed them onto the universe fully knowing they would have the ability to convert as many people as they saw fit. It was hard to grasp that this old man was the epicentre of such unspeakable evil. But was he really evil or simply misguided and in mourning?

The Siren Moons were well known in the Angelic System. The moons were delicately named Siren because of the human story. Beautiful women who would wail and sing their alluring songs to the wayward seaman who could not help but fall prey to their beauty. In the end, it was their demise as well. The Siren Moons were alike. They emitted a low frequency that lured most ships toward them and nearing the magnetic fields would tear ships apart.

Down below on the crimson planet Risk, nearing the planet Jelec, there were old cities unlike those of the glittering planet Vern. Unlike the pristine look of the cities on Vern, these cities were boarded. They were aged and dilapidated. They were the colour of red rust and many windows were broken or boarded. There were no signs of people. "This city's gone to the dogs," muttered Hariot, tufting dirt with his foot. "What happened here?" he asked, miffed.

Jathmoora picked up a ragdoll, its face cracked. "War. The Generation War to be specific.

This was a Gaul outpost before the local systems seized it. It is still running, if not a little slow," she said. The two looked up as the skies lit with fireworks. "The Siren Moons. So, the Mistress has ensnared yet another one."

Hariot was a biologist, a lover of plants and a maker of medicine. He had his own hydroponics bay. Making medicines with breakthrough plants was his job aboard the city/ship Mystic.

His appearance was at first startling. He looked so…well, alien. He had three sets of nostrils, gleaming eyes that had membranes instead of eyelids, and long encompassing fingers; his skin was mottled and seemed to have the ability to blend into the background, though he had not mastered the ability fully, tending to half shift to the background with one limb still his natural color.

He would on occasion wear clothes when viewed in public to better acclimatize to everyone's ideas, but he was used to running around the ship naked. He was the kindest, humblest creature around. His race was known as Jubulark, meaning "unknown" and they were considered unsociable almost hostile, if one was to go by the rumours.

Jubulark was a made- up term given to something they knew nothing about. He was very different to the rumours. He was kind, which flew in the face of everything his race was known for: tyranny, violence and dominance. Their whereabouts were just as unknown as their entire history.

Jathmoora was half alien, half human. This she knew. She also knew the disdain that people generated when faced with a half human half alien. The humans distrusted any alien and the aliens thought humans disgusting—dirt. So, belonging neither there nor here, she cultivated herself a ship by detaching one of the sections from the Hub.

She had peculiar traits, like bone encasing braces that encapsulated her hair. Her face was angled differently than a mere human, sharp edges and no real softness. She had been a performing sorceress for a good ten years when a blossoming romance with a monk left her diminished and slightly broken. But she was not without her flame, the rekindled ember that blazed in her heart.

Interspecies relationships were frowned upon. Some said that the diluting of an alien with a human would sully the strong genes of the alien species and bring only disease and weakness to them. Aliens were viewed as superior. Humans were the bottom of the food chain and to taint the line with human DNA was viewed as abominable.

Jathmoora knew what they all said behind her back on the Hub. They called her 'scourge'. They hated her and viewed her as weak. Only when she displayed her full powers did they back off and instead of hating her, feared her. She had no place to go but away. There was no place for her at the Hub, with their closed minds and irrespective ideas.

A strong voice can often be triumphed by the many whispers of the weak
—Unknown Archives

Ivan's bloated body was later found by the scout ships scouring the site. "Home base, this is Scout Ship 1. We have found what appears to be the remains of one Ivan Hobb. It doesn't look pretty, madam. He is burnt to a crisp."

A curt voice echoed throughout the ship. "Well, lucky for us, we don't care about pretty. Now retrieve the body before the Parliament sends their hounds."

The scout ship's light turned and hit the body of something else. Revolving around in space, the face turned to them and the pilot yelled rather girlishly. "Ah, home base."

Ivan's inept body tumbled in space before large, pincer-like claws scooped him up. "Dr Rain, we have him, but there is something else here," he said. "It's another body, madam. But it is unlike anything I have ever seen."

"Perfect. Retrieve that too. Meet you at the rendezvous point. Rain out."

It was raining. The doors swooshed open and red heels stepped out, the drops of rain lingering on Stella's shoes.

The corpse was encased in a special glass. Upon closer inspection, the skin could be seen. It was scorched but somewhat intact.

"Looks like we have our work cut out for us, boys," said Rain.

Her pointy heels clickity-clacked into the room. She stopped and turned towards the second case. "This one first." She ran her hand over it as though reading it. "Arrangements can be done for Mr Hobb once we have started. He will be given a respectable funeral and remembered as a patriot to humanity."

Though she said them, the words sounded dry and without context.

Welkin: a world of wonder, mystery and grace. Within the glowing clouds were city structures upon rock pinnacles, unlike anything Sean had seen before.

These structures were called Empyreans and there were many scattered throughout the world's great sea. The pinnacles were crowned with a fanning nest of forest trees. It was beautiful to look at, as the roots draped around the pinnacles snaking their way down toward the water.

"Your world is beyond anything," Sean said. "It is...magnificent."

"Be careful of the—"

Before Sean could do anything, a flock of Seraph males equipped with golden spears flew up to the ship, directing Sean to a platform. They were buff and golden like gods. Sean felt rather mundane compared to these flights of fancy.

"Do not be alarmed. They are our warriors—Seraphs. They will guide us to a landing platform."

Like he had anything to worry about. He had a whole bloody spaceship.

There were certain factions that constructed the race's echelon: The Elders, the oldest, The Seraphs, the younger and more proud males, and the women, the more subdued Angels.

Seraphs, the warriors who patrolled the skies, watched for hunters. Sometimes they could take down an entire ship, but they would have to be in numbers and heavily armed.

Thorn made it to the lower atmosphere of Welkin with a few encouraging warning gestures from the big puffed up Seraphs. Even up here Sean noticed the amazing luminescence of the clouds. He hadn't died and still found heaven.

As he descended as instructed he saw how everything was tinged in gold, bathed in a warm light. He saw the platform and made for it.

"Over there! That's the one, the one with the kinks," Celeste said excitedly. It seemed that she was happy to be home even though she had been dreading it all this time.

Sean stepped out onto the lowering ramp, stroking his Decanter, the exhaust sending plumes of mist around him. The bold Seraphs made way for landing and did so with grace and precision. Before Sean had time to assess the situation, Celeste came tumbling out the ship and jumped into the open arms of handsome males just dying to get a hold of her.

Sean teased his gun a bit more when someone approached him. He wasn't sure what to make of all this. The young nubile men or the fact that Celeste was all over them faster than a spreading rash.

The man was in a robe and Sean couldn't detect any overhangs such as wings but he did see a hand extended towards him. Sean waited before shaking it.

Just as the man pulled back his hood, Celeste came over. "Sean, this is Shartoon."

"Uh, I have heard of you."

There was an awkward silence then Shartoon's oaky voice rang out. "All things good, I hope. Celeste, who is this gentleman?"

"This is Sean Caleb. He is my partn—" But before she could finish, one of her Seraph buddies grabbed her and pulled her up into the sky.

"Fly with us, Celeste. We have missed you."

Sean looked back to Shartoon. "So…" Sean balanced on his toes and then back down again, hooking his fingers into his belt.

"Yes, indeed." Shartoon placed his hood back on and made to leave. Sean assumed to follow.

Celestial Beings had a religion: they worshipped the stars of the sky, saying that they were gods themselves to be revered. Sean had the fun task of listening to Shartoon talk about it all night.

Eventually, the discussion came around to the topic of the Old Timer, the said oldest star in the universe. This perked Sean's ears and roused him from his slumbering stupor.

"It is said the Old Timer is located in a flexural part of space. It is also said that the star is our salvation, that it will have all the answers we have been asking from the dawn of time. Some say it is even sentient."

Now Sean had heard it all. Sentient ships and now sentient stars. He wasn't sure if he could take on all these "beliefs"—or bullshit rather.

"Alas, we forbid our kind from seeking out the Old Timer. We believe secrets should stay secret, which is why we stay in the catacombs cataloguing every detail of our making. No one should know the mysteries that make them mysterious. What would be the point?"

Sean looked to Celeste and she had her head down. He knew how she felt about Shartoon. This must have been a sharp reminder. He wanted to go over to her and comfort her but he knew such displays would bring the attention of Shartoon or worse, the sharp spears of her buff comrades who hadn't desisted with their dagger-like stares.

The world that is heaven is not on our Earth but far away in the interlacing stars we look to every night—Unknown Archives

The dinner continued well into the morning—at least it seemed like morning. Sean couldn't tell with it being so golden all the time. After a while, the glistening columns and warmth grated him. It had somewhat lost its appeal since the frosty entourage. It was still amazing but he longed for his own bed on his own ship under his own rule.

Sean felt like he had already overstayed his welcome. He did however like seeing Celeste so happy. He was just jealous of the puffed- up peacocks around her like a harem of men.

He had never met anyone like her before. Granted, she was another species but that didn't matter—not to him anyway. It made her more special and he wanted her all to himself. That made him selfish but it also made him determined and focused.

Sean pulled away from becoming overrun with emotion and instead reached for some dried beef to better discourage his nagging jealousy that urged him to stroke his decanter more fervently.

Just as Sean was about to bite a piece, someone nudged him, seeing that he was an off-worlder. "That is Belarith Skin. It is the hide of the flying Drasks that grace our skies," said the man with a flaky smile. "They need constant shedding for their new skin."

Sean stopped there and then, dropping the not-jerky and instead sticking to the succulent fruits he at least knew were of less conspicuous origins.

Shartoon's wise old voice wafted toward him and he had to stifle another onset of yawning.

"The Old Timer is so old we think it is the first star to be created. Back in creation stars were young but through age, we think that this star has developed layers. It has become something else." For someone who shunned his people from undergoing the Rite, he sure went on about it a lot thought Sean.

"And that brings us to the Rite of Undula, and the fact that that Rite is forbidden because venturing out to the stars to find the oldest star is foolhardy. There are more hunters out there than we can point a spear at, and to break the mystery would be like breaking our religion. That is why there will be no more discussion about the passage."

Shartoon was protesting about undertaking the quest and yet everything he said made Sean want to undertake the rite. Sean and Celeste exchanged a stare. Anyone caught in between would have caught fire.

After dinner, Shartoon caught up and somewhat cornered Celeste. "We thought that the hunters had gotten to you, but I must say that was your fault. You are so young and naïve at times. Did you really think that you could undertake the passage without my knowledge?" he said rather derisively.

Despite the disdain in his voice, Celeste chose to answer quickly and precisely. "I do not pretend to hide it, Shartoon," she quipped fierily, "but you forget I am not a teenager. I am nearly one hundred folds old. And you are not my father!'"

Seeing Celeste in distress Sean intervened. But Celeste took off and as he broke out into a wild run after her. Shartoon's large body blocked his path. Shartoon paid concentrated attention to Sean, a mean scientist upon an ant.

He disclosed snappily, "A human. Never thought Celeste would stoop so low as to ensnare such insipid company."

That was it. Sean had had enough of this blathering man. Before he could stop himself, he was grabbing for his gun, but Shartoon began to laugh and that halted his attempt. "Ah, at last, the human shows us why we disdain the likes of them!"

Huffing and puffing, Sean chose to holster his gun and instead continued to run after Celeste, promising himself to finish what he had started here.

Back at the Parliament, the heads talked amongst themselves like chatty cockatoos.

"You can't hope to think that we can keep this under wraps! The people of Earth have a right to know..."

Bradshaw took a prominent step forward, causing Harold's moustache to quiver in protest.

Harold held a hand. "No need to be pushy about it, Bradshaw. The people will know something. But you can't expect them to easily digest everything that we have held back? We have held back the gates and what you're proposing will crash them down, and possibly cause more havoc than that which you hope to prevent."

Harold always had a way with heavy- handed words. He was a preacher but to Bradshaw that was hardly worth an ounce of respect. Words needed meaning, power, not empty promises or delayed threats. And that was all he was doing: unexpectedly thwarting him with mesmerizing sentences. Whatever happened to just trusting people with the truth? He swallowed what Harold had to say but he did so with no such pleasure.

"Perhaps when you are older and wiser you will come to understand the great responsibilities we have to undertake in order to preserve one's race."

As if engulfed with great ego, a smirk worked Harold's chubby features.

Dr Stella Rain. Leading scientist in Xenology. She had an abundant history with Harold behind closed doors. No one dared risk asking her about her sordid past with the great leader, unless one wanted a scolding stare that could render the most composed man to a puddle. She had a reputation for her harshness and her fidelity with men.

Stella was a self-proclaimed cougar. She could not help herself; it was her drug. She had lost her youth that seemed short-lived, and was now entering the idea of younger men simpering at her heels.

Most people would talk to her with their eyes firmly glued to the ground. No one dare meet her fiery gaze. Stella Rain was one of Earth's leading minds. She had brilliance. She had too. She was a scientist, but that also meant she lacked compassion at times. And that led to one of the ghosts of her past resurging in her dreams.

"Ms Rain?" quibbled a young pimply- faced scientist who had popped one too many pimples. Hearing the meek voice, Stella Rain tiresomely looked at him, causing her spectacles to slide down her nose a bit.

Upon recognition of this young boy, a small smirk worked her rigid features, sending the boy into fits of giggles.

"Pray tell, what may I do for you uh ...?"

"N-Nathan."

"Ah, Nathan. What is on your mind?"

There was something flirtatious about the way she talked, moved and tilted her head to the side.

"The p-preliminary tests have come back. We found something of interest. The burnt corpse may be vampiric. What we have ascertained solidly is that it appears to have a sex—female."

"Did you know that this is a top- secret project funded under the Parliaments' nose? Now I know that what we do is important but it is best we keep these fun little facts to ourselves. Don't you agree, Nathan?"

By this time Stella had her long red nailed finger under Nathan's quivering chin.

Nathan gulped in acknowledgement.

When in doubt about the right path forward, look back at the prints left on the path behind—Unknown Archives

Sean had managed to find his steps in between the boughs of one of the many great twisting trees that made the Nest Forests. It was a funny feeling balancing in the cradle as wispy clouds skirted the balls of his feet.

Celeste assured him he would not fall, but he grasped her outstretched hand nevertheless, always wanting an excuse to touch her soft porcelain skin.

Celeste leaned against a trunk, lightly letting go of him as beautiful flowers dangled near her face. There was light here: a soft dim glow that highlighted her demure features— defining them even more than they already were, if that were possible. She looked every bit the goddess, as her hair and feathers were illuminated by a glowing halo.

"Sean, I can't say how sorry I am."

Sean pretended like he wasn't enthralled by her beauty with a slight shrug of his shoulders. "The man seems to have it in for me," he said, recalling the matter.

Sean had to tell her he was sorry, even if deep down he wasn't. The man was her family after all. The man had said one too many insults. He didn't mean to hit him and break his nose. Sean had then been banished from the interiors of the Empyrean City instead finding refuge on his ship or here where no one would find them together.

"For the longest time, we have seen humans as…well, a sort of vermin race." Celeste averted her eyes. She didn't like talking about his race like that because it was like she was talking about him like that.

Seeing her discouragement, Sean gripped her fingers, interlacing them with his. "It's not your fault. It's your upbringing—I mean, it's not that you have a bad upbringing. I mean to say, you don't know things…I don't mean to say you're stupid or anything—"

Celeste looked serious for a minute and then her face cracked into a wide smile and the unease dispelled between the two. "You're so cute when you're nervous. Is that what I make you, nervous?" Now she was being coy.

Sean started to feel a hot flush prickling his face as well as other sensations. Why did it have to be so damn warm here? "How long you've known Shartoon anyway," he said, hoping the change of subject would cool him without the quick access to a cold shower.

"I've known Shartoon all my life. He was there to lecture me, criticize me. He is an Elder and as such requires respect from Angels such as me and Seraphs alike. As an Angel, it is my duty to be dainty and look after the Seraphs like we are bound housewives. But I never had my feet on the ground; I was always looking up, toward the heavens."

"You don't like him, do you?" he said.

"No, not really, but I tolerate him. In fact, he kind of is like a father to me since my own father died a while ago."

"Oh, I am so sorry." Sean suddenly felt like a dick. How could he be so overly forceful to pry?

"Don't be. I hardly knew the man, so I guess I don't really have the right to mourn him."

Sean knew that feeling only too well. He never thought his tears were warranted when his father died.

Celeste continued on. "He is set in his Elder ways. But he is truthful about most things and for that, I listen to him. Then again, he can be wrong about a great many things as well."

Sean realized he was tilting and before he knew he was slipping. A quickly placed hand saved him from diving off into the clouds. This action brought Sean and Celeste nose to nose as the sun rays peeked through the foliage.

A strange array of fluttering bird-like creatures passed over them. Both enjoyed their blissful moment as they melted into one another, intertwined as one within the boughs, their lips meeting at long last and meshing together as a parade of birds burst out from the surrounding leaves.

No one knew where they had disappeared to. Sean and Celeste spent the rest of the day inside the Nest. They forgot about the world outside and lived in their own. All they did was a kiss but it was enough—too much—and Sean was afraid where it might lead. And this was too good- a- thing to ruin with his raging hormones.

The horns sounded and alerted Celeste to join the world outside. As Sean came out of the shrubbery, teasing out twigs that had found their way into his hair, there was the cold reception of the house of Ballast and many sharp, sharp spears pointed at him. Shartoon stood in the middle with a hard face and crossed over arms.

"Come, my child. We have some duties to attend to," he said as he swung a wide arm around Celeste, breaking Sean's contact with her and leaving him to the mercy of the jealous Seraphs.

Sean hurried after her but the spears made it difficult to pursue. Shartoon turned back just in time to say, "Not you, boy. This is a family business."

Sean twisted his tongue around and managed a slightly bitter, "No problem." He made way back to his docked ship, noting the bandage across Shartoon's now broken nose and let out a small laugh.

"You don't understand, Shartoon! He is different. He isn't like the other humans. He is strong."

"Of course he is different because you have love blinding your eyes. He is a man with one idea in mind. You should have stayed here. You should have listened to me!" he shouted.

Celeste was taken aback. He had never shown this much anger before. "Is this really about me or is it about my mother?"

Shartoon stopped ranting and sank onto the edge of the bed. He straightened his hood and turned around so he was staring straight at Celeste. "I don't know what you are talking about." He feigned ignorance but Celeste knew him better than that.

"You know exactly what I am talking about." By now Celeste was in front of Shartoon, blocking him from the door. "When Father died you were there for Mother—a few too many times if you know what I mean. I am not your daughter and you can't tell me what to do! My mother cared for you—she did—but that doesn't automatically make me yours."

Shartoon felt his heart break. He had loved her mother and perhaps because that love was never reciprocated was the reason behind his disciplinary ways.

"She should have listened, too. You both are the same. Both of you be damned!"

With a flap of his cloak, he was gone. Celeste concealed what tears were running down her hot face but there were too many to hold back.

Bringing up her mother uprooted all of her buried emotions. Her mother's curiosity was what killed her. She went out one day and flew higher than the Seraphs to see the sky up in the ether. She was warned to fly lower but she continued and before anyone knew, she was skewered by a hunter's barbarous spear. In a vain attempt to seek revenge her father was stricken too and both plunged to the depths of the nadir.

Sean knew something was up when Celeste practically tackled him to the ground. "What is it?"' He clung onto her, feeling her shake. That bastard Shartoon had said something to upset her. He wanted to race out there and give him a piece of his mind and a revisit of his knuckles. But Celeste was so upset, he knew he had to stay here and console her.

"We have to leave. Now!"

The honeymoon was over. Reality had settled in between timed sobs from Celeste. "As you wish."

He stroked away a runaway tear and tucked it into her hair as he planted a kiss on her forehead. He would do anything for her; go to the ends of the universe for her, and he would make that trip twice.

With war there are causalities but without it, there are those who are thrown against each other in a vain attempt to justify that war is right—Unknown Archives

Stella leapt from foot to foot, drinking her umpteenth glass of scotch. Her heels were put up on the shelf and she danced around the office barefoot like a ditsy teenager. Memories started to swim to the surface thanks to the lubrication of ale. She held her head like the memories physically hurt her, or possibly it was the scotch taking its toll.

The forest was dark in northern Canada. More than bears were in these forests according to the locals, who reported seeing a strange silhouette up on the cliff, hearing it howling. Its chilling cries pierced the moonlit skies and terrified local villagers.

The unit was sent in to capture this legend, but when they got there they found something they weren't expecting. It was definitely something—something they couldn't identify. Only someone like Stella Rain, who was the only xenologist anywhere, could.

Week 1: personal log of Stella Rain

"Subject is sedated. We have identified it as the female of its species. Remarkable features: its elf ears, its small pink feathers. And, of course, the most striking of all: gargantuan white wings that broke the arm of one of the soldiers that brought her in. Blood samples and skin scrapings have been taken. The boys here have jokingly called her Natalie, named after Nick's ex who broke his nose. I am sticking to this title. Harold was wrong in thinking I would just slip away. Now I have proof. Proof that I wasn't wrong. Natalie is everything I have been working toward. She is the answer and I won't stop till I know everything."

End entry.

Week 5: personal log of Stella Rain

"Tests are continuing. Natalie does not want to talk or can't—we have yet to determine which. I want to know more. Her condition is deteriorating. She will not eat anything we give her. There is just not enough information without her talking to us. I wish she would just communicate. The things we could tell each other…"

End entry.

Week 8: personal log of Stella Rain

"It is a dark day indeed. After weeks of her refusing to eat or talk, a turn of events has left me with stained hands. I don't know what happened. There was no order, there was just.... Oh god, what have I done?"

Incomplete entry.

Personal log…deleting.

Personal log…deleted.

Stella had been so immersed in her flood of memories that she failed to notice the shards of glass now embedded in her hand. Blood oozed from the wound. She wiped her hand with a cloth and wound it tight.

She noticed the tears developing and wiped them away hatefully. She would not be weak. She would not let those memories rule her. She was Stella Rain. Need there be anything else said?

Kroden was a warrior once—a man of strength, a Gaul, and yet he was now ridiculed in Stations across the galaxy for leaving his rank. He left the fight and for it, he was a laughing stock.

He bore a visible scar clean cut across his left eye but the inner scars were the swirling turmoil in his gut.

Gaul were bigger and more muscular then Taroks, their sworn enemy. Gaul had flat noses with blue skin and wet looking blue locks that were usually shoulder length, common in most males.

Kroden sat at the bar on Station Alpha, drinking his sorrows away with each glass of Haldo Gin—a tonic alcohol beverage commonly known for its lurid properties.

He slipped further and further away from cruel reality. Kroden's vision started to swim as he focused on his own misery. Maybe another; just one more to subdue the emotions of ridicule and embarrassment.

Kroden reached the bottom of his glass. The unpleasing urine-looking drink sloshed over the sides as the alien bartender poured another. The taste was beautiful despite the piss appearance; hard liquor that could render a full Gaul unconscious within a few hours.

Station Alpha was alive with different races, pilots, traders and every assortment of life imaginable—often the crud beneath the fingernails but almost civil. Kroden flew back his last Haldo before passing out on the ground, thoughts leaving his brain as his listless mouth formed drool.

Most just left him making a wide circle. Everyone on the station knew about their recurring customer. Even though he still wore his armour, in their eyes he was no warrior, just a drunkard.

Kressangah had returned to the Order in shame and embarrassment. She had allowed Boris to get away with it, get too close to her, touch her.

The Order was an institute located in the crevice of a rogue planet devastated by meteors and stabilized into an oblong orbit around a nearby sun.

Anyone that came here were exiles and had nowhere else to go and nothing else to lose. They were dispensable and therefore made perfect assassins; either the job got done or they were cut down in their line of duty.

She had hoped to kill him and be done with it, but she only managed to escape with what honour she had left. She may as well have been shackled, haul the chain and ball that was the weight of her failure.

Kressangah did not like failure. She punched the passing wall to better vent her frustration and a crumbling indentation was left. Kressangah dragged her feet toward the large amber doors, her knuckles smarting. Opening them, the telltale squeaking alerted the human servants to vacate into their hidden chambers. They knew not to be seen unless commanded into the open.

She took a deep breath and removed the training sticks from a compartment. She would train until the sun set and her sweat dried.

The Live Wind was buzzing outside. Taroks knew to stay inside and the windows automatically erected force field shields to prevent being eaten alive, though it was a rare occurrence; Live Wind preferred corpses. Some vegetation still existed on the rock, but since the break from its original orbit, the lone rogue was a dangerous place to live. Every minute was perilous for numerous reasons.

The constant desire and need to work toward a complete moment of Serenity was every Tarok's dream—their inner goal, their inner conflict. They were agile creatures, though their fight with the Gaul race made them brittle-souled creatures that would not allow such enlightenment as Serenity to besiege them.

Taroks were rimmed around the head with crescents around the side of their faces, thin tendrils hanging off the sides. They had stripes along the rim. They had violet coloured eyes with colourful lids that were used to deter enemies. And they were small in stature. But when they moved, they were like snakes, able to bend to unbelievable feats.

Everyone knew about the Taroks' philosophy dribble and their Tarok tea blends. They liked to think they were superior because they were gifted with words and mixing herbs.

Kressangah stood in the middle of the empty arena, a large symbol etched into the grain. She knelt down and traced the outer edges of the symbol with her finger, the meaning impacting her deeply.

The sun bathed the room in a warm wash of light. The Live Wind was common on most arid worlds, minuscule bugs in the millions swarming at certain times of the day, but here it was magnified. They could hibernate when food sources were low, becoming solid inanimate objects, which was why they were in the billions.

She kept her head on her knee, the soft billowing curtains a small comfort. Yes, she had loved him, she thought angrily. Kressangah began training hard, forcing herself to her feet to better beat down her feelings with violent thrusts of her hand.

25

In the eye of the beholder true beauty springs; to the eyes of the ugly, only envy grows—
Unknown Archives

"Madam?" The lean silhouette of Stella Rain cast a shadow across the scientist tech. "The tests are conclusive. The creature is a blood drinker. From what we could analyse with what brain matter was left, she was in a state of complete madness, madam. No doubt she lost control of her shuttle and ploughed into the station, taking also the life of poor Mr Hobb."

Seeing that she was intended to show emotion, she quickly shrugged and shook her head in feigned dismay while fighting off a beating headache. "Yes, a poor loss that one. I will go over this data in the privacy of my office."

Sometimes when Stella Rain was alone in her office she would stare at the wilderness outside and wonder about Harold, wonder about the girl she used to be and if indeed that really was her.

She would never admit to the feeling of love. It was too soporiferous and hardly a thing to devote her time to. There was too much out there in the large universe to worry about such an insipid thing as love. She had a reputation to uphold after all. But sometimes she would just stand in front of the window and gaze out longingly, wondering what path she could have taken and whether indeed he paid her any mind.

Then like a lightning strike, she was back to her brittle self, shaking her head of the clogging thoughts. She took to her tumbler of scotch, the bitter resin taking her away from such turbulent thinking.

She was a heavy drinker ever since her departure from Harold and it was the only thing holding her together. She was a hard woman—she knew this. But why should she worry about emotion if she was so hard? Because she wasn't. Inside, way down where no light shone, she was that young girl who looked at men with starry eyes and hoped.

Harold had been in love once—a long time ago if memory served right. Stella was a beautiful woman. He loved her free spirit, her youth and vibrancy. They should have stayed together, should have been together forever, but somewhere in the haze of love, something else emerged. A mind heavy with other thoughts; domineering thoughts.

She was contacted and the next day she was working in a secret department on the research of alien life. He was heart-broken that she had taken that path but not much later he was given the opportunity to work for the Parliament.

He ascended higher and higher while Stella dropped to the floor. His regime ensured that she would never make a single discovery. And so that young love blossomed and died. Still, often he would sit at the window and wonder. Was she thinking of him? Was she happy? But the thoughts were short and held no substance, simply ripples in a puddle soon to turn to shadow.

Ring. Ring. Ring.

Stella Rain answered the plax in her hand. "Yes," came her curt voice.

"Stella?" The ice of her heart melted.

"Harold?"

"So, you haven't forgotten me completely?"

Stella held the plax close, absorbing his features. He had become bigger, rounder, yet she was hooked to every creased line. "What's the reason for the late call?" The clock landed on 12 a.m.

"Straight to business. That is why I chose you, Stella."

"Chose me? What are you choosing me for?"

"A project. A chance to finally not be held back, to see all that you have ever wanted."

Stella thought that perhaps her scotch had been a bad batch.

"Stella, are you still there?"

She cleared her throat. "Y-yes, I am. What do you propose?"

'Well, I have in my warehouse ships being constructed and in their last phase. Completion is soon. I have yet to choose a commander. The men picked need a leader to lead the Crusade through the rift."

"I thought you would have chosen someone else, someone—"

"Not completely competent and talented beyond compare."

Stella's voice hitched. "Okay, Harold. I'll bite, but if this is some kind of ruse or joke you won't be the last one laughing. I have become sharper in my dwindling days."

Stella imagined a smile.

"Glad to hear it, Stella."

The plax went blank and Stella couldn't feel her legs. She was numb. At last, she would be free to do what she always wanted but was never allowed. Whatever the reasons for this, she wasn't going to turn it down—not for all the gold in the world.

"Bradshaw!" The bellowing voice of Harold could be heard like thunder. Bradshaw was lit in half- light as he headed toward Harold, his head cast down. "Would you mind explaining this?"

Harold waved in his face a plax. A news link broadwaved all over earth about the conductors and their effects on the human mind.

"It is time the people knew."

"You think that you have control? Are you a leader? Because making things happen behind my back isn't leadership, its betrayal."

Harold wasn't humanity's greatest specimen. He only thought of blinding humanity from the truth. It seemed that no matter the issue, Harold always resolved it with his own quick fixes, never considering into the equation what was best for Earth.

"I am sorry, sir, but I believe that Earth has a right to know."

"And blowing apart their world and causing mass mayhem is good for them, now is it?" he said, trying hard not get too overwhelmed.

Bradshaw felt a wave of ice. "I guess not, sir. But the truth would have come out sooner or later."

Harold took the plax and smashed it underfoot.

Earth was deteriorating unless something was done soon. The core would burn out and reduce the planet to a cinder. Harold was just hastening the end. Humanity's future lay beyond in the stars. But Harold was so scared of facing the wrath of the aliens he had forced out of their galaxy he would rather hide in a corner. He knew they were waiting somewhere, contemplating their revenge on their wronged ancestors.

Harold never used to be so hell-bent on power. He once was a young man, many moons ago, and in love. But he soon became old and brittle. He didn't care about anyone anymore. He sat in his throne and no one could ever take that from him. A man moulded to its structure to be fossilized with the times.

Amidst the specs of dust coalescing in space, are memories, DNA, life of pasts, echoes forever—Unknown Archives

"Please, sir. This is the ship Mantra. Please come in…come in…sir, this is the Mantra."

All communications had ceased. Days passed into weeks and then weeks into months and the New Fleet were lost and without any rations, lost on the other side of the Rift—reserved too little more than a few crates of tasteless packs of Trite and Pork; all that could sustain them through the cold bitter space.

The one called Taylor shrugged in doubt. "What have we got, sir?"

Zias, who had become severely emaciated, held up two packs. "We have banana and beef, or pork and trite."

"Honestly, sir. Who made up these combinations? Someone with no taste buds, I'm guessing. Did the message get through or have we got too much interference?"

"No interference, Taylor. Whoever's on the other end just ain't picking up. I think we may be stranded here."

"Banana and beef."

Zias chucked Taylor the packet.

What was left of the fading man was now a withered husk, his receding hair now almost completely gone. The once stoic and bold man was now a blubbering mass reserved to the last of desperations. He dared not tell the others of how hopeless they really were.

This pale shadow had no strength of character. "Harold. This is Zias again. I hope you are getting this. Harold, you sorry sod. I know you sent us on a suicide run but please we are going to die here, all of us. Repeat: Zias Zechariah Davis requesting immediate extraction. The Mantra and all accompanying ships have failed to do as commanded and now are all inert. There is something different about these ships in this galaxy like they have their own calling—but you knew that already, didn't you, Harold? We are not in control of our ships and we are low on supplies. You bastard, I should have known better than to accept this mission. Repeat..."

Overcome by dehydration and impinging madness, Zias slumped over the console, unconscious, hands drooping over. The crew was defenceless and had no manner of hope caught in the ambience of the Siren Moons. Their calls were left unheard and became the corpses for the crows, the magnetics ripping the ships to shreds.

Zias came to consciousness rather rudely. The ships were listless hollowed husks floating in dead space. The consoles inside the Phantom sparked dangerously. The rest of the fleet was strewn across a wide section of space. All of his men, gone. "Taylor? Landon? Mack? Alistair?" But their blood was spattered everywhere and what had happened was painfully clear.

The ferocity of the ships tearing apart sang the obvious, and yet he remained alive. Why was he spared? "Computer, location?" But the computer was off-line, everything was dead and he was but a ghost in the twisted metals of the ship. Why was he spared? He deserved death more so than his comrades. Why would God—if indeed the creator existed—spare him from a life he no sooner deserved?

Harold leaned back in his chair. The signal disconnected and his rigid features were ever more prominent.

He steepled his fingers together, an ugly smile working his less than desirable features.

"It is for the best, Zias. It is the only way we can rise from the ashes." There was a knock at the door. "Come in."

The automaton named Carlton sat opposite Harold.

"We have lost communication with Zias and his team. Reiterate this to the public for me. 'In a valiant effort to make contact with life outside Earth, the New Fleet has been destroyed by the aliens that once shared our solar system. There have been no survivors. I plead with you to listen to us when we say we are better off alone then integrating with these so-called friends... We placed our trust in the ships they gave us and look what has happened? It was their ultimate deception. Give us vessels to make the journey only to have those gifts turn on us. Among the men sent was Commander Zias Zachariah Davis, one of our brightest. We plead you to listen to the Heads. WE are stronger united as one people. Yes, we lied to you but only to safeguard you all. All is not in vain, for we the Parliament have our own ships, and shall launch a Crusade through the stars to the place of our fallen brethren where sweet vengeance shall rain upon their sacrifice. We have enlisted the help of leading Xenobiologist Stella McCartney Rain. And though her humanity shall make its mark upon the universe.' Enact code 11-649. You are dismissed Carlton."

As though entrusted with some golden cup Carlton nodded fervently before being dismissed.

Harold had served out the New Fleets death sentences and he had no second thought on it. He didn't care anymore; all visages of humanity were gone, scoured from his soul. He would no sooner look upon them as insects. "It's alright to be the devil because the devil does what no man can: that which needs to be done." And he walked out the office ever self-involved.

Stella spent the next few days packing until she was left with only a few boxes of her personal effects. "It is done and dusted, I suppose." She looked at her office one last time and felt a pang of anxiousness. Could she do this? Was she able to take on the responsibility? The office lights dimmed and turned off for the last time.

A monster can recall the pain they've visited upon their victims by becoming a victim themselves – Unknown Archives

The blinding light was the first to hit his eyes. Then Zias felt the familiar sting of a hand smacking him hard across the cheek. He blinked, dumbfounded.

"Who are you!?" Her voice was so forceful.

Words seemed so foreign to him as he tried to speak. "I-I... am Z-Zias. My crew…we were… we were attacked."

"Yes, the moons are wrathful."

He looked up into her face and was taken aback. She looked...different? But his lack of strength prevented him from moving. He shivered as he discovered he was naked. Then he felt where plaster things had been glued onto him.

"Jathmoora, you can't do this."

Hariot sounded sincere enough but his words were whispers.

"Has the Hub sent their agent in the form of a haggard human?"

Hariot had feared this. All contact with the Choc-ra had caused Jathmoora major paranoia.

Zias felt so tired but just as he was lulled into a feeling of security he was rudely shocked back to reality. She was electrocuting him. Hariot backed away looking undeniably frightened.

"I asked you a question! Are you here to take me back—back to all the ridicule and laughing, to that cesspool they call civilization?"

Hariot couldn't believe what he was seeing, hearing, smelling. (charred flesh was less than pleasing)

Hariot couldn't stand witness any longer. He took a few steps forward and grasped Jathmoora by the forearm tightly.

"Jathmoora! No. He doesn't know anything. Didn't you hear? All his men are dead and he will soon follow if you don't stop now."

Jathmoora calmed for now but the storm of anger still swirled tumultuously.

The after-effects of the electrical currents running through his already ragged body, made his teeth clench and his breath halt. "I-I know nothing! Please, let me go." But his pleading may as well have gone unheard.

Hariot could bear no more, and unable to stop Jathmoora, left.

"I say again: who are you and who do you work for?"

Shock. Shock. Shock. They came in quick succession, one after another. This time Zias was almost crying, teetering on the edge of a complete meltdown. "I am Z-zias Zechariah Davis. I am a, a diplomat from E-Earth."

Jathmoora halted like she had been frozen in time. "What?"

"I…come…from…Earth." He was shaking jerking like a stunned ferret. Jathmoora left him in a puddle of his own drool.

Harold syphoned money for years, mastering the DED project. Dark Energy Drive. This new source of energy would bring them in from the dark by harnessing darkness. These ships would be greater and more powerful than the last lot. Unlike them, he had nursed these from infancy. He knew what to expect from them—their habits, their patterns—and once more they were only machines, no intellect or infernal alien intrusion. Just pure machinery for him to wield however he wanted.

Harold told Stella to meet him at the facility where he had the Fleet of ships waiting.

When Stella saw the ships, she became awestruck. "Harold, you have been quite busy."

"Yes. As you have."

Stella became deathly quiet. And her smile faded.

"Don't be glum Stella. Frowning never looked good on you. I am the Head and there is nothing that goes on that I don't know about. Your secret facility is safe. And I haven't shut you down for one good reason. I need you."

Stella felt his hand on hers and she felt a slight rush. "Harold..."

"I need your expertise. No-one else on Earth has any data or information on what we may be facing out there but you do. I made it a prudent decision to name you leader of our Crusade for validation of the people. If they knew one of the Heads had left, the Parliament would be viewed weak and become vulnerable to insurrection. So, I had to make them and you believe."

Stella ripped her hand from under his. "You, you slippery snake! You knew I wouldn't work for you, so you gave me my dreams on a platter knowing I would take it. And now I am to serve under one of your hound-dogs?! Who undoubtedly will be acting under your orders?"

"Bradshaw wasn't keen about the role. But he fell in line. Just like you will. I hold all the keys darling, for this is my kingdom. We prepare to leave soon. I have organised lodgings here within the Parliament. Don't want you disappearing now. A pleasure, as always."

Stella looked crushed. A woman who trusted no man trusted the one man she really shouldn't have.

It took quite a long time for Celeste to come out of her room. Sean could tell she had been crying, her eyes red. He didn't want to pry, to open up old wounds. Celeste made her way to the passenger seat.

She dumped herself beside Sean and gave a tired sigh. "Where are we?" she asked.

Sean had to get back to the present; he had been lost in her throes of beauty. Even when she was sad she was beautiful. "Not sure. I told Thorn to take us away immediately. I didn't enter any specific coordinates. I knew you just needed to get outta there."

"Thank you."

Her face broke out into a smile and Sean felt that tug, the tingle that let him know she was all his and she could rely on him.

"No problem. I got this ship all figured out. Well, kind of. There is a lot that I don't know. Thorn is holding back. I don't know why."

"A lot is unknown about these ships. Did they have lives before us? Who created them? Why did they end up in a foreign galaxy, stranded?"

"Ah, origins. The questions that plague us."

"Sean, I want you to know that you aren't a distraction to me. You are a lot more than that. I had a terrible fight with Shartoon about you—about a lot of things. He feels like he can control me." She grunted. "He infuriates me and yet I still love him—love him for caring so much that it makes him impossible. But Sean, you are so much to me. I don't care what happens in the future. As long as you're in it, I am happy."

Sean captured her face in his hand and stroked her cheeks with endearing care.

When we see the evil we have made, do we feel guilt or compassion, or any emotion other than pure elation?—Unknown Archives

Mayes laid down on the couch. Zias' attitude perplexed her. First, he wanted to grill her to a puddle and then he let her go without any hassles. What was his game? she wondered. The Parliament did nothing but return her to her house like she just had tea and a friendly chat.

"Ginger, come here sweetie." She suppressed a most urgent cough. She patted her cat, who purred.

2 weeks later...

"Mayes, we need you. We need our leader." Adrian was his name and he was very determined. Mayes noted how pestilent that was. She hadn't seen him in months and then one day he turned up on her porch pleading for help.

She felt terrible about it all but what could she do? The Protesters were planning an insurrection. She didn't want to disappoint them so she willingly accepted. "The Leader is mad. We have to take him down."

Her men were waiting for their general. She may have been once but was she now? No sooner than the thought passed, she had locked her door, the fly door shutting behind. And there they were shouting and waving their banners at the perimeter of the Parliament.

"Ban the Stripping! Ban the Stripping!" That's how it had started. Now the problem had grown larger. "False prophet! Lies. Lies."

Mayes was unsure of who started it but before long she was one in a wave of people, climbing the walls, overpowering the guards. As quickly as the storm had started Mayes was locked up.

In the detainment cells, Mayes tumbled her nervous hands in a twitchy ball.

"Mayes, what are we going to do? I have a family. I can't be here," panicked the young pregnant woman nearby in the darkness, a protuberant bump noticeable in the shaft of light. Clearly, the glaze of wild freedom had died from her eyes and now desperation was seeping through instead. Now guilt wormed into Mayes.

Mayes turned to the woman called Evelyn and placed her hands on hers, a distraction from her constant fiddling. "I know that. We all do. I didn't intend for this to happen. I—"

"What did you intend?" came the angered voice of a young man hidden in shadow. She knew that voice only too well.

He walked into the shaft of light, angles cut in interesting ways. "I mean, did you think we could win? That we could be heard? Wake up; we are nothing but hurdles in their way. We had no chance," he said despondently.

Mayes looked away, casting her eyes at the floor, the minuscule dirt so interestingly detailed. "I hoped to make a stand, a point, yes. But Adrian, don't forget you were at the gates too, voicing your own disgust," she said harshly.

Adrian withdrew and sunk back into the shadows, easily defeated. She could understand his frustration, but to place blame on someone who didn't even want any part in this wasn't going to get them out of this mess. She shouldn't have been mother hen to these kids. And that's what they were. It was reckless on her part. So, she looked again to the floor, the swirl of dust, the turmoil of her swirling mind.

The ships rose up like a vision into the heavens. Just as they departed Earth and entered the rift, there was a mighty crack so loud it seemed to shake the Earth beneath. Everyone fell to the ground from the immense shock. The skies ripped apart as Detachment Palaces descended.

Panic and chaos unfolded in quick succession. Harold for once was speechless. The amount of fear that had suddenly accumulated on his face was nothing short of remarkable.

Just a few seconds ago Harold was spouting the biggest crap ever heard, about instilling strength and becoming giants. Where was Harold's strength now? He didn't seem like a giant now.

Harold like everyone else scampered to get away from the hordes of Raiders descending out from the Detachment Palaces. Earths prime defenses, the pulse ropes, were gone. The message about them being fried never got through, at least not until it was too late. Harold sent his Crusade through the rift with laughing happy faces. Now there was only fear and tears around him.

Carlton was cowering behind an upturned car as the Detachment Palaces landed and blew them away like toys, having a total android meltdown. "Systems overload. Requesting maintenance. Overload...too many unknowns...cannot calibrate....cannot...."

People scattered into the sewers as the surface littered itself with hungry Raiders.

"Feast my brethren!"

Meanwhile up at the Skeleton Stations.....

Pop, pop, pop.

"What's happening?" said one Skeleton Master. The chair in which he sat began to tremble. "I don't know!" yelled another man from another Station. Skeleton Masters were being gyrated out of their chairs.

Nine canisters deployed and opened from shut shoots from all nine stations. They began to glow.

"Where did they come from?"

"What's happening?"

"Is everyone seeing this?"

Communicational chatter was rampant across the system.

The ground of the Earth ran red with blood.

Havoc had arrived to those unbeknownst to the absolute catastrophe raining outside.

Mayes only felt the flames when they were inches from being incinerated. She knew she needed out and the guards were too occupied and couldn't help them. They were on their own.

Mayes touched the straw with her feet and let it fall through the cracks leading to a hidden trap door. "Come on! They aren't going to help us. We must help ourselves."

Adrian was left banging at the door. Mayes outstretched her hand, leaving the trap door open. "Come on, we haven't got much time, Adrian."

Flames started licking outside the door entering underneath. "The Parliament is on fire! The people are on fire!" screamed Adrian, who backed from the door like it was searing hot and popped down with Mayes.

Evelin started groaning, moaning; she was having contractions. Mayes ran and skidded on her knees to the pregnant girl. "We should be outta here soon. Just hold on, Evelin." What was she gonna do? She didn't know at all. She had become so entrenched in shit she didn't know how she was going to get out of it again.

They escaped to a woodland scrub. Looking back, Mayes saw the flames eating the Parliament, and up above the Raiders escaping into their Detachment Palaces.

The flames seemed to be angry and intent on burning the Parliament to ashes as though sentient, as though commanded.

Perhaps it is with the soft touch of a friend that we realize we are not alone
–Unknown Archives.

Kressangah noticed the light outside, slightly obscured by the mass of minuscule bugs swarming. The morning had come swift and she was oblivious to the time passed, as if she were deep in a trance that often came after a massive training session. She noticed with a pang that she had not even made it to her bed. Overcome by exhaustion, she had surrendered to the floor last night.

The arena was a place of destruction, a mashing of bone and blood spillage, yet it was the centre of their Serenity. True irony. The red ring around her neck was itching and her throat slightly hurt. She rose, noticing drool that she had left on the floor.

That had never happened before, succumbed to sleep without seeking the comfort of her bed. Boris must have really gotten under her skin. Kressangah did hate him and yet she continued to see good in him, a forlorn shadow that did not exist.

She didn't just grow frustrated with herself, she was embroiled with disappointment. He had promise. It was minuscule and pretty much nonexistent, but it was there. He had the ability to love—as crazy a notion as it was—because he did at a time love her or maybe she imagined he did?

It was a crazy time. Kressangah remembered only too well. It was five years ago when the war still raged with unbridled hatred. Kressangah had made her stance. She told her superiors what they could do with their orders and in doing so she had been exiled to this god forsaken piece of shit planet.

It was only when she heard Kroden had been dismissed, stripped of his rank, that she slumped to the darkness fully and wholly. She embraced the darkest parts of her nature with plies of Haldo.

She remembered seeing Boris for the first time. His chiselled jaw, his strong physic. In a weirded- sense he reminded her of Kroden. And to an extent, he served as his substitute. But she soon realized that they were nothing alike.

She was lucky to make it out alive. Boris had a terrible temper—almost unbearable to experience. But experience it she did, so she ran and covered her tracks, so he may never see her again. And yet she had gone to see him. She had to bring up the past, dredging dirt and all.

Boris wanted to hurt her, meant to even, but he also lusted for her with a passion, a crazy unmanageable passion that couldn't be called such a sentimental thing as love. Kressangah knew that no matter the sparks between them he knew nothing of true love, of caring and sensitivity, of actual humane tenderness.

His way of loving was to be violent and squeeze the love out of you like juicing a Codaos Spike Fruit. He knew no better, and yet she hated herself for feeling sorry for him, for feeling anything at all for him—a man not worthy of her love or her faith.

The energy shields erected buzzed louder. The Live Wind was swarming heavily this time of day as it did all days. She scratched herself bloody, she noticed. Kressangah suddenly stopped scratching as the creaky doors opened and in its epi-centre was someone's silhouette. She could almost hear her heart skip.

For a moment she thought it was him; an ache in her heart. But a soft oaky voice floated toward her and she felt at ease, comforted. "Hello, child. I hope that I have not come a moment too late." His figure came into the full light.

She looked up into his heavily- bearded face and relaxation dawned on her fine but haunted features. "Hello old friend. Gerof, what are you doing here?' she added. They braced for a meaningful bow before hugging.

Gerof was of the Laranie race, a large furry biped assimilated to that of Star Wars' Chewbacca but more humanized and gifted with speech and well versed in English. He walked forward and his tufts of fur along his elbows swung outward. It gave him the appearance of a wise holy man with billowing sleeves.

The sound of the swarming was a distant hum.

"Thinking about something that should have dissipated by now?" he said reassuringly, taking a seat at the middle of the symbol. He noticed the troubled look on her face. He knew her well enough to know when something was wrong.

Kressangah ventured a smile, tilting her head to the side and trying her best to cover the ring. Gerof softly caught her hand. "Tsk, tsk, what barbarian dare lay a hand on my child?" Kressangah loved his voice. Always had. It was tender, and it was his. A voice that made her want to surrender all her secrets, even ones she knew she could never tell.

Gerof extended his hand a second time but it was not gentle enough and Kressangah involuntarily flinched, a sharp image of Boris's hands enclosing around her neck springing to her minds-eye.

She then smiled nervously to apologize for herself, but the cat had been let out of the bag. "It's nothing. It was an accident. Yes, a mere heat of the moment accident," she lied almost as much to him as to herself.

He gave a dismayed shake of his head. "He must be in your head rather than your heart if you can excuse his vulgar behaviour. Accident indeed, my child. There is no excuse for that sort of behaviour. You know my views. If I have been distant lately or in fact absent, it is because I know I haven't been welcomed here but whoever did this should pay—no matter my views," he said a little more angrily than he intended. Gerof stepped back to give her breathing space and seeing the discomfort he created started to wander around.

"But alas, this is not why I have come."

He brought his hands together in a symbolic brace. "The deterioration of the Order has come to my attention. So many conflicting sides. The Generation War cannot go on like this; more than bloodbath, more than a stupid conflict of sides, people will not only lose their lives. They will be destroyed infinitively," he said.

Sometimes she thought he had more philosophy in him than the whole of her entire people. Taroks were very philosophical people and for a Laranie to quote, it was most respectful.

Hours had passed. Kressangah decided to stand, the aches of the floor making her groan as she cracked her neck. She too paced, the swarming thinning, the hum dulling as noon arrived. "Yes, it is true. I hate to say, it but your fears were well justified—the Order is crumbling. I should have left here a long time ago when I knew everything we believed in was misguided. I should have gone with you," said Kressangah. "Maybe then I wouldn't be flinching at a simple gesture of love," she said, looking away abruptly, tears welling in her eyes. She could feel his concern. She wrenched herself free of her anguish with a shake of her head. "I know I can't rely on you. I have to have my own legs. But that is what I tried to do here. This was home, but it isn't any longer. I will tell them I am leaving. It is the only right thing to do."

The swarming seized and the energy shields went down, allowing a bout of wind made by artificial pumps to upset the curtains and the ambience between them.

Gerof paced and then went in front of her and delicately grasped her chin, upturning her face towards his and directing her stare into the twinkle of his eyes. She always loved his eyes. "Child, you are always welcome to join me. I have come to see that my children do not end up in the caving hole the Order has fallen into," he said.

"And soon we will be homeless, hopeless and alone immigrants living like the cockroaches, like Krelian Gypsies," she said, slightly backing away from his delicate touch. She could not even stand a simple amount of touch on her skin like the precipitant were barbs.

Gerof knew of what she spoke of. The Order was a place for exiles that had no place in Tarok society or on their homeworld far in the Satanic Region.

"Rotting from the inside out, we have no other choice," he said. The two stood in sweet silence, a contemplation working between them.

Taking measured steps, the two went through the doors and down the passage way mired by columns eaten by virulent Frost Vine. The might of the Order was not that concrete, a waning strength but still it held, for the moment, just like the pillars.

At the end of the open doors, something was amiss. Kressangah slowed her steps, allowing her enough time to brace for what she was about to see. The wind howled and the Order was a deserted, hollowed shell. Specs of debris and splattered stains sang the obvious.

Kressangah knelt down hard on her knees. "There was nothing you could have done," came his distant voice, his haggard mass nearing her as comfort. "They wanted this. This was their only way to reach true Serenity, for they knew they were never going to attain it," he said as comfortingly as he could, though he held back his own tears.

"Mass suicide. I am alone.' She started to sob in between shallow breathing.

Gerof knelt down. "No child, you are not.' Gerof tried to bring her back up but she seemed content to stay on her knees so he did too, both huddled in a mass, blood dripping down the walls.

She had slept through a mass suicide and awoken to horror. No one would know what happened here; only the residue of blood would be left, the live wind stripping the bodies and consuming every morsel. It would be stories untold save for the splatter on the walls.

A man pities another who has slumped to the depths of desperation but when that man is in the same position, the successor only laughs at the woes of the man who offered him no help in the first place—Unknown Archives

It took a lot of persuading, but finally, Gerof was able to get Kressangah to leave with him. Gerof was always a man of generosity. He was hoping to save all his children but only came away with one and perhaps the most important one.

He loved to display all sorts of objects on his ship of prolific significance. It soothed Kressangah as she skimmed her fingers over vases and miscellaneous items from all corners of the galaxy. It softened her grief.

She looked out the view screen to see the Order shrink into nothingness. It was her home for the longest time and now it was but a tomb. She could feel the knots in her stomach untighten.

She started to see that there just might be a life outside the Order. Maybe this wasn't an end but a beginning. Granted, she didn't want to leave like this but the universe always seemed to have things in order—perhaps this was simply meant to be. After all, not all of life is glorious and beautiful; there is going to be horror, there is going to be pain and there is going to be grief. That is life; that is the order of things.

"What did you do, Gerof? After you left us. What did you see?"

Gerof chuckled to himself a little as images of his past flashed in his mind. "I saw the universe. And child, there is more to it than we could have ever imagined. I come not with just trinkets and stories but with a warning." Suddenly the softness of his lines tensed and he seemed serious.

"What is it, Gerof?"

He placed a furry hand on hers, a symbol of caring but also of preparation. "We all come to an end as you well know. Well, now it is the universe that is nearing death."

"The universe can't die. The theory of it having age has only ever been a theory—nothing else."

"Oh, but, it is more than a theory, young one. I have seen it. Cracks in the galaxies, seams coming apart."

Kressanagh needed a chair; then she realized she was already sitting in one. She momentarily looked away. "What can we do then? If what you say is true, how can we stop what is meant to be?" she said, realizing all that had happened was simply trivial.

"This isn't natural. This is a mistake. I won't lie, there isn't much we can do." He sounded like it was already set in stone.

"I am no scientist. I bring the good word, but on my travels, I saw a lot of strange, wondrous things. I also came across Sprites that seem to have oozed from the wounds forming. Child, I have more bad news before reaching any sensible good news. They are by no means nice, these Sprites. I am sure we can find something like the Wave of Retribution to wipe them out before they wipe us out. If we destroyed them once, we certainly can again. And perhaps slow or even stop what's happening."

No hatred. No malice. Serenity. The Taroks had worked years to obtain this level of being, but no Tarok had ever obtained it or witnessed it—many even doubted its very existence. What was it to be calm, to be content and needed, wanted? No one really knew why we were here—was there some hidden reason?

Taroks were doused in philosophy. They believed with every ounce that life was needed and that they were needed. But the real reason—the reason you get out of bed, the reason you do your tasks—wasn't to fix yourself, it was to matter, to have a reason to be alive. But Taroks were always self-evolving. They wanted to be better. Each day they tried to better themselves. Some didn't believe in it. Saw it as meaningless. But a war was upon them and the old one swept under the rug. Everyone knew that something was coming, something even their heavy beliefs couldn't protect them from.

Kressangah could see their faces, each of them clear in her head. They had come to a dark realization. They saw no Serenity. They saw an abyss. And it consumed every morsel of them. She knew them well. She laughed with them. She cried. She was their friend and yet they had chosen to make this decision without her.

Was she spared because she was truly enlightened or was it just a decision they made on their own? They had spared her and she would be greatly thankful, but still, the sting, the hurt of not being with them to stop it in the first place hurt more than any relief she sought.

For the longest time, she was at the end of a scope. She was an assassin, a lethal killer. But when she took lives she didn't see them as people, she saw them as lights being doused. It was sad. Perhaps they had realized it too. Perhaps they saw the lights and in turn their reflections that were ghastly upon viewing. A mirror. And it cracked. It hurt them in places they never knew it could. It hurt their souls. And the only way to escape it was to die, to end the turmoil of life and seek eternal serenity—peace via death.

Even the smallest contribution can have a lasting affect – Unknown Archives

Kroden lay in the pool of his own saliva. His head throbbed. The liquor was dry in his mouth. He stumbled over to the table and pulled himself up. The surly bartender just gave him a scowl. No one cared that he was hurting. No one cared for his turmoil. No one saw him. Ever since that day he had become a shadow.

"Hey, bartender, you seen a young short Tarok around? Beautiful. As beautiful as the day, as the sun. She is the prettiest creature in the universe."

The alien bartender looked down at him, chewing his toothpick lazily. "Nah."

Kroden hung his head. Of course, she wouldn't be here. Why was he hoping? Why did it matter? He had thought about her every day since that day. It was love. Had to be. Or perhaps he was the most pathetic being of all—one who was delusional.

Feeling the lingering uselessness, he shuffled to his room. He saw his armour in the corner, unused. He once was glorious in battle. What was he now? He sat at the end of his bed. Why was it that he ended up here? He was a general, for Christ's sake! Now he was a bum drinking himself into a stupor.

Memories hit him hard and sharp....

"We got them fleeing. Run through the dead, finish off anyone still alive." The Tarok general was mighty in stature and demanded obedience.

Kressangah was different. She was younger for one. But she was also different. Some how she felt that all this was for nothing. She listened to the general but not once did she believe in what he was saying. All she could do was say yes. To obediently follow. She knew nothing else. "Yes, sir!"

The field was littered with the blue blood of dead Gaul. She felt no pity or remorse going through the dead. She had, in fact, killed most that she stepped over. There didn't seem to be a soul alive.

And then she noticed it: a wiggle. She headed to it, curiosity baiting her like sweet fruit she needed to taste. She placed her gun at the Gauls' head but he was dead and then she faced with the Gaul underneath and a live firearm.

She saw not the enemy. She saw glimmering eyes. Piercing eyes. And she felt her finger wane. She felt her stomach lurch. What was this? An unknown emotion. She needed to fire. Why wasn't she firing? Was she shaking?

Kroden looked to this Tarok about to blow his head off. He had never seen a creature such as her—reluctant. He had laid waste to many a Tarok but this one was different somehow, changed. He could not quite place it. Why was she not blowing his head off?

Even as she pointed the weapon at him he felt at ease. Something told him not to go for the blade hidden behind his back.

Kressangah felt her whole world lurch. She slowly lowered her weapon, opening both eyes to see this man, to view this new world she had entered. She offered a shaky hand, unsure.

Kroden seemed to move in slow motion as he reached for her. When they were nose to nose they were lost together, fuzzy outlines in a bold and sharp world. The bodies of Kroden's men and comrades faded and they arose together into an embracing light until harsh reality brought them back down.

The general could be heard over the mound. Even this far she could hear his grating voice. "Go. Run! They mustn't know I let you go," said Kressangah.

Kroden smirked suddenly. "What about me letting you go?" He couldn't believe that the field he was on was about to be filled with heavily armed Tarok and he was still making light of the situation.

The carnage and corpses melted away. It was just them. She smiled. It felt foreign to smile, but she did and it felt wonderful. "Go!"

Kroden caught her fingers one more time and then ran in the opposite direction. He never forgot her face. She let him go and he had let her live.

He awoke with a thud to the ground. He had inadvertently nodded off. He wished he could see her again, tell her all that he knew. But he doubted that day would ever come. He returned to his bed and felt the sheets, surrendering to a turbulent sleep.

The creation made by the creator shows reflections of both creator and creation as the face of true nature is revealed to all—Unknown Archives

The universe was even more mind-boggling than initially predicted. The Colossal Galaxies that once existed were mighty super structures. The Rifts merely the byproduct of the galaxies drifting apart but something else existed—something even more mind-boggling than them. It was a threat that no one could have foreseen.

"'You can never hope to grasp the notion of the universe breaking apart. It is forlorn and beyond your understanding. And yes, even the dreaded Raiders would run for cover as something even worse comes out the darkness.'" And so it was said by some unknown scholar, his existence capsulated and put in storage in the Library of the Unknown Archives to collect dust as it were.

Deep in the unknown parts of the universe laid darkness. True darkness that held terrible intelligence. The Dark Matter that accounted for most of the mass in the universe was more than enigmatic, it was unknown. The only thing people knew about it was that it existed, but even that was put doubtful.

Dark Matter Entities thrived in their territory—the Voids—littered with Dark Matter that no light could refract. Also known as Sprites, these creatures were no dainty creatures, they were brutal and lethal. Most travelled out of their territory and into heavily civilized galaxies, tearing at society, planets, ships, and stations.

The life that people knew was going to be ripped to shreds. No one had encountered these things before, and any who had were never heard of again. The time for fear was neigh. These things came out of the darkness like nightmares and now they wanted only one thing: total annihilation of anything biomass.

They believed in a higher plane—a plane of energy. To them, beings of organic origins were nothing but a waste of space. So, they would rip into you, mesh into the flesh, and force the blood out of your pores. It was amongst the most horrendous sight ever beheld by man.

An eerie sound came across the universe in bouts of waves like solar winds. But these bouts held information and hidden language.

Translation:

"Why do they think the universe is accounted for 80% dark matter? Because the universe was not meant to have matter. They are a mistake, an obstruction to true existence. We are simply finishing what started eons ago."

Something like mad laughter filtered through the rest of the translation as waves of Sprites gallivanted across the cosmos.

Gerof darted from one sparking console to the next but everything was fried. Kressangah nursed a bleeding cut but that was nothing compared to what would befall them if they didn't get out and get out now.

Kressangah could feel his fear. It was tangible. Confused and a little scared for both him and herself, Kressangah took Gerof by the hands, trying to steady him and looking him in the eyes.

His eyes were always the window to his soul. In them, she could see all that he was and all that he could be. He was wise, he was bold, but right now she saw only a glimmer of that, the rest was pure fear. "What is out there? What is trying to get in?" she said fearfully.

Gerof's lip trembled as he said, "Sprites. They are death. Only death is not even as bad. We must get this ship going." And with that, he wrenched his hands-free, not cruelly but more in a harsh rush.

Outside, the ship was surrounded by these ghostly shimmers. Their shape was that of a butterfly with huge sails for wings, but they were no beauty to be admired. They were trying to seep through but suddenly they were distracted by something and disappeared, leaving the ship heavily damaged.

Kressangah, heading for the bridge, could feel her legs buckle and she fell forward as a piece of loosened bulkhead skewered clean through her body. She yelped.

There were fires erupting everywhere. Gerof could feel the heat and he could hear her screams but the smoke was making it hard to distinguish her. "Kressangah?" But the intensity of the flames was too much. He squinted and tried to shield his eyes. A wall of raging flame lay between him and her. Then the world started to dim. The fire roared and then…darkness.

The stars held sway over more people than they knew. Stars had power. Stars were magnificent and yet so many didn't know a thing about them. Space and stars were one, they congealed to be one. And in subspace was a substance that glued the universe into a coherent, working machine.

That substance had a name: Choc-ra. No one knew of this power, for it was as elusive as it was questionable. Many disbelieved the claims that it even existed but exist it did. There were a talented few who knew about it and used it smartly. To some, it would seem like sorcery, but to the more competent, it was a source of protection and a window into something incredible—to touch the zenith.

Jathmoora the sorceress. She had left her Hub for a better existence. The Hub was a collection of ships patched together. Crafting herself a ship from that Hub, she chose to leave, no longer appealing to their ideals.

She travelled the stars, ever searching for the reasons behind the Choc-ra. Its existence called for a reason. Why was it there? She knew it was for more than just magic tricks. It held a purpose like every living organism; that is what she believed it to be.

Only one other had accompanied her on her travels. Nothing was known about Hariot's origins, only that she found him in a cracked pod floating in space left for dead.

"Jathmoora, why are we passing through the Bezner Mines?" Hariot asked while pruning his succulent, which gave a small moan.

She was a tall woman with jutting features. She had bone protuberances on either side of her head that encapsulated her hair.

"They are remnants of the War. They have been inactive for years. This is a shortcut."

"I would prefer the long way if it saved being blown up. Things happen, you know, Jath."

The cactus gave a small whirr and Jath smiled. "How is Jerup doing today?"

"He needed his hair cut but he still wants to grow. I just hope we don't have another incident." And by incident Hariot was referring to the time when he took some Space Weed and it grew unchecked through the ship, clogging systems and burning out wires.

Hariot smiled nervously. She knew why she kept him. He was young, a baby when she first found him in a pod, lost to the elements of space. She guessed he had been dumped. Nothing was known about him. His species. Their world. His name. Nothing. All she knew was that she had to keep him safe.

He was a strange looking alien—as strange as they came. His lip was set in a groove and he had a long, pointed tongue which made eating an entertaining event.

Show me your bad side and I will give you a taste of mine, you get what you are given
– Unknown Archives

Raiders were poetic in their barbarism, like a perverted idea of Shakespearian devilry. Raiders balanced poetic and savage brutality with precise balance. They were silky with their words and managed to make killing sound reasonable and dignified, a habit of satisfying one's thirst and enriching the soul—if only they had one. Or a conscience. They only knew pain and pleasure; they knew no distinction between the two. For the longest time, they stayed within the darker parts of the galaxy.

But now they had wandered further into the bright of the universe, wandered closer to their food source. Their time was at an end. Raiders thrived in cold space; that was their territory. Their Hive Ships possessed mucus doors that made it disgusting to pass through but practical as it enhanced the cold in which they thrived.

"We have seen much in our infinite lives." The Raider Horde Chief addressed his horde.

No one dared go up against a Hive Ship for fear of its Detachment Palaces that were the front to their assault, a hold for their menace. They would land on planets like marching ants. A Hive Ship was nothing when compared to the many puzzle pieces that made the whole structure and through space, they travelled as one massive machine.

"We have come out of hiding for we are in need of our wine. I see them and I hunger. But something out there doesn't want us to have our fun. We have been sidelined by these things. They don't relish the hunt like we do, they are just killing machines. And we are just as likely to be killed as our food-source. I am afraid our 100 year wait has come sooner than I'd like. We must enter our sleep and wait till the galaxies restore themselves."

The Hive Ships had managed to gain a foothold on many planets. But their time had come to a close as a greater evil came into play. The Raiders were not prepared to face such beings. If they were to face death—a concept most unknown for a Raider or the wrath of Dark Matter Entities—they would forgo their immortality and embrace cold death. One evil knows its time is done when another shows its face.

They fled in hordes. No one complained of course, but it did raise the question: why were they leaving their only food source? And the answer: to embrace 'the slumber'. Every hundred years when they had nearly decimated an entire galaxy they slumbered in their pods in a dark part of space until the time was ready for them to return to their replenished food source. It was too early to go to their slumber but they had no choice. They would not dare go against Sprites.

The tides of war come swift and knowingly, but the ripper comes even swifter, unknowing of who to take first—Unknown Archives

The hodgepodge that was the many conjoining spheres that made up Station Alpha were bombarded from oncoming objects that could not be classified. "Evacuation. All personnel evacuate. Hull integrity failing. Evacuate. All personnel evacuate," said the cool unstressed voice as panic broke all around.

The station deteriorated fast and almost all evacuees were getting to pods or docked ships or simply crashing into each other to reach them. The station was one of the oldest habitats in the galaxy and now it was being attacked relentlessly, crumbling from within.

All those nights his door had shut with a shuddering softness as deafening as the roar of a hurt dragon but at least a dragon could breathe fire and not cold condensation as she did. Now Cleo was finding her life in true jeopardy. She knew not what to do.

Boris grunted awake and grasped for his net disperser, his one and only love. Flesh beings meant nothing to him; they were the utensil. The alarms were blaring. Boris couldn't think to accept that he needed to get off this station and pronto.

A large bang made Cleo gyrate out of bed as she fell into a heap on the floor. Boris wasted no time in taking her up in a sheet and slinging her over his shoulder. He didn't care for her protests, her kneading her knuckles into his back.

He just needed to get off the station. He knew she would not speak up, for she could not speak. She was mute—thankfully. He darted out of the room and just in time as the bulkheads came crashing down on the bed they were just in.

Panic had broken out everywhere. He pushed passed elderly, young, he didn't care to be careful or considerate; all concepts skimmed over his thoughts like a pebble over water. Boris even bashed someone over the head for stopping him, pleading to be taken with him on his ship. Finally, he threw Cleo down, noting that he had actually knocked her unconscious, and blasted out of there as the station crumbled to bits. "What a shithole."

Cardvia was fast becoming stronger with every moreish bite. She was not proud of the massacre but she was starved and nearing death and pretty much driven to it. She was so in tune with herself, yet sometimes she felt like the bloodlust overtook her better judgment.

The crewmen she inadvertently murdered were not to blame for Shakik's error but they paid with their lives. What could she say? They were delectable and by no means innocent.

Cardvia had been dosed with injections for weeks at a time, weakening her, crippling her mind. She was starved and poisoned to such an extent that when she had the chance she gorged herself on every living thing on that ship. She did so with no reluctance. None of the crew had a chance against her ferocity.

She saved Shakik for last, and he whimpered like a baby.

Now alone on the ship, Cardvia was faced with cold, harsh reality. After being imprisoned for the longest time, she was now free to venture to wherever she wanted but she had no idea where to start.

For now, she was numb, frozen to the moment while all around her the dead people gawked at her with wide-eyed expressions. She had slaughtered an entire crew—over forty crewmen.

After fighting for so long, she couldn't fight back the real her. The monster that she so hoped would not awaken had risen. She had become the darkness she vouched to not bring Shakik too.

He only wanted to have a place in society but she stole that from him. She snubbed his light. Cardvia felt guilt ensnare her and pull her down to the dark abyss. Something like sadness racked her body.

Why should she feel guilty after what that evil man did to her? She was trying to rationalize the massacre, make it better on herself, but she had done it. She had steeped her skin in blood and now the only blame was left with a bitter taste of metal in her mouth.

She needed to get somewhere. She needed to fly away. She hadn't been a pilot in the longest time but it came back naturally. Her species were known for their superior piloting skills as well as their unseemly appetites. Perhaps the latter more than the rest.

In the end ultimate power overrules us all - Unknown Archives

Sean could hear Thorn all the time. Celeste wasn't happy about him always being preoccupied, but she ought to have known that this was bound to happen with the melding of mind and metal.

So, she searched the many rooms of the ship instead. Her white wings were folded back as she slowly cantered down the winding corridors, skimming the walls with her perfectly manicured hand. She wore no shoes. No Celestial Being adorned such things as shoes or clothes; their feathers were all the cover they needed.

Though she appeared humanoid, she glowed with an internal light that was far from ordinary. She radiated perfection.

She finally stopped at one door that was sealed shut. All the others were empty with a few boxes filled with miscellaneous stuff. This door though, it was sealed shut. She tried to pry it open but she was no wall of muscle. "Sean?" she called over the comm.

"Found something?" he called out.

"Maybe. Could you tell your bestest buddy to open this door? I think it is stuck."

And no sooner said the door opened, making a small shusshh of relief.

"Happy hunting."

Celeste gave a cough as the accumulated dust hit her. "Lights." But they were busted so she grabbed some flashers from a panel along the corridors.

All along the corridors were panels with compartments for flashers (tubes run by the moonlight and lit up the darkest of places).

She moved in with the flasher held aloft in front of her. It looked all ordinary so far but she wanted to know why this door was shut. She continued to search.

A few hours later on the main deck - "And in the darkness, we call. But to no end do we realize that we are at peace because we have reached that which we do not see: death."

"A little bleak, isn't it?" Sean cast his eyes back to Celeste, who placed the aged book down.

"I found it in one of the rooms. This ship is massive. And I think it is true—the truest thing we know. Death is peaceful and after fighting, clawing your way through life, when you hit that dark you welcome it."

Sean knew there was another reason he liked her: she had depth. She had scope and definition unlike any broad he knew. He wished he hadn't forsaken his own women but he couldn't help it. She was stellar.

"Would you like me to go on?" Celeste asked, seeing that Sean had drifted off.

"Please," he added with an inclination of his head.

"They spread throughout the stars like locusts—like a plague—and only when we realized what they were did we quiver. To know one's end is to know what lies ahead, but without the threat, we have no purpose. Evil is what keeps us alive—without it, we are numb, we are dead."

"Who wrote these?"

Sean looked slightly perturbed by this darkened view on the universe but also slightly intrigued by the mind behind it. The words held weight and that was something he hadn't seen in a long time.

He always had a simplistic view of the world. Kill. Have beer. Get girl. But now it was erupting in layers.

"It doesn't say. I mean, it does but the name has been crossed out. They almost ripped through the paper," she replied, indicating where.

It was soon discovered that the room that was sealed was filled with ancient texts and prophecies of a doomed universe. There were also plaxes with countless retellings of events that took place years in between. Some spoke of a terror unlike anything released into the universe. Others talked of the universe and it splitting in two. All of this was a bit farfetched in Sean's view. But still, some of it did resonate with him.

With what we know and what we hope to gain, is there ever going to be a time where we are successfully satisfied?—Unknown Archives.

The room was no longer sealed and Celeste could go forth and explore the many wonders to her heart's content. Meanwhile, these days Sean was locked up in his room, surrounded by towering piles of plaxes heeding all the same warning: some unknown threat that would engulf the universe.

Celeste loved to retrieve the plaxes for him and trundle down to Sean's lair.

"How could it be, Sean?" she said.

"How could what be, love?" he said, stroking her hair as she lay cusped in his legs.

"That we know nothing of these cryptic messages," she answered. She held the plax, waiting for Sean to reply.

"Maybe…" he said and grabbed the plax, "maybe we aren't supposed to know. When whatever happens happens, it will have been preordained—fate."

"You, a believer? I didn't think that possible, Sean." She leaned back on the bed she was sitting down. It made Sean rather uneasy so he cleared his throat.

"I just think that with everything we have encountered, maybe there are things unexplained that we hold no power over," he said.

Celeste sat up. "You don't believe that! We can't be powerless. The rite of Undula is the reason for everything. The star will hold the answers, Sean. We must go there," she insisted.

"You really want that? To go to a place that could very well contain more dangers that this mysterious threat?" he said.

"I believe the answer is there. You can come with me, or you can stay here."

Sean thought he dedicated a hmph. "Okay," he teased. "But only if you stay on this bed and see what happens when you suggest such bold things."

A smile reached her face.

Who knew what else lay dormant within the many unexplored rooms throughout the ship. Celeste, after her spell with Sean, decided to venture forth. She didn't find anything of interest, though she did pick up on a few things.

Thorn was a big ship and she felt like he was hiding something. She didn't have any proof or sound reason but some rooms were sealed. She knew that he could undo that but yet he did not. The rooms remained sealed and the secrets behind them so. It puzzled her.

Ever since Sean had bonded with Thorn she knew he would be out of reach at times. She didn't blame Thorn for it—or even Sean—but it did bring up the subject of shut doors, hidden conversations. Just what was he telling Sean and what was Sean not telling her?

Celeste wrapped up in her silk sheet and sat down beside Sean. She held a plax in her hands. "So, the seeds of creation past were dispersed across the universe—hidden. They help us. They will help us keep the galaxies together for a storm is about to hit. Beware of the storm."

"Do you think your dad actually went through these?" she said suddenly curious as to whether he did.

Sean looked away as though watching a fluttering bird. "No, Celeste. I told you, I don't know a thing about my dad. He may as well have been a stranger.".

Celeste could feel the shard off that comment. She should have known not to bring up the subject.

The ship wandered the wastelands of space, the destruction of the past Wars evident everywhere. Scattered civilizations, destroyed cities, cratered moons.

The plax slipped a little in Celeste's hand so she awoke with a start. She had been going through a lot of them and dozed off.

"No one can tell if this is real or a dream. One would hope for the latter so none of this could have transpired. What if it is real? What if such nightmares exist? How can anyone fight? How can anyone have a damn chance?" she told Sean waving the plax fervently.

Sean was silent. At first, Celeste thought he hadn't heard her.

"Is everything okay?" she asked.

"Sorry. I have been thinking about my dad. I keep rehashing everything he ever did and everything he didn't do. I just can't come to an understanding. It has nothing to do with you. I just think that this ship is one big reminder that he isn't here with it."

Celeste put the plax down to comfort him.

"Maybe he just had to do something."

"God knows what my dad did!"

Celeste realized she had hit a nerve when he basically lifted her up in the air and planted her down with a thud. She went to apologize but her lips sealed as she saw Sean put up a hand before she could. "I wish I could fill you with answers but truth be told, I know very little about my dad and his ventures. He didn't bring us along; he left us on the world without truth or reason."

"I believe now that you are quoting someone from that book. I didn't mean to pry."

"No need. I never expected my dad to be some hero or something. I only ever wanted my Dad to be my Dad."

"How we wish so much from our parents. But it is only when they are gone that we forget the reasons we were so terrible."

"I do not want to be angry with him anymore. I am tired but he keeps antagonizing me from his grave."

"Perhaps he is trying to make amends for the times he missed out."

"Would be nice if he were here to tell me that in person."

Celeste smiled and the suns burned brighter. She was the very vessel of perfection. Sean could feel himself falling apart with every breath she breathed. She was his everything.

He felt like an arse for getting angry with her. If he ever hurt her he would make sure he punished himself. He would have her—no, he would claim her. But he didn't want it to sound like that. He wanted to win her with his personality, not his brawn like he did with so many others—too many, he thought fleetingly. So, he leaned over and kissed her eyelids.

Sean was sure Thorn was hiding something from him and even his beloved had alerted him to this.

He went into the room that Celeste described. Indeed, it was stifling in here. He spotted the books, old and dilapidated piled hazardously in one forlorn corner. They were close to complete disintegration.

As he scanned the ones underneath, he came to realize they were in an alien language. Celeste could possibly translate but then the ship rumbled. "Thorn? Celeste? What's happened?"

Sean heard Thorn before and now as he heard him he could tell there was hysteria in his voice, or what surmised as a voice. "Sean, you might want to come up here," came the panicky voice of Celeste.

Sean came in at a gallop and stopped with a skid. There were so many of them. Hive Ships. "What are they doing?"

The ships were moving and interlocking. "They are becoming super structures. A singular entity. They are meshing their components to better become formidable again. This isn't a good sign, Sean. If they are trembling it is for good reason."

Perhaps that storm had finally hit.

The mind is as unknown as the visages of the universe hidden in darkness
—Unknown Archives

The Hive Ships had no retaliation against the might of the Sprites. How could one fight against something that moved like ghosts, wisps in space? In the Satanic System, Hive ships had dwindled to a thousand. In the Dark Horse System, there were none at all. And here in the Angelic system, numbers were dwindling fast. No communique came from Le-chuisa system—dead space.

Eric had heard of this and started mass production on his dolls—his soldiers—straight away; he was afraid of losing his children. Eric didn't believe in defeat. He knew not these Spirits in space and cared not for how they were destroying. If they were non-matter then he had no hope of understanding them. He worked with DNA and touch, not with imaginary phantoms he could not think to grasp.

Sandy had been her name—or was it, Sandra? Eric had to repeat what had happened to his wife multiple times. He would get his trusty AI Charlie to tell and re-tell the story. Each time Eric would see a picture in his mind of what she possibly looked like and each time he felt a gap between what was real and what wasn't.

In fact, he had rare days where he could see her entirely. Her details were slipping from him like water in cupped hands. As time passed, all visages of her existence would slowly be erased.

His memories were dissolving and he was losing his mind. But all of the brilliance could not be diminished. He would be great again and his children would be proof of that at—least that was what he told himself.

As he tinkered at his bench, his eyes screwed up in concentration, he requested the story once again with glee. "C-Charlie, my dear friend. Do you recall that lovely lady I met when I was young and sturdy and not this faltering mass?"

There was a tsk in Charlie's vocals before he responded with an extra cheer. "Yes, master. I do indeed. It started long ago…"

And such would go the time, filled with stories of a woman he had butchered in a fit of mad rage. And each time Eric heard the words he believed them wholeheartedly. A momentary feeling of joy—or what could be called joy—filled his heart every time and he was happy again, at least for now.

Eric wasn't always mad. He was once a thriving man in love. He married young, he had kids young, but somewhere along the line, he lost himself to the dark parts of his brain. He suffered chronic blackouts.

No medical intervention could help him, even though he tried. He was lost in anger and frustration even though his wife Sam tried to comfort him night after night. His kids would ask daily what was wrong with Daddy.

Sam had no answers for them. She lay, one night, sound asleep, the kids snuggled next to her after complaining about nightmares. Eric, the man, was gone. He was unaware of his actions in that moment.

Before long, he sat in wet, sticky blood, holding a butcher knife aloft; his children and his wife had been stabbed countless times in what could only be described as a wild, frantic attack.

There wasn't much left but a heap. The pain, the confusion, the anguish he felt were beyond anything a human man could bear, so he blocked it out and never blacked out again. He buried his memories deep and never again felt the emotions he felt that night.

The human brain was an unknown entity. To date, there still wasn't enough research on our full capabilities. But for Eric, the truth was simpler. In us there were monsters. He had become that monster and now trapped in overlapping webs of brilliance and madness he became lost, a man not quite a man but cultivated of his own accord. It was a trap. He had reached the apex and returned broken—brilliant, but broken. And that was how it had always been. The wall between genius and madness ever indefinable.

Living life on bullets, blood and the drink, Sean knew almost nothing else when a Sergeant. All he knew was out there was the enemy. Sean had never had time for a serious relationship. In fact, all of this relationship stuff was very new to him; foreign, alien.

Out there during the flits of war, all that mattered was your own arse and not getting too shot up. Now that he was retired, all aspects of his mind had to be reevaluated.

Since his time with Celeste, every moment was joyous; a wondrous adventure to uncover, and in doing so he was discovering himself—parts of himself he never knew to exist and given the right time might even take over him entirely.

He never wanted to feel anything else. He never wanted to be anyone else. He was so much better when he was with her. She was the better part of himself—the self he saw in the mirror hidden underneath those roughish looks he had used on so many women but it was his insides that had drawn Celeste to him. Go figure.

Celeste slept soundlessly in the silk sheets twisted comfortably around the both of them, entangled in both skin and fabric. He turned to the right and met the pointy ears of his lover.

He delicately touched the edges and now saw the smaller details. Her wings lay softly over him like a second blanket. Last night was a galactic explosion; a supernova of its own volition.

Nothing would hurt her as long as he was there, as long as he was breathing. He turned and saw the decanter innocently seated on the counter. Anything in his path would meet the end of that barrel.

Life was different now; it had a different meaning. He no longer had the cross strapped to his back and he tasted sweet freedom like wine poured by cupid.

In his ear, Sean could make out Thorn—a slight quiver. He was being courteous. Thorn understood the relationships of flesh beings more so than other mechanoid crafts.

Sean and Thorn didn't really have a language but a rhythm of feelings and patterns that made out a sort of language. When the two communicated it was like the sharing of souls, an imprint of one's thoughts. The shape of what that person was feeling was left on the other. Celeste called the process back-bleed. When he asked about it she often grew silent.

Sean slipped out of bed and grabbed his trousers. Celeste slept intertwined within the sheets. Sean smirked, realizing that she probably needed to regain her energy as he slung his decanter into his holster. Shirtless, he made his way through the corridors, the dim lights adjusting to his eyes sensitivity. "Thanks Thorn."

Nothing do we then seek when the end is near. To stay here present is all we can hope to accomplish in our small world—Unknown Archives

The glittery city world of Vern approached ahead. Downing the ship, Boris made way for a docking platform. He usually avoided such heavily populated planets but he felt the more people to choose from, the less likely those things would focus on one lone hunter.

When Boris stood, he stopped and cast his view instead upon Cleo, who was bleeding through the quickly placed sheet. "Errr," he semi-grunted.

He made way for a local medical hospital, carrying Cleo over his shoulder like a bag of potatoes rather than an injured woman. When the doctors fixed her, the nurse had something else to report. It was something that caused Boris to damage the wall next to her and frighten the nurse back behind safer partitions.

Boris just didn't need this right now. He was on the run, forced from his destroyed home and now he had to worry about a friggin' baby! This shit was just too much. He didn't waste time and picked up Cleo. He didn't give an arse's freckle about the stitches.

Cleo lay in the other room on the bed recuperating. He could feel the lethal and dangerous hunter inside him beckoning him to do it. He itched for his blade but he couldn't. Was he so weak as to allow this undoubted abomination to live?

He couldn't take it anymore so he grabbed for his net disperser and went out into the night to hunt and kill. He left Cleo and prayed that when he came back she and the baby were gone, vacated from his life, sparing him the trouble.

Cleo awoke with a start. She groaned, nursing the side where the stitches had come apart. She looked around, frightened for a moment, not sure where she was. She could feel it moving inside her stomach.

It was alive and she had the unseemly task of birthing it and probably rearing it. She creakingly got out of bed. She was hungry and sore. Cleo wrapped the sliver of the sheet around her and went over to what she assumed was a bathroom.

She had been in Boris's service for nearly ten years—owned by him. She was his property; not his equal and certainly not the mother of his child. She needed a way out. Leaning over, she glanced in the mirror and saw the strain on her face.

She was physically beautiful but the beatings of slave life had subtracted any vitality she once had. She had cracked her jaw. She had shattered her leg in three places. There were scars on her back from lashings.

She was beyond broken. And now she had this life inside her. What was she going to do? She couldn't take care of another being. She was having trouble taking care of herself. She felt the hot tears begin to stream down and shakily opened the tap and splashed cool water on her hot face.

She looked to the side and saw the dent. She felt worry prickling her like needles through the skin. What was his reaction going to be when he came back? She feared to even think about it.

Feeling drained and physically in danger, she returned to the comfort of her strange bed, wrapping herself in sheets and praying and hoping he wouldn't return—or better: that this was all just a horrible and bewildering nightmare.

When the sky turned to ash and the ground shook, the only thing Harold hoped was that he would live. He didn't care about power, about his position, about any of the things he thought he cared about.

He had knocked on evil's door and they sent out their minions to take care of him. The only image that came to him was that of his sweet Stella. He remembered in those moments the times he spent with her when he was free when he was in love, a real man. What was he now?

The Raiders encroached on his position. He held back a yelp but his shaking and production of sweat led them straight to him. "Eh, boys. We got a porky one here. Who's up for dinner?" The Raiders were not merciful.

All that was left of Harold was his drained body. A man had heard the cries but arrived too late. He looked down at the lifeless body of Harold. He heard the growling of the Raiders and vacated quickly.

The light was just light, but how does one identify dark from the night? So many things are associated with darkness—in particular, the topic of evil. Dark is forever associated with evil, but the universe in all its complexities cannot be so black and white.

One thing is for sure: the balance is in a continual battle. Evil for all its nastiness is tempting for reasons unknown. It is its allure. Being underhanded seems to awaken the senses, stroke curiosity...

A small unidentified craft traversed the borders of the Kale Galaxy, not seeing what was happening to it.

"I'd decided to leave, to go to this strange place. I volunteered too quickly before examining the options before me. Now I've stripped my path and I balance on a sliver of options."

"Tesker, your pessimism is not becoming. You made the right choice. Those hunters are vile. I pray that this new home will be better—a utopia."

"Or it will be as fiery and hot as the hell we left behind? I know, not becoming of me. I've heard it all before. One thing you need to know about me is that I never lie, never extend the truth. I am blunt, but hey, that is me."

The visitors turned tail as soon as they saw the barrage of Sprites coming like a wave of terror.

Tesker spoke. "Perhaps not this galaxy."

When is morality questioned: when the resolve for the intention is no longer good or when the outcome is nothing but immoral?—Unknown Archives

Duration: 0600 hours aboard the isolated post 33-B.

Random chatter

Hey, you heard about this? Apparently, we're becoming crowded with outsiders. Yer, there's another rift and we're getting refugees by the shipload.

Nope// extends sarcasm.

Well, it's true. I didn't believe it either but the source is more-a-less reliable.

Well, are they friendly?

Sort of, but they are peculiar looking; knotted skin rough like tree roots.

You're your own source, aren't you? Why am I even surprised? A Krelian is only as good as his word, right?

Raiders had polluted the planets like a seeping poison. Most residents still carried blades to fend them off; a clear serrated cut to the jugular was all that sufficed to destroy them.

Now that their numbers had reduced dramatically since the Cleansing, as it was now called, people had other worries to contend with. And no sword or materialistic item could kill them as they had no bodies in which to plunge the weapon.

But a few Raiders refused to go into hibernation and wished to still feed. These rebels were called Banshees.

"Spread out. The Sprites have done our dirty work. Feed and kill the survivors. We're not changing them anymore."

There was a whimper.

"Hold it."

The piece of the sheet moved. There was someone hiding beneath it. When the sheet was taken off, a young girl stared up at them with big eyes. She was half starved and cold.

Just as the Banshee was about to grab for her, she snapped at him with gnashing teeth and her eyes became dark; pure, undiluted dark.

"She's possessed! This whole town is possessed," he said as others came into view, brandishing rifles and shot guns, clearly possessed.

The Banshees ordered a retreat but just as they had slaughtered thousands they too met a most sticky messy end.

Tantalizing fruits, malted liquor, fine Clousa web silk: all these afforded luxuries never impeded with her diligent duties.

Lolalia knew what was expected of her as their empress just as much as she knew there was somewhere else she needed to be. Ever since she was little, Lolalia had felt the tug of the Moons, their magnetic pull. They almost spoke to her, telling her to go and find her mother. But it was all about timing. She couldn't very well sprint off and leave everything without taking the proper measures.

But who could she trust to lead in her absence? Her sisters were too fickle to undertake such a responsibility. Burdened with too many thoughts, she laid her head to rest and hoped that the morning held more sensible prospects.

Feeling the impending prickle of the duties to be performed, later the next day, she sought the gardens and walked barefoot across the green grass. It was the only luxury she afforded —that and the Beimmion Pools occupied by the Balas eels, who snaked around her ankles and turned the mineral enriched water iridescent blue.

Lolalia waded in the lit pools. The water had youthful properties; a bath each day said to retract the skin to that of a twenty-year-old, but Lolalia simply enjoyed the eels' company and warmth of the underground springs.

Once she had gotten out of the pools, she went passed the Soolmar Bellflowers and then later rested under the Worm trees, whose leaves were ever sensitive to touch.

Sean had more than a mere connection with Thorn. Conversing with him was strange, to say the least. He didn't hear his voice, he more a less sensed his voice. In his mind's eye, he received a river of indescribable notions, images and sensations. That said, it was disconcerting the day that communique was abruptly severed.

"Thorn? Thorn!"

But there was no response and something most unusual: silence.

Celeste's worried wails reached his ears. Darkness took over. Panic arose. Then it happened.

Splatters of blood worked their way up the walls. A shiver travelled down Sean's spine.

Flashers highlighted the way as he plunged into darkness. He couldn't find Celeste and the pain deepened in his chest like a splinter working its way in. He followed little dots of her blood like following breadcrumbs.

At last, the trail ended. It was not to a pot a gold.

The blood was concentrated here at an empty pod bay, the pod gone.

He felt nauseous. He cast his eyes down and a single feather lay there stuck to the blood. He picked it up and a torrent of tears came flooding down.

She was gone. She was hurt. He sank to his knees, uncaring of the blood he was getting on his clothes.

He held the feather aloft, the Flashers highlighting it dimly, the only bit of her he had left.

The ship shuddered. The things were still here. And then something summoned them away. Sean should have felt relief. But all he felt was a pain as his ship and heart lay in tatters.

Shellcone Spiral - neighbouring galaxy

"To lost friends and absent enemies." All the Krelians stood and charged their glasses. Together they looked like a united family as they sat, scraping chairs noisily. "We welcome our new partners, the Clugugun race, whose hospitality and kindness has seen to our rise in the echelon of society."

The Clugugun race were of coral evolve. They didn't eat but consumed the nutrients through the air so the feast was kind of wasted on them but the notion was ever noted. Once again, the glasses were charged, the complacent faces of the Clugugun portraying rudeness but their continual nods to the speeches making a subtle hint of understanding.

"Just coz you don't eat doesn't mean you have to be an outsider," a boy said next to an equally young Clugugun girl.

At first, it was like the girl didn't hear him, then she turned around to meet his gaze. "I am Cassaky. I am glad that you invited me."

"You see passed most things people see first. No bullshit. That's what I like about you. You're a precious friend to us. Whoever talks down to you isn't on your level and should be demoted to an acquaintance."

The girl Cassaky's face erupted into the first smile he thought she had ever experienced. It was obvious that the art of smiling was lost on her. The Krelian boy found it most endearing.

"Such ungelded fondness for a woman you only just met."

"What can I say? You captured my interest." Everyone dug in save for the Clugugun, who sat idly by observing the eating habits of the Krelian Gypsies.

Some people are here like a flash of a shooting star and then gone; others are like suns that burn brightly for years to come—Unknown Archives

Transmission intercepted 0800hrs borders of Dred System
Code X-N10 cracked
Loading….
Loading…
File decrypted

"Time is irrelevant. Days bleed into one another. I have no idea of the world outside. Is it still there? Is there still green? Seems so long since I've seen green. Everything here is white—perfect but too perfect for my taste. I miss dirt. The sterility is getting under my skin. I don't have long so I will attempt to be brief.

I guess my journey starts a hundred years ago. I had acquired a vessel and attempted to explore as much of space as I could. Needless to say, it was a fruitless task. The universe is indeed vast, but just how vast I was about to find out.

I had always thought of this universe being the only universe. So, you can imagine my surprise when that notion was contradicted. During my travels, I encountered something—something I still carry with me. I have a swath of the universe before the big bang. Turns out our universe isn't the first. The big bang resulted in the obliteration of the old and the birthing of a new one. Technically no evidence of the previous universe should exist but it does. I have it.

Unfortunately, my curiosity led to my captivity. There are creatures old and ancient that believe I shouldn't have this. They are what you might call the police of the universe. They talk but I don't understand them. They have been sort of friendly but alas, I am stuck in this dimension, out of phase place—whatever you call it—and I am going nowhere. Huh, nowhere is where I am. I can't even tell you my coordinates. It's like I went into a whirlpool and Kansas is far, far behind. This is my last- ditch effort to tell you so you know. If one universe can die then what is there to stop that from happening to ours? Whoever receives this, more fragments—or seeds, as I call them—remain from the pre-universe. They are out there; diminutive, scattered, but out there."

The reputable seeds were sewn. Cleo was with child. She hadn't noticed the time she was away with Boris but when alone with a mirror she saw the jut, the telltale bulge that told her she was with pregnant with a half-breed, a possible monster.

That morning he didn't return. Cleo thought for a second that she was free but just as an inkling of a smile began to form, the door burst open and with it the quick appearance of a frown.

"Haven't you left yet?" Boris chucked his net disperser down and she jumped. "Don't worry, if I'd wanted you dead you would be. Just don't get in my way and we won't have any problems."

Always fear. That was all Cleo knew and breathed and lived. She had hoped briefly one time that she could free herself of the pain, the turmoil. She was so close to ending it all, but she couldn't. She didn't know if that made her brave or insanely cowardly.

Ever since Boris was born he had blood on his hands seeping into his very soul. The death of his mother was accidental yet he felt like he was no longer an innocent the moment he cried. Killed during child birth, his mother wasn't the most honourable woman, but she did not deserve death and yet she died, killed by her newborn son.

Boris was unsure if he was aware at that time, conscious of the choice he made, but ever since then he was cast into violence and moulded in brutality. He never had the tender touch of his mother, never knew love as a nurturing thing. He only knew a hard life—everything else was hidden from him, unknown, alien. So, in a way, he was just as innocent as a child, for what is innocence but ignorance. His ignorance was his virtue hidden behind a mask of cruelty.

The right to be innocent was snatched from him and now he did everything he could to fill the void in his heart with every misdemeanor he could commit.

Family. He didn't need it, he didn't value it and most of all he didn't know it.

Boris watched quietly in the corner, darkness enveloping him. He was mesmerized by how serene she seemed like no bad dreams invaded her. One thing he could say for sure was that he could suffocate her right now, the pillow lying innocently to the side.

Boris heaved a sigh. He was bad and he didn't care. He was more than that; he was evil, dark and sadistic and worse of all he loved it, rolled in the elixir of it. Yet a small inkling, a fraction of himself yearned for acceptance. For his dead mother's acceptance, and for Cleo's love even. It was enough to make him sick and he wrenched his fists and started pacing the room, uncertainty wracking his body with unwitting pain.

Boris had this sort of thinking before when Kressangah was in his life. Kressangah had hope for him. Who was she to hope for him? She saw flits of potential and that was what drew her back, time and time again until she finally realized he was no man to be redeemed; he was an evil to be feared.

He glanced to the corner and saw his Net Disperser. That thing—object—was more a part of him than any person. It was an extension of his malice and his tool for violence, his one true companion. That was his family: to exact vengeful wrath on all weaker specimens. He knew that. Hell, he had always known that, but he didn't want to acknowledge that something else was missing.

It couldn't be sentiment. He hated sentiment. He spat on it. Yet every night he went to sleep with a niggling thought that he was not the man he could be. He wanted to just take that pillow and suffocate her, end the misery.

Or did he think ending her misery would somehow stop his own? His problem would be solved but to no end would he feel resolved, so he let her breath and let her fetus remain alive...for now.

And he blazed into the night seeking comfort in alien brothels and bottoms of shot glasses.

Cleo stirred. Boris hoped she would not wake to find him leering at her. He would hate for her to think he actually cared. He quickly made way for the exit.

Cleo awoke to a noise but when she shook the grublantern to illuminate the room it was to emptiness. She imaged she saw the back of Boris. Overcome with tiredness she returned to her sleep never the wiser.

As Boris walked the glittery streets he thought back to the attack on Station Alpha.

Those things were not evil, they were purer than that. Even he had to admit they scared the life out of him. He was all for mayhem and cruelty but he rather liked the material world, the feel of someone gasping for air. He by no means wanted to see it destroyed; he wanted to manipulate it, squeeze it for all its juices.

Cleo was just extra baggage; in no way was he saving her or tying himself to her, rather he'd tie her to a big rock and plonk, be done with it. He was not grounded; he was a wild beast to be feared.

Morning came swift and sharp, the light from the sun blaring in her eyes. Cleo pushed back the sheets she had inadvertently twisted herself into. She was scared when she glanced down. There was blood.

What could that mean? She felt fear prickle at her. What if he found out? Would she be deemed irreparable? Would her life be in danger?

Suddenly she remembered the first time she found out she was pregnant. Images flitted through her thoughts. Though she wrangled with herself over the morality of what she could do, she doubted she could willingly cause harm.

She didn't want the child, but destroying a life—that was something else entirely. But could she make him mad enough to kill the baby and spare her from the guilt generated? A thought. A niggling, awful thought.

No prouder can a father be of the offspring he has fathered no later can he mourn the failing of his upbringing on the fruits of his love—Unknown Archives

Mayes could fight her way through the brush but she couldn't fight her incessant cough. She was captured by Adrian, who shared an endearing smile.

She was getting worse as the night descended; the cold acting as a catalyst. She didn't care about herself at the moment; all that mattered was Evelin and the baby. She needed to get her to safety before the baby came skidding out onto the ground.

Evelin's distressed voice could be heard ahead. Mayes hurried forward. "It's coming, Mayes! This child wants to be born."

Mayes saw an alcove up ahead that suited as some sort of shelter. "Up here!" she said.

The fires consumed the Parliament and humans everywhere were scared, hysterical, but all screaming ceased as soon as the light hit them.

An instant memory wipe and they wandered about aimlessly at first and then started asking what they were doing. The biting into necks, the pouring out of blood, alien vessels descending, everything had been erased like a bad dream and all that was left were news reports of a massive outbreak that had caused mayhem.

In the sewers, the tunnels led nowhere else. A man had his hand raised, pipe in hand. He was so tense he was afraid to let go of his weapon. He was going to bash that creature to death; he never felt such rage before.

Luckily, the creature before him turned to ash before he could do something. And in that moment, he realized one fact: what the hell was he doin holding a pipe? In the sewers? He dropped the weapon and walked out rather lost himself.

Mayes knew she had technology implanted into the stem of her brain to prevent the Wave of

Retribution exacting its effects and erasing memories, but where did that wave come from? And who had deployed it?

The days leading up to Harold's passing were filled with confusion and apprehension. When Stella heard about what had happened on Earth she was devastated. She had not loved Harold for a long time but that love had been there, left its imprint and so she was affected. So much so that she remained the rest of the time in her room swishing the gin in her left hand and crossing her red heels, over contemptuous.

"Can I come in, Madam?"

The slurred speech of Stella filtered through the door. "Y-yerss, you can come in-n."

An official-looking man stood in the doorway, his brooch with the insignia standing out on his left breast. Upon seeing the young man, Stella approached with arms wide, almost spilling her remaining gin.

The man stepped back in anticipation. He grasped her wiry arms and put the drink aside whilst fighting back Stella, who was attempting to kiss him.

"Miss—no. Stella. Stella!"

As the volume and sternness of his voice hit her, Stella's eyes blew wide and she looked like she had just been slapped. She threw herself out of his arms and stomped back into her room, taking care to lock it.

"Miss Rain?" The man knocked on the door. She did not answer so he attempted to convey his urgency through the door. "There is a problem, Miss Rain. As we left, the rift shut closed behind us. And Miss Rain, that is not the worst part. We have arrived to some sort of war. There are ships strewn everywhere and lost detached transmissions claiming of ghosts that can possess. We are stranded and without back up, Miss, as the rift closed and took half of our men with it. Who knows if they survived. Over 500 men, Miss."

Without anything else to add and the silence, the man disappeared down the hall and the strangled sobs of Stella could be faintly heard.

Sean lay beaten—not outside but pulverized inside. He was an eager pilot. He was also overconfident, cocky. He made dangerous manoeuvres that didn't just endanger himself, but the ship and Celeste. How he wished she was here. He did not know he was suffering from black-bleed, not until his link to Thorn was severed and the silence loomed, shrinking in on his mind.

It was like suffering from withdrawals. She had tried to warn him, and now that coupled with the loss of Celeste sent his mind into a turmoil of the cruelest kind: utter loneliness. At the stern,

Sean had felt like a rowdy cowboy as he worked the vessel like it was a part of him, a smooth device of death weaving in and out the fabric of space like a thread through a needle. It wouldn't have been half bad if he wasn't clearly displaying signs of back-bleed. She had warned him, he thought violently.

He pictured her minute details like drinking in a masterpiece. It was like he had painted her, every stroke to his whim. He had seen his madness building day after day and could not confront it. Where was his caution? He recalled what she had said about back-bleed.

"When the bond occurs the pilot become one with the ship's essence and with it the feelings of power and control. It will be like pure ecstasy. It becomes a bleed- over of the memories of the ship, a powerful creation inside the mind of one human."

She said it was like powering an AA battery with a nuclear bomb. Perhaps this detachment was for the better. That he could abide but his severance from Celeste he would never accept.

Two days earlier…

Out in space, debris floated around them; the debris of Detachment Palaces and Hive Ships, possibly the ones they saw before. "What is this?" said Sean.

"Something got to them. It is weird; the debris is whole, not segmented into pieces by a laser blast or live fire," Celeste started. "Perhaps these things are worse than what we first predicted."

Sean realized the seriousness of this discovery and came crashing down from his ship high. As far as he knew, the Raiders were the bad asses of this galaxy so for someone to crush them with their fist. Then another thought occurred as the continual back chatter with Thorn muttered in his ear. "What are Sprites?"

"Who told you that...? Wait, never mind."

Celeste knew only too well how he came by that tasty information. "They are kind of a disaster that befell civilizations aeons ago. They are very dangerous but hardly seen till it is too late."

Sean spoke first. "I know something. Yes, those logs. This is the threat that pilot was talking about. If such a threat could exist we may be more fragged than we initially thought."

Minutes were muddled as a great booming shattered them to their knees. Sean was overcome by some sort of force, gripping his head like it might split in two.

Suddenly Sean spoke, his voice distorted. "What is that? There is something. They're—they're inside me. I can't…can't get them out—"

Sean rocked into consciousness. He had fallen asleep—or could it be considered sleep when it was so marred by hellish nightmares? The ship was still dark, only illuminated by the Flashers, who were going to need a moon's light soon to repower. He would be left in utter darkness. Another sadness.

We often try to recreate the way we were when with that person but when can two halves be whole when one is gone?—Unknown Archives

Inside the locket was the only part he had left of her: a lock of her beautiful hair. Robert knew she would be given the Passing upon her passing. But he needed more than just the acknowledgement that she had moved on. He needed proof that she really did exist so he kept her hair as a memento. She was floating around out there resembling nothing of a person.

He kept the locket on his person always. He didn't know breaking into the secured facility that day would be so easy or that stealing an unmanned ship would be even easier. Obviously, the report that the "unidentified outbreak" was just a cover story for whatever really happened.

He knew not to trust his memories. He had kept a record of his life the day she died and he saw gaps. There was something the Parliament was hiding from him, from them all. He knew he wouldn't be able to find out now with them dead so he made way for somewhere he might just have some degree of hope—out in the unknown; a place that was denied by the Parliament.

Well now the Parliament was no more and the rules didn't matter. He was dishevelled and unclean for the first time. He had lost all manner of self and went out into the unknown, stumbling from foot to foot.

He did know that whatever really happened must have been major for him to get past the security defenses without even so much as a shot fired.

Several hours before the destruction of Station Alpha....

On his way toward his apartment room Kroden flitted in and out of consciousness, briefly lying there bruised and bleeding. He had been bashed...again. He wiped the dark blue blood from his nose, smearing it over his chin. He spat out the clotted blood forming in his mouth. His jaw on fire.

Kroden made it to his door after a delayed detour, pausing at each wall.

The doors hissed open and Kroden stumbled inside the dark to his messy little flat bed. His breastplate armour lay scanted to one side; his red skirt lay on the chair and his dagger in its sheath lay on top.

He had forgotten the man he was behind that gear. He had dissolved into a puddle of piss not even worth killing, just injuring and left to scamper into a hole.

Catching sight of himself in the mirror as he rattled the grublanterns, Kroden ran a finger down his scar. He had gotten that for her. He had bared all the pain and anger for that one girl and now he would probably never see her again. And that crushed him more than any fist to flesh.

Kroden was beaten countless times on countless stations. The assailants hadn't even known him. They just knew about him and that was enough for them to lay into him. This out of the way station called Station Alpha was no paradise; it was a shit hole inviting the shittiest people around in the universe to infest it just like it was infested with Halo Rats. The innards of the station would be chewed out within a couple of months, rendering the station inert. But it mattered not—another would be built in its place.

Kroden succumbed to sleep. He started to dream: Dillis stood with his hand draped across his knee staring out at the setting sun, red merging with orange like a river burst forth from its bank.

"Kroden, come see this," he urged. There was a strange echo: a clear giveaway that this was a dream.

Dillis was a short astute man with a ruler straight moustache. His rank was clearly displayed on his left breast pocket with a distinguishing insignia. "This is what my life has amounted to; what I lived and breathed for years—a turn of events that will herald a new age," he stated stoically.

The epic moment was marred by the dead around them; dead Gaul with their blue straight strands of hair stuck to their dark blue blood on their pallid faces. Kroden could not help but look away, sickened.

"Despite the repercussions of what you see here," added Dillis upon seeing Kroden waning, "we have taken steps forward. It was not wise to believe that the Generation War could finish so quickly and yet its regime has weakened."

The younger Kroden, absent of his scar, took a moment before tearing his eyes away from the dead fellow soldiers. "Why should you care what becomes of us? I mean, I am an orphan—what would you know of it?" he said a little more derisively than he intended, momentarily forgetting the higher- ranking officer he was addressing.

Dillis gave a knowing smirk. "I know more than you think, Kroden. And I also know the sacrifices to be made. I care for people that are not of my kin—that differ from my kind statistically and politically—because I was brought up in a human colony. My parents were human. I learned all there was to learn about Earth and the Old Fleet and a forgotten era so magnificent it makes all of us seem like itty-biddy chess pieces. Come with me, I will show you what I mean."

Kroden fast forward his dream, ever making noise and tossing around in his white sheets. They were in an encampment now—Gaul prisoners of war.

Kroden glanced up at what Dillis was drinking. Dillis caught his inquisitorial glance and smiled. There was that strange echo again. "It is the sap of the Gundagar trees, the ones we passed earlier. Brilliant qualities. You'll find Gaul are very resourceful—more so than you have come to believe. Strand them on a lifeless desert world and they will thrive. That is their nature and that is one of the reasons I believe they deserve our friendship. We could grow with them and learn along the way," he said. He took another sip.

They are not inferior as we have come to believe. We have to reach out and make them a part of our lives and dispel any further bloodshed. I have spent many a day mourning lives I have snatched away in the name of our cause. But it is a worthless cause, no closer to the serenity we aspire to reach than the darkness that encompasses us. If anything, we are moving farther away from the complete serenity we wish to achieve with this needless bloodshed," he said with clear distaste. "Thank you, Nesda," he suddenly said to the Gaul woman parting with the empty husk shell. "There is a lot we can learn from each other," he said, motioning for both of them to rise.

"And this is why you do this? The Golden Days?" added Kroden, not sure of the term but hearing Dillis talk of it.

"Yes, Kroden. It is our only hope." Both went to the end of the cliff and watched the last of the sun sink down in a marriage of red, orange and a burst of purple. A most auspicious dusk.

Kroden awoke with a sudden jerk, the station falling to pieces around him. Nursing a thudding headache, probably from the metal lain away from him, Kroden clumsily made it to his armour.

Everyone was in a mad panic, running every which way as he exited his room and fastened the last latch of his armour.

"The Raiders; they will engulf us all!" screamed one woman fleeing with her son, who flicked his snake tongue at him. The Golden days was a noble dream but the arrival of reality shook the very foundation he stood on.

Portions of his dream were coming back to him. He shook himself steady. He needed to get out. He dashed back inside, grabbed his gear and left in the herd of people cantering toward the escape pods.

Kroden noticed something. They weren't being attacked by Hive Ships; they were being attacked inward by some sort of ghosts. Maybe he shouldn't have had that drinking session earlier.

When Kroden got to the promenade with all the other aliens going the other way to escape pods, he saw that the assault was coming from some things swiping in and out of the metal—an unseen threat save for a slight distortion that moved through space and metal like silk. "They have come," one stipulated with his arms flailing wildly with some sort of bacteria on his face. "They have come!"

Kroden realized that most of these residents had come from other galaxies. They obviously knew something he didn't. Whatever they were, they moved like ghosts in space. They could travel through solid objects and apparently into people. A person next to him spat blood as the being inside meshed into her skin, forcing the blood out the pores.

Kroden made to save the woman but she was no longer sane—gone as she writhed in convulsive fits. If he stayed here he would die—or worse: become possessed or whatever by these horrid things. He had to get out of there, now; now was the time for cowardliness. Bravery would only certainly get him killed.

And then with clear perception, we realise one true, clear fact: we are alive, need there be anything else to add?—Unknown Archives

The canisters returned serenely to their dormant state. It was like nothing momentous had happened when the truth was exactly the opposite. Earth looked also peaceful. The people on it were just ambling about, unsure of what they were doing or how so many people were suddenly dead.

The Parliament was ashes.

Zias looked around, blinking. Where he was, he could not tell. Something was embedded in his skin and he cast his eyes down to see tubes running from his arms and legs. What was this?

And as though his thought had summoned her, Jathmoora made an appearance in the doorway. "I see you have awakened. Her voice was so calm but in a way threatening beyond belief.

Zias tried to move but each time he moved electrical currents jumped into his body and he was shocked. He looked at her, exasperated, needing an answer, a reason for this torture. "Why are you doing this? Where am I? Who are you?"

Jathmoora moved inside like a graceful woman of status. He flinched at her advancement though he knew the devices on him were delivering far worse damage.

"I am Jathmoora and you are on my ship. Keep your voice down. I don't want Hariot to know about this." She knelt so she was eye to eye with him. "I am doing this because on all accounts I know nothing about you. Where do you come from? What do you want? So, I believe it is my duty to ascertain any and all information from you. This is not my first choice, but times are hard and I can't afford to take any risks."

Suddenly Zias looked forlorn, scared even. "Look, I will tell you what you need to know. None of this is necessary." As he moved his hand in a gesture a jolt was delivered.

"Perhaps. But this way you can't afford to lie. Now, tell me about Earth? A place you said you come from?"

As Jathmoora left, the screams of Zias echoed in her ears. She felt bad about it all but threats were appearing everywhere. Now was not the time for pesky emotions such as empathy. One had to be hard in order to survive. She was doing the right thing. She was. Truly.

No order. Chaos bled inward, creeping like snaking rivers coursing with the slain. There was no hope to evade these creatures. No army was there to stop them. Everywhere and everyone was cast in darkness and there was no hope of finding the way out. Most had evacuated the galaxy and left for better chances. What they didn't know was what was happening was happening to the entire universe. There was nowhere to run. No hole to dive into.

Some valiant hero was supposed to manifest himself but no one relied on the help of some wayward stranger. It was everyone for themselves and in that bred an ugly side to the psyche. Everyone was stealing and making way with what they could. There was no thought to order or even common decency. All of that was erased, gone with the blood of those possessed.

The tremors of the universe could be felt everywhere by everyone. What could be done when so many horrible things were happening on all fronts? There was no relief, no pause to collect oneself and discover what to do. Everyone was becoming unreasonable and taking from those who could not defend themselves. It was horrible beyond belief.

The hive ships had all but evacuated. Now they ventured to their sacred space where they would slumber until the galaxy had righted itself. If only they had known the severity of what was really happening they would not have slumbered.

Hidden in a corner of the galaxy, this sacred space was never visited and contained no life so it was perfect for them. Like clusters of sacs, the ships gelled and hung in space like seeds waiting to spring forth.

Boris came bolting in like he sensed there was trouble. He looked to the sheets soaked in blood, exasperated. He hissed through his teeth and before long rage overtook his features. He had Cleo up against the wall one handed, choking the life out of her. "Listen to me and listen good! If that child is dead you are as good as dead too."

He let her go and he disappeared. Cleo was left coughing, rubbing her bruised throat. Hot tears exploded from her eyes. Just when she thought she was safe it all came tumbling down around her. False security. She fell for it every time.

Boris was seething; a hot trembling anger threatened to engulf him entirely. Why did he care for that thing in there? Because it was of his seed? No way! He would never begin to think to love it, to even tolerate it. But perhaps there was room for using it. An idea formulated, swirling in his corrupt mind like a storm. He could use the child; cultivate it into an ultimate hunter. Boris cracked his knuckles and neck. The thought was tantalizing.

Desperate people often resort to desperate measures but in the end, the desperate receive nothing for their vain efforts—Unknown Archives

Selene was Boric-kay, a related species to the Borics. They were of separate strange appearances yet both desirable for their individual looks, often attracting slavers to their small out of the way worlds.

Boric-kay had small faces framed with hair and bristles or quills intertwined—not quite as reptilian as the Boric race but ever so alluring with their exotic looks, though not subjugated to slavery like their cousins.

"Selene, are you coming?" exclaimed a monk up ahead over the hills of the southern continent of Sadie—less bogged and more pristine on these upper parts. They were located near the swamps but here it was just plains.

Selene twirled around, catching the smile of her mentor who approached with hurried steps. She met with a gaunt-looking alien who wore a leather cap enclave to his head. "What were you doing anyway?" he asked, curious.

Selene tufted her toes in the dirt. "I was fending off would-be robbers." Her cuts could be seen and clearly, the others would be appearing worse. "You know eventually my appearance is going to get me killed. I don't know why I just can't be a man. Forget that I am a woman and enslaved to the impulses of the opposite sex. I just want to not be like this," she said like her looks were an affront to any male's eyes when the truth was painfully opposite.

Maud looked at her, almost scanning her. She hated stares; he knew that. "And what do you suppose we do about that? Radical gender replacement? I hear the aligned planets of the Satanic System allow such brash procedures." he entertained touching her sores to better assess the damage.

"Uncle! You're so sarcastic sometimes."

Selene grimaced, no longer amused but rather annoyed and wrenched his hand away. She picked some local flowers, ground them in her hand and applied them to her cuts herself.

She was so beautiful on the outside, yet a brute at the core. "Wish I had the balls to do it. Maud, come on. We have places to be and people to see," she said overly sweetly like she was a girl with braids and sweet disposition and not the foul mouthed little terror he had raised.

Selene had packed her belongings—she owned little—and made her way to the Way Station. Maud caught up to her. He had no possessions at all; it was part of the monk way: no possessions allowed.

She placed her bags down, ready to board. "I wish you could accompany me," she said, the city-ship Mystic in the background. She seemed saddened. "I know that you have done everything in your power to make my life better than it was. I thank you and shall always think of you as a father."

Maud smiled and was shocked when she came at him with open arms. She never had personal contact, at least not this personal. She hated it, said it was too sentimental and girly.

"I know you do, but I have my path to follow—as do you. Just don't let her get under your skin," he warned.

"We both know that only applies to you, Uncle. I think she is a great mentor," she said.

"Go on go before you say something I would rather not hear," he said, shoving her inside the vessel.

"Goodbye, Maud," she said. Suddenly her heart felt heavy, weighed by grief. She would miss him terribly and knew not if she would ever see him again.

Boris was a hunter through and through but more than that he was a cold- blooded killer and Cleo knew if he found out about her predicament, her life would no longer matter and her children would be in jeopardy. But did she really care about that? Did she care what would happen to this thing growing inside her?

Cleo rubbed her bulge tenderly, eager to scratch it out of her. Thick tears streamed down her face, forming stains on her cheeks. Cleo hadn't said a word in what seemed forever. Actually, she never talked. Not even when she was a child. Some debated whether she could or if she even had a tongue. How could she be a mother when she lacked the basic necessities to communicate? She would never be normal; she could never be a mother.

Boris returned at night. He seemed calmer but Cleo did not wish to test his mood. She had gotten rid of the sheets and now calmly ate a sludgy soup of some kind. Boris said nothing, not even by way of a stare.

"Make sure you're ready in the morning," he said suddenly. "We're leaving."

Cleo could not talk; she simply shook her head.

"Here, take this." And Boris chucked some sort of bottle at her. "It will help." He disappeared into the other room.

Cleo was by all means bemused by his behaviour. He was what you would call a hot and cold person. But this? She didn't know where to start. This was an act of kindness, but she didn't understand. He was harsh and deadly but could it be that there was another side to him, one that had not been able to flourish? She shook her head. He is a killer through and through, she thought. She took the pills and finally surrendered to sleep.

So here she was: alone with her murderous lover in a shady apartment; she was a tag-along but there was nothing that she could do to cut the tether. What could she do about it but stay along for the ride and hope she didn't end up on that wall? Now pregnant, she was in even more danger than the countless rapes before.

Cleo stifled a sob as she heard the clinking of Boris rechecking his Net Disperser. He seemed so calm. She was finding herself more fearful than when she thought she had lost the baby. He was not to be trusted. She knew the killer inside. He was up to something, but what she could not know.

That night, Boris lay next to her on the clean sheets. He knew that he wanted this birth to happen. He knew that he was not a changed man as some would have come to understand. He was what he was always meant to be: ruthless, cold, and relentless.

He would pretend to be good, to care. He would do what he had to in order to make sure Cleo birthed this child. And before she knew what was happening, he would act and take her child. No amount of talking or thinking could change his mind. Deviant he was and deviant he always would be.

Flames and fire forever intertwined, for there is no distinction between the two
—Unknown Archives

There were theorists out there that speculated the existence of other universes existing outside our own. Could there really be separate walls that define us? The galaxies are held with cohesiveness but when that glue disappears all manner of chaos unfolds. Does that mean that we unfold with it? Was time "time" or was it a ripple effect in a very large pond.

No ripples last the duration of their journey—eventually it pitters out. And so, it is with space. It is stretching the length of it ever expanding. No one can expect to live forever but those romantic enough encourage the notion. The stories we tell ourselves allow us to sleep at night, the wishful thinking of the possibilities, but like those ripples, eventually, there will be nothing left. Only the still water.

The System Le-chiusa ran unchecked. The Sprites were gone but what they left behind made even the most resolved man shudder. Is this what awaited the poor souls in the Angelic System? Worse?

The universe now had cracks in it, widening and becoming more precarious. The maggots writhed through the holes, rifts that before lay dormant. Space/time was irrelevant. Space travel was instantaneous but the price was easily steeped. No one knew the fortune they had perhaps a million years ago; time was fragile, precious, but now the sands trickling down were thinning. Time was nearly up.

"What do we do when the tide is stronger than us?" asked Zias.

Jathmoora looked down at this man she had tortured and she felt the prick of remorse in her insides and it made her squirm. "I do not know." She removed the pads that stuck to his skin with a satisfying pop.

He was now beyond emaciated and wasted to nothing, dwindling to nothing. She tried to help his haggard mass but he refused it.

Hariot had refused to talk to her when he looked into the room. Before Jathmoora could explain, they had landed on planet Sadie and picking up her niece. She managed to escort her niece to the room before too many questions could be asked. But Hariot. He didn't give her anything. He had seen the darkness in her and it scared him to pieces. So, he locked himself in the hydroponics and did not come out.

Zias was in the room leant against the wall. He saw Selene and reached out his hand in desperation. "Help me!"

Jathmoora tried to explain to Selene but she backed away from her like she was contagious with some plague.

"I cannot attempt to convey the sorrow I feel for the pain I have caused you. All I can say is nothing. A sorry would be more a taunt than an apology."

The small eyes of Selene blinked in astonishment. She took off before anyone could notice her tear stained face. She was tough—at least she conveyed herself as such—but the fifty seconds she saw in there tested even her own concrete faith. She was after all a girl—a girl rife with emotion.

Mayes couldn't believe what she held in her arms—the tiniest of life. The cry pierced the cool morning. Evelin held her arms out for the baby. "Here you go." Mayes grabbed her jumper and braved the cold to better accommodate the life she had delivered into this world, the dimness of the fires dying in the background.

"We'd better get you two to the hospital."

Evelin was so happy—a little starved, but happy to see those eyes. "I will call her Mayes if that is okay with you. I have decided you are to be godmother to young Mayes."

Mayes was beyond flattered but eager to get out of there, her shins protesting as ever. "I would be honoured. Now, how 'bout we get out of here and get you two to a hospital."

Mayes didn't stick around in the hospital. Blue coats freaked her out. She was a nurse once but never again. She said her warm well wishes to Evelin and was glad to hear the baby was doing well before she made a quick exit, coughing violently.

Mayes was happy to have reached home in one piece. She longed for her couch. She didn't even bother with the television, her rasping cough following her. She was wiped. A meow caused her to look down and see Ginger affectionately pleading for her tin of tuna. "I forgot to feed you, sweetie."

Before long, Mayes allowed herself to sleep, Ginger curled on top of her chest, a half- drunk tea sat upon the table.

0800hrs before incident at the Order

"You are the essence."

"HA!"

"You are swift in battle."

"HA!"

"You are the product of your devising."

"HA!"

Kressangah awoke with a start. The images still floated in front of her. Her colleagues who lost their fight. Looming beside her was the Laranie—Gerof, his soft hairy hand on hers. It was a welcome comfort and a much-needed one. "Bad dream?" he stated.

"Last moments with my people. I really...I don't know whether to be grateful it's over or—"

"Child, it is far from over. We have staunched the wound but the infection still spreads. The Generation War is a stigmatic pond. I do not know if we will ever run the same but there are far worse things happening in the galaxy at the moment than to concern ourselves with trivial wars."

"What do you mean?" Gerof looked away like his eyes were glassed with water. He did not answer her, for he would have to inform her of the reason he came to her in the first place. Kressangah hadn't seen him this serious since they had that spat on Regel 14 when he told her to forsake her duty and leave with him. Yes, I should have gone with him, she thought bitterly.

The ship headed further into the Satanic System heading toward the edge of System Le-chiusa. He was about to tell her when everything rained down on them, the ship beginning to tremble and the sensors displaying gravitational disruptions. That could only mean one thing: the truth had come banging on their hulls.

"Gerof, you getting these fluctuations? They are all over the grid." The ship was beginning to shudder and shake and before long it was on fire. Gerof could not find her through the thick flames. A bulkhead came crashing down, blocking his path to Kressangah who he had seen up ahead screaming in pain and in one flash darkness it took him. That would be the last thing he would ever see.

Pain is what makes us real so when we stop feeling does that make us unreal?
—Unknown Archives.

The great and esteemed Sultan was a vile and perverted man with thick porky fingers. He had a great appetite that did not just portray to food. He would advance on his fostered granddaughters and try to seduce them, snaking his hands around them like they were his harem. His particular favourite and the most mouthwatering delicacy was Lavinia, who was his own blood, his daughter. He knew no border of decency. To him, all women were culprits and easily devoured.

Everyone knew he tried to kill his only daughter when she denied him and for the first time raised her hand against him. What he didn't fathom into his plans was that his daughter had already birthed a child she hid under her cloak who was then taken by the Sultan's guards. For her betrayal, he devised a much crueler fate than death for her. He killed the father in front of her and then condemned Lavinia to the Pits for a lifetime of torment and cruelty holding in his hands his new replacement.

Lolalia gazed longingly into the velvet midnight blue skies, the wind whipping her fine hair back. She loved to stare out at the stars at the open window. She turned around in time for an airborne vase to hit the side of the window. Loud, raucous voices could be heard drifting in. She made her way toward the commotion warily. She passed servants scattering to their hideouts, opening secret compartments in walls.

"You can't keep doing this, Vivien!"

The one called Vivien looked ready to pounce; she was even pulling out her hair.

"What is going on?" came the meek voice of Lolalia. She was always so soft spoken. That was probably why so many people underestimated her.

Vivien cut her a glance as sharp as glass. "This doesn't concern you!"

"Well, I think it does, considering that was my mother's vase."

"Dear Mummy. She is dead. Why bother with her memory?"

Hot prickles of tears stung Lolalia's face. Why were her sisters so mean to her? She was gifted with Kind of Heart but that also meant that she was extremely raw and the single stab of cruelty would send her into vibrating tremors of sorrow.

The other sister, who was less mean but ever conceited, spoke. "This isn't the time, Lolalia," said the one called Candice in a slightly kinder voice, but not by much.

"Candice, you know we have to do it. I don't care if she finds out. Maybe she should know. Yes, I shall enlighten you, dear sister." Her smile disturbed Lolalia greatly.

The one called Candice hid her face in her hands like looking at Lolalia would suddenly cause her to combust into flame. "Please, Vivian. Don't do this. You will rip this family apart." But her voice was just white noise.

"Lolalia, you hated our grandfather. Why?" The question was just flung at Lolalia, who was quickly overridden. "I will tell you. He did not kill your mother. He sent her to a prison transport—you may be familiar with it: The Pits.

He was a pig, a vile wretched thing that didn't deserve rulership over this planet or life itself. So as faithful sisters we did our duty. No Sultan, no empress, and no line but there is the little trouble of you, who by our records is of his blood. So, you see the trouble."

Lolalia realized what that implied. She stepped back and then started stumbling away as Vivien came at her with a hidden knife.

"Vivian!" came Candice's hysterical voice. Obviously, she had not foreseen this act unbecoming of her radical sister.

"She has to be rid of! The Crotch line is tainted. We are dying while their blood still runs."

Lolalia managed to gain some distance before heading to the ship bay. She needed to leave but the tears were obscuring her vision. She wiped her face hastily and stumbled over her own feet, looking back to see one of the human servants' dead, sliced apart. She quickly recollected herself and sped to the nearest ship she could find.

Vivian cut through a pile of people, slashing one in the arm. She was beyond a hurt soul; she was lost completely, swallowed by the gaping hole of despair that came with years of abuse.

Shouts from the injured man and Vivian brandishing her weapon fell to a dull hum as Lolalia fired up the ship. She was naturally attuned to the way technology worked. She figured out how to use things quite easily and right now speed was of the essence.

The events of what had just happened swirled around in Lolalia's heavily burdened mind. Was her mother alive? Was she the Sultan's heir? She knew looking back at the small planet that she would never be able to return—not with a wild element like Vivian running around. She thought with a pang about the future of her people but then she could only think of her dear mother suffering in that place. And no sooner said, she was gone. The planet Jelec diminished and fell far behind. Even though she felt her world disappear, a new world opened up—the world where it was just her and her mother. The Siren Moons with their power guided her even out here. She knew she had to find her mother. That was her sustenance; she needn't anything else.

"I think you should go in there."

"Why? Who's there?"

Dillis tried to tell Kroden and then decided to let him see for himself. Kroden eased into the room like he might disturb the dust.

Her body lay there still and perfect. His breath caught in his chest.

7 hours earlier on Station Alpha…

Kroden managed just to get into one of the last pods, never assessing why it was left— a detail for later. He didn't get far when his pod was picked up by another ship by which he had lost all consciousness—work of the Haldo he slammed down earlier.

He had tried to send a beacon out but in the midst of it instead met darkness and awoke next with a nudging pistol at his head. "Wha? Who—When?"

"I can answer all three. You escaped near death. I am your saviour, very lucky and I just saved you from a decompressed pod. Nice flying, by the way."

Suddenly the figure focused into clearness and the line between reality and dream had shifted. "Sarge?"

"That's right, son. I remember when I met you. You were a meagre orphan; pliable, menial but the war changed everything, every person that came into it."

"I am not working for them anymore," began Kroden but was overrode by Dillis, who had the stage.

"Oh yes, a lot changed over the years." He had not taken away the pistol yet. "You're lucky to be alive, son."

"Is that going to change?"

"You don't appear affected or worse, possessed. Sorry 'bout that. Precautions. When I heard about your elite soldiers, I wasn't sure if the orphan I taught would still be there. I take it you know of the situation?"

Kroden tried to shake the fuzziness away. "Barely. What were those things?"

"Things that make the war look like a picnic. Come."

Kroden accepted his hand, a far more acceptable offer than the cold nozzle of his pistol. Precaution? His Sarge sure had changed over the years but then so had he or more so changed back.

47

Wounds cannot heal if the infection has spread–Unknown Archive

Cardvia washed the last of the blood from her skin but she feared it had seeped further. No amount of scrubbing would remove the blood from her soul if she ever indeed had one. She was on the ship—a dead ship. She didn't want to leave because she felt if she left the ship she would know then it was all real.

Cardvia spent hours moving bodies to the bays to eventually space them. Not a traditional sendoff but at least she wasn't stuck with them gawking at her with their pallid faces. All around her the piles of mounting bodies was making her feel sick.

She wished so hard that she wasn't what she was. She could understand why she was the last of her kind. Her species couldn't survive as parasites. But what could she be? What else was there out there for her? She was driven by bloodlust; it owned her, made her its bitch. And to try to be something else was fighting against her nature. And yet, she clung to that hope with every fiber of her being.

The ship started beeping. Clearing the console and smearing blood over the screen, Cardiva viewed her impending doom as the ship closed in on an asteroid field. Cardvia snapped to reality as she realized the ship was in the vicinity to approaching asteroids that weren't any ordinary asteroids.

Was she already out this far? Surely not, but she knew before even checking the sensors. Devastator's Edge. They were erratic asteroids that made a field riddled with holes, and worse, infested with Snapping Moroi Eels, the universe's biggest anthropoids surviving in the vacuum of space.

The Snapping Moroi Eels would have her for breakfast. That was sweet irony: something eating her for a change. She couldn't stop the momentum of the ship; she was on a direct course to being the main banquet.

If the food was what they needed then food was what she would give them. The bodies all set up nicely in the launch bay and Cardvia strapped the explosives the other side of the hatch. She slammed down the panel and gave the Moroi Eels something to chew on. The Snapping Moroi Eels jumped out of hidden holes and chomped down whole bodies.

They loved meat and didn't mind the taste of metal to get to it but for them, the taste was more bitter than usual as she detonated the explosives she had managed to strap to the bodies in record time. She was sure they would have a few cracked teeth by now. The path before her was clear.

Cardiva may have avoided death for now but eventually, it would claim her. She didn't believe in an afterlife. To her, everything that had a pulse would eventually succumb to death. It was a cycle and to think that we could avoid it was greatly stupid. Cardvia didn't fear death because she knew the facts. She knew there was no heaven, no hell, but a span of nonexistence. The universe was much the same. It too had an age. It would end one day and perhaps all the atoms would return to the box it came from.

Sean was left on a listless ship, looking at blood stains as awful reminders. He went into the room that meant so much to Celeste and read for hours, lost in the words he imagined her reading. "We could not have anticipated the extent of their malice for we only thought them sprites. But these beings come from darkness and know nothing that accompanies light. They are pure hatred—hatred for everything in this universe that is matter. At first, we experienced bouts of gravity fluctuation and then the radiation started. I escaped in time though staved not my own death to record this but that of my crew. If anyone is reading this then please know that these things cannot be stopped. I have never in my life time come across such undiluted evil. Old Timer, protect us."

Sean felt the tug of tears deep in his navel. These books spoke the truth and it rang clear in his ears. What could they do against such evil? Celeste was gone and he doubted he would ever see her again. And that doubt manifested into fear; a fear he could not contain. His baby, his sole reason for being, was gone and only the company of despair was left in his cavity of a heart.

The end of days draws ever nearer but still the world rotates like there is no end in sight – Unknown Archives

Reaching for another drink, Boris swayed to keep himself stationary. The baby was alright. Cleo was alright. But was he alright? Hardly ever. He knew deep down that he should have killed them both but something got in the way—something even he could not have foreseen. And it wasn't love or compassion. It couldn't be.

The planet Vern was soon out of their sight. Boris knew he had to fly away but how far was far enough? He didn't rightly know.

The screaming came so fast the glass slipped from his hand. Boris ran to the screaming. It was time. Cleo was going to pop. He stood there, not quite sure what to do. This was all new to him and scary as hell.

She couldn't talk but man could she scream. Boris wanted to shut her legs so the baby wouldn't come skittering out but there was no time. He grabbed what he could and made her comfortable. He didn't even think of what he was doing; it just kind of came naturally.

He then realized what he was doing and came somewhat to his version of senses. He let go of her hand as he was holding her, comforting her. What was this woman doing to him? For years he had abused her, used her like toilet paper, and now he decided to be chivalrous and noble. It was beyond him. He strolled away and left her to painful contractions.

He didn't care. No, he didn't care. So why was the hair on his arms sticking up? Why was there a knot in his stomach that hadn't been there before? Why did this shit even matter? Nothing mattered. Only sex, violence, profit and his own life. He couldn't believe the train of thought. It was stupid and he would not even allow himself that. He decided that he had to leave her and wait it out. He did so outside, leaning down the wall and feeling his heart—which he considered was shriveled up—pump with every scream. And then the cry pierced the air.

Boris took off his saturated top; they were passing the twin suns of Planet Macabre and the heat was penetrating the hull. He squeezed the shirt into a bowl. The sweat tinkled hitting the metal sides.

Hooked on the edge of the mirror was a tribal-looking root carving. Noticing it in the corner of his eye, Boris grasped it lightly with his clawed hand. A memory swam back to him and suddenly he wasn't on the ship but on Planet Isis, his birth-world.

The ship's shaking dropped him out of his reverie. He clenched his fists tight. He would be a hunter, ruthless, and meticulous. This soft sentimentality was for losers, not for vicious animals like himself and he tore the carving and threw it away. Once he paid off his debts he would be on his way to making fortune on a station that was ideal for his lifestyle. He would be carving his own fate free from petulant emotion. And Isis would be in his rear.

Boris had squeezed the t-shirt so dry his hands were chaffing. He returned to reality with a burning sensation to his fingers. He dumped the shirt into the bowl and made for the pleasure room. He strode with determination, with gusto, as though pulled by a yanking string. With a fiery spirit that could not be contained, he strode to the alien prostitute and unsuspectingly planted her with a kiss.

"W-what are you doing? Usually, you just go for the goods, Boris."

"Shut up."

The piercing cry of the newborn baby roused Boris with a shuddering smack against the wall. The doors slid open. He took a moment before cautiously stepping in. There were muck and blood everywhere but in her arms, was a baby, clearly half alien. He couldn't help it; a smile visited his face.

He made to approach and grab the child when the ship shuddered with an awful wrenching noise. The lights flickered. Boris knew this wasn't good. The baby cried. The ship shuddered and Boris acted. He saw only one option: Abandon ship. He saw two people: Cleo and the child. He realized he was becoming infected with emotion. This was his time to be the brute he was and not wilt under the loving eyes of Cleo or the child she had birthed. He ripped the child from her arms. She was weak and could not reclaim her. She was hemorrhaging and succumbed to unconsciousness.

Boris stopped just as the door swished open, the baby crying in his arms, Cleo unconscious, and the ship collapsing around them. They would come. They would come and they would rip her to pieces. He should have been glad. What was this infernal thing he was feeling? He hardly knew. He acted fast and grabbed a handful of Flashers. It was a wives' tale. He scattered them around her, not caring if it would work. She was doomed either way. Then he left with the baby in hand.

The ghostly shimmers of the Sprites invading the ship crossed him. Having past experience with the entities, he dodged most of them holding a Flasher above the baby. It was like Kryptonite to them. He took one last glance as the door closed, leaving his slave to the wrath of these things. But in his arms, was a baby and looking down at her something happened inside, like a tick of the clock or the spring of a mechanism.

At the end of the days, would living have been worthwhile or just a time spent dawdling around the universe aimlessly? –Unknown Archives

Zias lay unconscious. A heartbeat came back to him, thumping in his ears. He opened his eyes wide, blinking away the haziness. Where was he? Then it all came back to him in a flooding headache.

All around him were sparking, damaged consoles and his crew...they were all...dead. He hadn't moved from his last predicament except now he was nursing a sore head. What had he hoped, that an angel would come down and swoop him to safety? There were no such things. Outside, bits of his ship orbited two strange moons emitting some sort of aura.

And then suddenly a jerking memory came to the surface. A signal that they had picked up moments before chaos unfolded. He heard it before their ships inserted control. The signal somehow pulled them towards jagged rocks, luring victims to their death. But he alone had survived. Only him. It didn't make any kind of sense and what was worse, he didn't know if he deserved a second chance. Not for the type of person he was.

Thudding awake, Zias saw the bowl of food in the right corner. He dragged his limp body to it, stuck his finger in, and brought the horrid sludge to his lips. His hands trembled and his mind turned into the substance he sucked into his mouth. He was alive and staved off death for a second time but he feared it was all too late.

The hours melted into one another. Zias accomplished some measure of sleep while Jathmoora was away and then Jathmoora came in. She held a plax in her hand. He was still traumatized and shuffled back like she was a repellent of some kind. His eyes felt heavy but he managed to somehow open them.

Jathmoora had entertained a hope that he would wake from this living death. She had to show him, wake him up somehow. He was close to delusional but once she pressed to play his eyes opened with wide attention.

Images flashed by in quick succession. The plax played scenes from another galaxy, one not familiar; recordings from security feeds on numerous stations and trade ships. A similar burst of energy like the legendary Wave of Redemption rippled across the galaxy, causing something to happen. It was unbelievable. A moth to a flame.

"They are referred to as Dark Matter Entities. They came to pick off the dead when the Raiders attacked. Then the attackers became the attacked. The Light Conductors are dangerous on numerous fronts but the most potent are the fact that it invites these vultures. And I hate to admit it, but they are far fearful than the Raiders. To the Raiders we are food; to the Sprites, we are in the way. These things come along and infest the galaxy. The Raiders are a pest but these things—these things are pure evil," she said. "That galaxy is now inhabitable. Rifts have torn it to bits. Fortunately, no one knows the whereabouts of the devices, lost long ago by the Ancient Ones." Suddenly she saw it, the twinkle in his eye. She had struck a chord; she had unearthed the truth.

That was his secret. That was what he was holding onto. She continued despite his discomfort. "The Raiders will drain every morsel of blood till this universe is but a dry husk and then the Dark Matter Entities will descend and pick off the survivors. They will have their part: us out of the way, free reign on the universe. I want to know about your world, and about your goals. Tell me, what has happened over there that makes you detonate a device in my face?" she said, wincing at the reminder of a fresh abrasion on her right cheek. "Do that and the pain will stop. I promise." She waited for him to reply but as Jathmoora looked into his face, it was still, inanimate. He was dead inside. She had broken him. Those images were the last straw for his sanity. She had let him peer into hell and it swallowed him whole.

Dark insidious seeds that had been sewn aeons ago threatened to bloom and sprinkle their deceit like toxic pollen across the galaxies. The Coalesced Galaxies, AKA Super Clusters were once conjoined, but the tear of them drifting apart left Rifts: a phenomenon both amazing and mind boggling; its creation went beyond anything science or humanity could grasp. And so a tie between the Kale Galaxy and the Milky Way Galaxy was made and there was a door to whatever wonders or whatever evil.

Why was it that the galaxies drifted? Was it natural? Was it age? It was a scary thought but theorists were starting to come about the revelation that the universe wasn't as limitless as some believed. That it had a limit, a point of end. And these Rifts were only the beginning. A sign of what was yet to come. Who then could save them? Were they redeemable?

Who knew what dark threats lay waiting in the corners of the Voids, spaces stretching between each galaxy? A door had now been opened and evil would snake its way in just like it had done so many aeons ago and threatened the future of the Ancient Ones, a race thought to have died long ago but remained, if not in a different skin.

What was known about the Ancient Ones was limited to a few rumours and hearsay. People's descriptions of them varied. Some said they were large and menacing and others proclaimed they were dainty like the Celestial Beings. Anyone's portrayal was up for interpretation.

A crew flew past the sacred grounds. "Something deep and disturbing down there. What do you suppose it was? All that's left is debris."

"Whoever built the ships would know the answer."

"Too bad they're not around to ask."

1000 years ago.....

"Daddy, Daddy! let's play Wraith and Runner."

"Not now, hun. I am trying to fix the systems on these ships. You've been watching those old Earth show transmissions?"

"What are they for?"

"Well, you know about the epidemic? I think you're old enough to know that our top scientists and engineers have created these vessels for our souls. We'll be seeing the universe. While our bodies will be different, we'll survive."

"Wow. I'll be a ship."

"No, sweety. There are occultations for the young. Only the old buggers like me are affected."

"So I won't see you?"

"No, sweety. But it is the only way our voice will be known."

"I'll miss you, Daddy."

"I'll miss you too, munchkin."

In the madness, can it be that we are consumed by the evil we have learned to stay away from or is it that it still finds us in the times of pure darkness? –Unknown Archives

Sean was asleep and flashes of events shot past his vision like a movie reel.

No sooner had the darkness come that Sean found himself slumped over, drained of all willpower.

More flashes. The last precious moments with his love. They were of horror.

He started to get angry with himself, clawing at his head like something was squirming inside. Celeste tried hard to keep his hands tucked to one side.

He was starting to scare her. The lights shut down suddenly and her fear amplified. Darkness had swallowed the ship whole, heart beat in the distance.

"What's going on?" she said in a small, timid voice.

Sean still scratched himself madly. She tried frantically to stabilize him. He was sinking to the ground, overcome by what she could only see as madness.

Perhaps the depth of space was too much for him, or her worst fears had come true: the ship had taken over his mind. "Let him go. Don't you dare take him from me!" she shouted to the ship.

She could see nothing, hear only the thump of her own heart. Celeste grabbed Flashers from a compartment, flimsily grabbing at them and laying them like breadcrumbs throughout the ship. As she hovered one over Sean, she could see his pallid face, the sweat coating him like liquid. "What do I do, Sean?" The silence was a piercing answer, thunderous and ominous. Celeste was left alone and the ship was making odd noises now—Sean as well, as he seemed to be gagging on his very own tongue.

The ship Thorn tumbled through space inert, paralysed. There were no signs of life stirring within. The Dark Matter Entities were taking swift dives that almost looked like they were stealing chunks of the ship's essence just as they had done with the Raiders prized Hive Ships—and even their conglomerated construct could not withstand the onslaught of their might. The blood-curdling scream of Celeste echoed throughout the possessed ship. No one came to her rescue; no one heard her screams. The silence weighed heavy like an ominous presence.

Hours later, Sean awoke to wires sparking and fried consoles, blackened from short circuiting. He awkwardly placed his shaky and sweaty hand on the nearest console. He didn't care about the minuscule scraps of metal cutting into his hand; he was so engrossed with his thumping headache that he didn't even register the pain.

Sean tried to shake his head clear of the cobwebs but he felt weirdly claustrophobic. He then realized something more immediate. It was silent—too silent. He couldn't hear the ship; he was disconnected. And then he saw the trail of blood leading away from the bridge and dread took over him like a hard anvil.

Celeste's blood! He made a wild dash out and followed the flashers that led to an escape pod, the edges sprayed with her blood. And then he stopped as the beeping console advising him she was no longer on the vessel. Dear god, what had happened?

The ship was frighteningly silent and there was so much blood. Wasn't she on the ship? How could that be? Even if she jettisoned, he'd only been out a few minutes. But when Sean wiped the console clean of her blood that dripped over the sides he saw hours had passed; hours she had to spend alone, frightened…hurt? He could feel his insides expand, squirm. He had failed her. He had promised to protect her. And where was she now? God only knew.

Those logs weren't exaggerating. The nightmare these things unleashed was clear throughout the ship. Sean could hardly see but thanks to Celeste and the Flashers, he saw enough to get around. He didn't know where to start.

He didn't know the schematics for this ship. And without a direct line to Thorn, he was feeling the prickle of insanity at the back of his mind as pure sadness wrought his body in an aching cocoon then thudding to awareness he grits his teeth and clenched and balled his fist.

Sean awoke the sweat cold on his face like a sheet of ice. He was breathing heavy. Those things weren't in him. They couldn't be. He was alone, lost, and tormented by dreams. But for all the horror they showed, they also showed her. And he was losing her piece by piece, day by day. He let out a god-awful screech that could have melted the metal around him.

Jathmoora understood her curiosity. At a young age, Selene had demonstrated a bizarre affinity for morbid things. She saw someone bleeding and she wanted to know why and how and whatever other verbs she could come up with. They went into Jathmoora's sparsely decorated room and sat face to face. Aromas wafted through the air. It was a nice change from the clinical death outside.

"So, how was life on planet Sadie?" added Jathmoora like mad torture wasn't happening just outside this room.

Selene smiled knowing the underlying question to that sentence. "You mean how is Maud?"

"I don't pretend to pry but yes, how is Maud?"

"You should talk to him yourself. I know he would like to hear from you."

"I know, but we have a tainted past."

"Well, the way I see it if you love someone, balls to everyone and anything else. You want them, claim them." She was brash. Jathmoora looked at her as though with someone else's eyes. She was always tomboyish but she was also a rare beauty and yet so young, so naive. She had lost that innocence long ago.

"I wish it were that easy, child. But when you're older you will realize life doesn't become about want or have, it becomes about what is and what's not. And Maud and I were not to be." Jathmoora looked away suddenly overcome with strong emotion.

Hariot was the one to supply nutrients to Zias daily, though Selene often tried to intervene and help. Hariot made it a point to ground some specific dry leaves and place them in with the paste. He was not a doctor but he believed in the medicinal properties of alien plant life. There were noble prizes in waiting.

"He's been like that for ages." Maverick lacked the finer finesse of people skills. He came across as rude and unemotional, detached even. But he was the captain so his word went.

Maud was far away but he knew that Selene would be safe so he returned to the situation with a rather shaky nod of his head. "Yes, he seems to have taken your insults to heart."

"I merely commented that he stop being a pretty boy and embrace manhood."

"He is a Celestial Being and their appearances are well honoured in their culture. To ask him to not bathe just to save water consumption was to him a great scorn."

Maverick placed a hot hand on his head. He was fed up with having to coddle everyone—especially this flight of fantasy. He was after all his slave. Why was it important how his slave felt? Why did he have to be kind so he didn't hurt his feelings? He should jump at his command, not lock himself in the cargo bay and proceed to not talk to anyone like a sulking baby boy.

Maverick bashed at the door with his palm. "Stern, you open this door right now or so help me I will open the hatch doors and drop your bronzed arse into space!"

Maud was now shaking his head fervently with disapproval. "Maverick! Stern, there is no point to this. Please, what if we come to some sort of compromise?"

Maverick mouthed 'no' but Maud was insistent. Maverick heaved a sigh. "Oh, very well, Stern.

You may wash once a week but any more than that and you can lock yourself in the cargo bay with my condolences while you starve to death."

"In other words, he is sorry and would be grateful if you would come out."

The door hissed open. Stern came out, no look of appreciation, just simple relief that soon he would be letting cool water touch his densely dirty skin.

Maverick bit his scarred lip and rubbed his shadowed shaved head. "Bloody boy thinks he owns this ship." Since Maud had come on board there was less agitation amongst the crew. He hoped to instil some sort of peace after all that was a Monks prerogative. And it was working but for ticking time bombs like Stern who held resentment for Selisca being killed, there was a doubt that even his skills could be of any use before being killed.

When love has encompassed the soul will hatred destroy the heart, or has it become tougher through the hurdles of loss to ever be broken again?—Unknown Archives

Lavinia gripped the edges hard, mould and wet grit seeping into her nails as she scrambled upwards to lift herself off of the icy cold floor. Down in the darkness, she seemed to be without hope or light, all enveloping darkness sapping it from her very breath.

Gases would soon seep into her chamber and once again she would relive the torment of illusions and false hopes. Sometimes she'd rather the other option but if she took that path there would be no climbing out, just endlessly falling, tumbling toward an abyss so cold and dark that she stopped the thought there and then with a violent thrash of her head bouncing off the wall.

She was weak and growing weaker by the day. The food, if you could call it that, was nothing but the basic of nutriment paste, tasteless and bland. Without the needed sunlight and fresh air, with the constant coldness and assault on the mind, it wasn't long before one would crack. Lavinia eased herself back onto her creaky thin bed. She was stronger than that though. She had to be...for her.

These humans that manned the Transdrive Asteroid, they had no remorse. How could they even be human? She had heard of their duplicity; their kindness and their misery. Never had she encountered a human with this evil twisted mind, pure, undiluted. It was like they were possessed or something, sapped of all humanity.

But unfortunately for them, they were just plain human, the more horrid side exposed for all to see. Some said space did it, made them hollow inside. No one could know for certain; all that was known was to avoid them at all costs. They weren't always these shells. Once they were the most decent of people until life in space changed them for the worse and soon there was no kindness, only misery, a standalone muck that sucked shit in.

The sounds of the cold den they were in deafened her: slow dripping pipes, corroded archways, and infested systems with Halo Rats slowly gnawing, and the ominous oppressiveness of silence mixed with whimpering prisoners.

It was enough to drive anyone mad but if that was not enough, the humans had devised a gas infiltration system. Every hour on the hour, hallucinogen gases were pumped into each cell, snaking down the corridors and playing torturous jokes on the prisoners. There was no escape. Many died, succumbed to their own madness.

Constantly on the move, no one ever knew where they were and increased the broken psyche to not know where they were but constantly lost in mind and space. The part-asteroid-converted-to-prison was powered by a trans-dimensional drive that allowed them access to almost any plain ever conceived, all the nooks and crannies of the universe.

The prisoners were all put together but each alone. No one saw each other; no one cared. Lavinia felt like giving up so many times but one thought, one memory kept her going, kept her away from the edge though pebbles occasionally fell. The beautiful glowing cheeks of her baby girl when she first held her for the briefest moments were all that kept her from doing it.

That was what she lived for, that was what the humans could never take from her though they tried; they beat her, tried to break her spirit, but one thing about her Prosper Tattoo: she was Caring of Soul and as such had infinitesimal patience and courage. She kept that part of her secret, neatly tucked away where no amount of torture could touch.

Who knew how long the pod had been wandering space. The pod was finally in the hanger bay and shattered immediately as it had frozen hard like a cracked egg. The being inside was badly cut open, bite marks all over her, some sort of acidic erosion to her skin. Everyone stayed back except Maverick, who was immune to her screaming.

He approached her and scooped her up, not worrying about being delicate. He had witnessed this horrendous attack once before. She screamed in agony, a scream like someone's skin was being peeled off while they were still alive. He knew she was in terrible pain but the quicker he got her to where they needed to be the better. Like a Band-Aid.

The others followed in silence. At the Med bay when Maverick placed her down, the blood soaked through the sheets immediately. "We have to dress these wounds. Monk, do your job." As though something had crossed his vision, Maverick took off quickly, burdened by disturbed thoughts.

She was unconscious and the reason why soon became clear as they looked at the scans in the med bay. Maud cautioned them to her lungs. "She has ingested Flasher liquid—or Killer Honey as it is called—to induce a long sleep before death."

"Why would she do that?" said Stern, who had been allowed to roam the ship now. Maverick knew he wouldn't try to escape; he had tempted that fate before to no avail. He knew he wouldn't try it again. The universe was a nasty place and there were worse people than Maverick, though he doubted it at times.

Maverick uncrossed his arms. He was in deep concentration unlike the crew had ever observed. "Because she has been hit by Sprites."

"She has been hit by what?" repeated Stern with a little more bite than intended. This was close to home—one of his own. He had a right to be infuriated. She had been assaulted and God knows by what.

The ghosts of our past seem to come back to haunt us. Or are they merely warning us?–Unknown Archives

The wounds were extensive. Leaning in, Maud could see the degree of the bites. He tried hard not to retch. He permitted the callousness of Maverick; he had this life to care for. "Do your best, doc," came the winding voice of Maverick as his shape disappeared down the ship's corridors, a discernible tortured shadow on the walls.

Stern was quick on the heels. Maverick cautioned Stern with a strong stare before telling him what he needed to hear. Stern and Maverick stood opposite each other just before the bridge. "I saw it once in my galaxy. I thought I could outrun it. Stupid!"

Stern could see the battle raging inside. He saw Maverick at that moment not as a hard-arse slaver but as a damaged man with a sordid past. "They are Dark Matter Entities if you want to know; they reside in the depths of the Voids. No one ever sees them coming—that is until it is too late." Maverick became sombre and silent. None of his crew knew of his past and this was treading awfully close to those horrible memories—ones he wanted to be left behind.

"Will she survive?" added Stern. Maverick looked the boy up and down. Why would he care? She wasn't his mate. And why was he seeking comfort in this string bean? He guessed it had something to do with the fact that they were both of the same species. A bond. He himself had never known that bond. When his loved ones were taken from him he ran. He never thought anything wrong with that until just now.

After Stern had finished with Maverick, Maverick returned to the Med Bay to ascertain the damage. Maud turned to a most pensive Maverick, his gloved hands full of blood. "We must work fast. Whatever she did, these Dark Matter Entities are remorseless. She staved off death but if we stay here bickering she will succumb to it.

She probably saved her life without knowing it—something in the liquid forced them out, caused them to abandon her. She will die soon if I don't extract the Honey from her bloodstream, flush out her system before it causes immediate poisoning and death. The more extensive but less immediate wounds will have to wait."

Maverick nodded fervently. "The quicker, doc, the better." He allowed a smile of comfort before parting, deep in thought.

With the tonics and mixtures Maud had obtained from Hariot, a most peculiar creature, he was almost certain he could mend these wounds but he doubted that he could restore her to her full capacity. She had been assaulted, yes, but not just physically—she was mentally and emotionally tattered to the seams.

He left these perturbed thoughts to himself and dared not voice them until he had done all he could for her. He could face the wrath of Maverick when nothing else could be done.

First, he dabbed at the wounds. Celeste looked so hurt; the most horrendously hurt being he had ever seen. He took a sludge paste and smothered it over her skin forming a case or cocoon. Then he wrapped her in layers and layers of soaked leaves, thanks to his friend Hariot. It would be a solid 8 hours before the sedative would wear off and he could ascertain anything else. He decided to head to his room and pray. It was the most fitting thing he could do.

Deep in his dreams, Maverick went back to a time where he was most vulnerable. A time that he had thought he had buried long ago. It was just about to resurface.

Maverick held her hand right to the bitter and bloody end.

"Please. Don't. Change him at least. Just don't let him die."

Maverick was unconscious, lopping side to side, blood trickling from teeth wounds.

"He is a tasty morsel. But humans no longer satisfy our ranks. Why should we save him?"

"Because—because…" She was now crying, almost blubbering. "I need him. I love him."

The Raider's laugh was like jagged ice.

"P-please."

Maybe love wasn't meant to last. Maybe it was a big joke, but that didn't stop people from seeking it continuously.

Deep love, the kind that transformed, was always the carrot on a very long stick, always out of reach.

But Maverick and Raven had it in spades and even now as he bled on her clothes as the change set in, that love pulsed to its own rhythm. "I am here, my love." She held him close as the crippling pain of DNA reworking itself coursed through Maverick's body like electric currents. Darkness had encapsulated his mind, enslaved his soul, but in the background, was a voice so familiar, so comforting. It pulled him back from the precipice.

His eyes flew open. "I love you too."

Raven smiled slowly when he pulled back her head and sunk his new fangs into her neck.

The call of bloodlust was strong but Maverick pulled away, resisted before draining her completely. "What's happened to me?"

Raven clamped a hand to her neck. "I saved you."

"You-you made a deal with the devil."

Raven knew that to be true, but for love, she would have done it again. "I thought I was doing the right thing."

Maverick noticed the others, circling, snarling. He hissed at them.

"You have broken flesh."

"Leave her to me."

"Oh, twisted mind. Come on, fellows. Let's leave the newcomer to his meal."

As they left, Maverick sunk down to his knees. "I am different, but you don't know. And now I do."

Raven didn't want to look into his eyes. She had turned him into a monster. She didn't want to stare into the void, see that emptiness where his soul once thrived.

"Look at me. Raven, look at me."

She resisted as he tilted her head back. Then finally she saw. She saw it as easy as spotting the glint of a coin in the sun. "Maverick?"

"Yeah, it's me. Your situation has saved my soul. As soon as I drank your blood it happened."

No innocent deserves the horrors that visit them but in times of horrendous things it is only a matter of when –Unknown Archives

Later, Maverick returned to his room, winding down the corridors of the ship. He had managed to corner Stern and locked him in the cargo bay. No doubt by now Stern's hands would be black and blue from banging on the door. Maverick didn't care. The boy was too prissy for his own good. This would toughen him up.

Later, in the Med Bay.....

"A vegetable?"

"It is fifty-fifty. In most cases, the subject demonstrates autism or mental retardation," added the monk with a heavy sigh. Maverick turned away, seemingly hiding a troubled face.

The monk continued to speak. "Though a case like this hasn't been seen before. Well, from the ones I know, most never get to that stage."

The monk started pacing, his thoughts deep and troubling. "I am a man of faith, Maverick. I believe in a higher being: God, I suppose. But when I see these new things cropping up, I find myself surprised and to an extent frightened. Who knew such things existed?"

"I knew. Only too well, my friend. Do all that you can." Maverick slapped him on the shoulder before parting. The monk rubbed where he had slapped him and returned to his work on the woman, who lay peacefully.

Maverick gave a grave shake of his head as he walked away. The idea that helping was helpless made him feel terrible. It made his life crappier. He was no saint but he was also, no doctor. So, he allowed this petulant man to help. He was a pirate. A deviant. He cared only for himself. He cared once and that had gotten him nowhere. Second mistakes just meant you hadn't learned from your first ones and were doomed to repeat them.

He scammed people and yet this girl, this angel who had captured his imagination and perhaps for a minute his frozen heart, he could not let her die. Why he did not know. Nevertheless, he allowed the crew the courtesy of believing he was a semi-noble man. The girl who was eaten alive by malicious beings made his blood boil. He had seen it all before and hoped—yes, hoped—that he would not see them again. They had found their way to this galaxy, to him. Damn them!

Maud softly dabbed the fleshy bite marks. He did not want to cause her more pain, though she was out and probably suffered greater pain than he could imagine. He looked down at her intriguing exterior, shaped her ears with his finger. He had been around a long time but never had he the luck of seeing an angel. And she was a perfect angel. She was so innocent and yet she was subjected to the wrath of some things he could only describe as sinister—so sinister that a man like Maverick was a quivering mess.

Maverick had been standing in the background quietly observing. "She has severe trauma. It is not only physical. She probably has been reliving the last moments before she was savagely attacked," explained Maud to Maverick, who was puffing on his umpteenth smoke.

Maud touched Celeste across the head, tucking away unkempt strands of hair stuck to blood. "She does not deserve this," remarked Maud. "I have leeched the Honey before it could do its damage but we need blood. More blood was lost than I initially thought and she is becoming weaker. She needs—"

"She needs a donor." And before Maud could intercept, Maverick was moving fast within the ship to the cargo bay. Stern detested and knocked stacked boxes in the process. Stern was wriggling and non-cooperative but that didn't sway Maverick, whose arm wrestled him to the Med Bay. Maverick simply popped him one on the nose and he was out. He flipped his remarkably light body over his shoulder and made way to see Maud. In the Med Bay, after the monk chattered his argument in Maverick's ear, the transfusion began.

"Maud, I respect you. I know I don't act like I care sometimes but you have faith in things I could never even contemplate. You saw hope where I saw despair. I haven't been up front about my past because I don't want to share what happened. Just know she is very, very lucky. I have seen these beings before and their wrath is savage. Now proceed; I am sure that Stern will get over it. I will see to it personally."

"How do we fight these things?"

Maverick smirked suddenly. "Dear monk...what do you think I am doing here? We tried to fight and in the end, all you can do is run. Run until your legs turn to mush."

For the crew of Maverick, it was clear what the Sprites were capable of and what they had in mind for the rest of the universe, which wasn't a cheerful notion.

When we don't think about the other's point of view, we go about it raging and running full ahead and when we lock horns we engage in a lasting battle of who is right and who is wrong - the victor never certain– Unknown Archives

The flames came from all sides. Gerof lay unconscious. He was blocked and his hands were burnt from having to try to shift blazing bulkheads. The flames singed her skin and her howling was heartbreaking to hear.

Suddenly a loose bulkhead pierced through her torso. Kressangah was trying to get up but was pinned solidly, the ship falling apart around her, the sounds of the inferno raging like a terrible dragon. "Get out, Gerof. Get out while you can!" she pleaded. But she could not see him or hear him. She feared the worst. Smoke was filling her lungs and if the flames didn't claim her, it would.

The flames were acting differently than normal flames. The fact was they were being commanded. The Sprites were watching through Raider eyes, ready to slaughter them and dispel their wasteful matter when they were summoned through some telepathic link. The possessed Raider Hive Ships disengaged and the live fire went with them. They left in a rush.

There was darkness sliced by images of light. First blurred lines, then form, then finally a pieced together picture. Kressanagh's torso was bandaged, covering her breasts. She could still feel the pain of where the bulkhead had been rightly nestled between her ribs. She startled, almost ripping her stitches clean out. "Gerof!"

She didn't make it to the next sentence before an approaching hand landed on her shoulder, sternly pinning her to the bed. "Fear not, he is in the next bed beside you."

She knew that voice. She craned her neck to see his face hidden behind blue locks. "Kroden?" He had changed; the scar for one and the years evident on his face. "What are you doing here? What am I doing here? Gerof, is he okay?"

Kressangah groaned more from the shock of seeing her one true love alive then the pain throbbing between her ribs. "Yes, he is okay." She couldn't help but detect something in his voice that made her wary.

"What happened?"

"We were kinda hoping you could tell us."

"We?"

"Dillis. He is captain of this ship."

Kressangah eased herself into her top that lay to the side. She was so physically appealing. Kroden blushed but luckily on his bluish skin, it didn't show.

Kroden was a General; he remembered that much but still, a small part of his brain neglected to ignite what had happened that day. He saved lives, ended men; he triumphed in the battlefield.

Back in his days as General, legions marched to his order, to the beat of his drum. He had the unseemly task of sending men out to die, to knowingly allow them to smile and salute before their last hours alive. The days of his orphaned life were left as a shallow pool in his mind. He was now strong and commanding, a tower of muscle; not this meek skinny brat who knew nothing of discipline or vision. That brat still existed—he had just conveniently suppressed him. But it had all been for nothing, he thought as he started to feel that brat resurface. A brat with the beating heart of a boy in love.

"I don't know what happened. All I know is that was Nanite Flame we encountered. It's a notorious Raider trick. But I saw something else—something move through the air. A ripple. Maybe I had smoke inhalation but...all I know is I owe Gerof my life."

Helping Kressangah eat her porridge, he noticed that she was intent on leaving the bed so he discreetly pulled them close. She eased into her Chinese silk robe. She did not want to be bedridden any longer, though he would beg her to return to bed. Her wound still hurt but she didn't care; she suffered the pain. She needed to see Gerof. She needed to know he was alright and the assuring words of a man she hadn't seen in years weren't going to cut it. Her violet eyes blazed. She wanted to rip that curtain aside even if she had to go through a wall of muscle to do it.

"So, these Sprites, why didn't they finish you?" cut in Kroden's voice.

Kressanagah paused her attempt to jump over. "Maybe we weren't that interesting to them."

"They were relentless on the station."

Kressangah looked at him quizzically, suddenly curious. "Station Alpha. I heard about that evil. When we fought in the war all we knew was the enemy. We knew not true evil."

"Things I never even thought existed, Kressangah. They're real."

"I know. I have seen them. There are worse things out there than Raiders—at least that was what he had said."

Kroden looked away, a little perturbed. "Dillis. He saved us; he believes that we can end this war. He can save us all. He believes it."

"Polluting shit. That's what Gerof believed and where is he now?" Let me see him." She was starting to become panicky. Why was he so intent on hiding him from her?

"I was broken and beaten and you never came. You never..." Kroden began.

Kressangah's purple lavender eyes lit up and she neglected to continue toward the next bed. "You never told me that! You were beaten?" she said, as she tried t embrace him.

Kroden stamped his foot in anger for letting it slip and pushed her away. "I didn't tell you because I didn't want your pity! When I was inexorably discharged I could never go back to the life I knew." Suddenly he was quivering.

Kroden was angry with her for her blatant ignorance. She never knew. How could she? They had met for a few minutes but for her, it was an eternity. He had lost his whole livelihood while she continued down a doomed path.

"I had hoped that you would tell me these things before...before all of this happened," she said. "Gerof did the same thing to me—to all us students. He didn't tell us the truth. He left us and thought it was in our best interest. He was my mentor, and he left. But you—we—had something beautiful and you destroyed it because you were scared of what people might think."

"I did what I did because I had to! Because I believed it at the time. If I hadn't they would have found you and destroyed you. When I stopped you that day, when you had the musket pointed to my head, I realized something profound—something this man you accuse of polluting my brain instilled in me when I was young: we don't have to fight. There is another way."

Kressangah stopped for a minute if only to catch her breath and his encroaching hands she bound together with hers. She slowly breathed in and out to the timing of his breathing. "I am sorry. I know you have made sacrifices. Your eye...I am just on edge at the moment because"

"Yes, I heard about the mass suicide. They may have been misguided but they didn't need to end like that. I thought I could evoke some inkling of understanding but I could never understand what they went through. The disappointment, the failure.

My superiors knew what had happened that day, so they punished me. They stripped me of my rank. And the scar, little more than a gift from the soldiers I commanded who beat me down and called me traitor after my shameful dismissal."

Kressangah suddenly felt embers erupt in her chest. She lunged forward with a pulling magnetism and latched onto Kroden like well-oiled parts. "I should have known better. We only met for one day but I should have known you were a man of steel, not some blind sheep." Kressangah nuzzled into his chest and then tilting her chin up, navigated her lips to his for a long-awaited, deserved a kiss.

Her whereabouts couldn't be ascertained. The pod, while he was unconscious for a varied amount of time, could be on the other side of the system by now. He had no leads and right now no hope. Sliding his bloodied hand across the console—he had not been to the Med Bay to address his wounds in hours and the poorly made job was now seeped with blood—he didn't care about himself. Maybe that was careless and stupid, but he could think of nothing else other than what her last hours were like. How he wasn't there to comfort her. She was alone, scared, hurt. And what had he done to save her? Nothing but sweet fuck. The silence was unbearable. The ship really did feel dead and to an extent so did he. He didn't know what the point of it all was because if this was it if this was life amassed to—a world without her—he didn't want it and dark ambiguous thoughts penetrated his waking hours, his Decanter ever close. "Thorn, if you are there, please respond. Give me something, anything."

Nothing. Nothing but dead air.

Sean shook his head in dismay. This was hopeless. The ship was inert and tumbling on its axis with life support failing. If he didn't get some help soon he would die. Sean couldn't begin to list the many systems that were damaged or offline. But he had to start somewhere, to do something other than this inane wallowing. He wasn't dead—not yet—so at least he could put himself to work.

The engine was a piece of art, to say the least, but he couldn't make heads or tails of the inner workings. He couldn't fix it. He had no way of knowing what was what. Fly it, yes, but keep it under management...no.

Fed up with engineering, he headed to the galley with a quick stop at the Med Bay. He let reason take over. He knew that Celeste would be cursing at him for letting himself wither and die, so he dressed his wounds and stifled back the hard sobs. He did not feel like eating but he knew he could run on nothing so he actually ate something for a change. He was losing weight and his mind was strained. He returned to the bridge and sat down huffing. He didn't know how or why but he had lost himself in this ship, dedicated so many hours that seemed to be at the time important. And now the one thing that was most important of all was not there. He almost blamed the ship for switching his attention. He had lost Celeste and now he was blaming his disabled ship? He could have kicked himself. He almost swore outright when a beeping from the consoles called him away from his rage and reignited his coal black hope.

Sometimes turning the wrong corner can lead to the eventual right path
—Unknown Archives

He lay unconscious in the shell of his pod. He listlessly floated from dream to present, his oxygen levels beeping as it exhausted 50% and depleted rapidly.

Alarms whirled so loudly it hurt his ears. His legs were turning to mush running, but he didn't care. Not anymore. Turning the corner, he met a jumble of arms as scientist officers zipped around as though on skates. No time to offer a sorry, he continued on in a mad dash, leaving a rather vexed scientist to his scattered papers. He was a man of stature and appropriate manner once but now all had unraveled.

He held onto a pittance of DNA, his source of all his turmoil and the source of his tattered happiness. This would fix everything, make the hurt go away, and to some degree absolve his pain. He knew it would because it had to. Robert didn't know how he did it. Before he knew what was happening he had managed to secure a ship and evade any fire before security was sent to stop him. Did they even send security?

He wasted no time to find an answer and he was out of there. He had his own mission now—the only one of real importance. Whatever form she materialized, he would make his home. She was always going to come back. He knew that there would be a way—some way to restore her. Out there was the answer. The ship lit the skies and departed to embark on the greatest journey there was: that of love.

The Maker was no warrior, no great being of power, just an old fragile shell and yet...
He was in his station mixing and pouring chemicals from one flask to the other. He hummed

softly a tune that was unrecognizable but strangely warming. All around him in his lab were cylinders with half formed Raiders detracting the joy his tune embalmed. Evidence of his splicing was everywhere. Suddenly the computer chimed. "Inanimate object detected, projectile trajectory imminent," it sounded and repeated. Charlie's way of annoyance for he was of individual thought, no processed construct of embodied structure and law.

Stopping mid pour, his glasses askew, the Maker Eric hmphed. "That is funny, no object or ship has ever discovered me. Computer? Charlie, my friend, scan object."

"Scanning…object containing one life form—human, male...and evidence of the residue of a few unknown DNA strains. Instructions?"

Eric paused and then placed his vials down. Fresh DNA; that was intriguing. "Retrieve. I have been without a companion for so many years. Perhaps this being could provide some illumination as to why my Raiders are dying when they were built to be immortal," he chimed like a boy.

Charlie made a funny snorting noise like he was offended. "Oh, Charlie my friend, except for you. Without you, I would have gone mad long ago," he added apologetically with a tittering laugh. Charlie thought he had gone made long before then but concealed his smugness with a quick hmph.

The ship was frosted over with ice and looked like it had lost propulsion and air were at a cruel 4%. Clearly, the pilot did not know what he was doing, sending such a vessel this far out into space. Another mad soul. It looked like it had been through some battle or worse. The journey through space and the disengaged thermostatic didn't help matters. The poor soul could have been dead. But dead or alive, it made no difference as long as the DNA was intact.

The Maker defrosted Robert fast and there appeared to be no permanent damage or what they called freeze-dry when one is defrosted so quickly. Looked like he would have someone to talk to after all. "There you go. Up you get, boy. That's it, take deep breaths," he said, marshalling a drink in his hands as Robert continued to cough and splutter.

Robert was glistening with frost and shivering cold. He was quickly given a foil blanket like he was with his grandfather or something. He suddenly searched for something but it was in his hand; in fact, it had fused to his skin. He sighed with relief. "T-t-t-thank god you f-f-f-found me. The ship sss-topped functioning once we went through that thing. And me not knowing what I was doing dd-didn't help matters."

Eric smiled, busying himself with the flasks. "Not a worry, my friend. At least you are alright." Eric busied himself like his guest was simply making a house visit. "I am Eric or The Maker as some wittingly call me."

Eric went over and extended his hand. Robert paused then grasped it. The warmth, he wanted to leech it from his hand. "Robert. Robert Harris," he said as his chattering finally came to an end.

On Planet Isis, twin planet to Vern, the city gleamed in the night like glowing bugs. Cleo sat up in bed with sudden sharp stabbing pains. Boris appeared at her side. "What is it?" he said. Why would he care? She thought it was pretty obvious what he felt about the situation after his earlier outburst, casting the dent in the wall

Boris pushed her hand away and left his hand on her belly. She could feel his ebbing anger. He was a beast and this tender moment couldn't erase that hard fact. "The creature is growing horns or is very rowdy. The pain will subside. This is why slaves are conditioned for fear of this very outcome. Humans are not physically compatible to carry Claspher embryos; don't expect to survive the birthing process."

Boris never shared his thoughts with her; never opened up as a person. For that, he would have to bare his emotions and that was something that would never happen. She was merely a function for him. He hadn't forgotten that but the days were long without some portion of the conversation.

He left his shadow. Enough time had been spent. The need for the pulsating of blood overcame his brief interlude. And then a flitting thought: could he be caring for this abomination in her womb or the women who allowed it? He cocked his net disperser. Nah.

Boris had put Nina in the cradle at the passenger side of the ship, but for the life of him could not get her to shut up. He had to dock with a station soon and restock—or better yet, sell the brat for a good amount of Cretzins.

But no, he couldn't. His petulant thoughts kept darting back to Cleo, the mother of his spawn. Was she okay? Why did he save her life? Did it work? What did he care if it worked? He wanted to veer himself into the approaching sun but seeing a station to the far regions negated his previous impulse.

The Med Bay was in shambles but Sean managed to salvage some more supplies and bandages. He twirled the feather he had found at the pod chamber between his fingers. It had blood on it. He yelled in pain as the pressure he placed on his ribs was a little too plied. He tried to save the tears that would mingle with his blood. He had cried too long and he was tired of it.

Sparkling lights and wires made it hazardous to travel through the ship. Sean lifted what he could and returned them back to their original places, but most of the time he just moved them out of the way. The bridge was the worst—like a bomb had detonated. Whatever these things were, they were nasty.

He wasn't sure his ship or his mind would ever be the same. Sean leaned against the console that he brushed the metal debris off of before and tried to connect to the ship for the umpteenth time. "Thorn, are you there? Please reply," he pleaded. The exhaustion was evident in his tone of voice as it broke and cracked. But the ship was silent and dead.

Things had gone from bad to worse in such a short span of time. Sean couldn't help but think that this was worthless, pointless. He felt like this could very well be the end but in that time of darkness, a voice eased him back from the brink. The voice of his father, a ghost offering consolidation.

Sean never freely admitted it but he did think of his father often. Indeed, he had made mistakes and wasn't a real father role model, but something about him stuck with Sean. He was a proud and able man.

Sean knew that if he was in this situation he would not give up—not when someone he loved was at stake. And so, in that place of darkness, Sean veered himself to the course ahead, to the course of hope and survival.

He tried his best to mend his wounds but they were extensive; the Bionics would take a while to work and wrenching at his stitches didn't aid the healing process. They would heal but it would take an extended amount of time. He was grateful to Celeste for laying the Flashers. They were a pained reminder that she had tried to the very end.

It made the cleanup easier to know that she had thought of this before being brutally taken away and the lump in his throat eased. He tried to mend what damaged operational equipment he could but he wasn't a technician and he wasn't a doctor. He was a one-man team.

Every few hours he tried calling out to Thorn but as usual, there was no response. Where had he gone? Was he gone forever? Did his essence just evaporate? Sean steadied his pumping head. He needed to regain his thoughts. First thing was first: get the ship up and operational. That was the objective. His sanity could wait.

Maverick couldn't help but think back to those dreadful days; the days when he had people he loved who were then unceremoniously taken away from him, ripped to shreds, to atoms. Maverick was in his room, shaving. The blade moved smoothly across his skin with a rough Scritch. The Sprites were more than malevolent; they were truly and utterly alien. Their beliefs, their essential core was unlike any other sentient life in the universe. And what was worse: they sided with the darkness that had no side but its own apparent realm. But Maverick was neither dark nor light. He had no place, no side, just like those malevolent beings. So where did that leave him? Where did that leave her? Within the Dark Matter where the Sprites resided? In a place of non-matter?

Maverick had left her to her sleep. She no-doubt faced a tumultuous battle inside. He knew the horrors out there; he felt their constricting coldness like a coiling snake. He knew loss and the needless bloodshed. And worse, he had lived through it.

For the Raiders though, the need for blood was a river coursing through the universe. The Sprites cared for no such pleasures. Raiders tapped into that vein; they appreciated it as much as their wine. And yet as horrid as they were, they were the least of this galaxy's problem, especially when the fate of the universe lay in tatters.

Maverick later returned to her bedside, seeing the great discomfort she was in. He couldn't help but be withdrawn. It troubled him. She could not walk, she could not talk and she was fed intravenously. And yet she was one of the lucky ones. He knew.

Stern had been watching silently. He made no noise save for his wings that alerted Maverick to his leering. "What do you want, boy?" he seethed. He couldn't help but feel the anguish inside, let it spill out from him in bursts of anger and frustration. He had this slave to do his bidding but he did not share a liking for the boy.

"Well, considering you offered me as a living blood bag I do believe I have the right to be here to see if it worked. After the entire debacle, it would be a great disappointment if it were all for nothing. And remember, she is my kin. Tell me, were you going to drain me dry?"

Maverick snorted to himself. "I think we both know the answer to that."

For some unknown reason, this encouraged a smile from Stern, who had come to a weird understanding of the way Maverick worked.

When we feel for others; the empathy burning brightly in our skins, do we become connected with our inner selves or are we simply spreading ourselves too thin?
—Unknown Archives

"How is it that you know so much about them?" said Stern eventually. This was by far the most conversation he had with Maverick after continual cussed insults about his mistreatment.

Maverick waited before answering that. He didn't want to converse with this bronzed god but he somehow felt better talking to the same species as the one who lay bedridden. Somehow, offering some consoling advice would ease his burdens of seeing one in no state to offer any.

"Because my world was ravaged by them. We had no technology against them, no weapons, and I doubt there is any out there that exists against them. The Sprites want the rifts to tear the universe apart and live in a place of non-matter. So, if you are wondering if I am scared, no need to ask, boy. I am already shaking in my boots."

Stern felt resentment against Maverick. After all, the man nearly drained him dry to save this stranger's life. But still, he was grateful that his contribution saved her life, a being of obvious innocence.

Later, Maud made his way to the bridge to tell everyone, in particular, Maverick. "She will be scarred but with enough skin grafts, it won't be noticeable. As for her mind, she will have echoes of what happened to her forever. She should be able to reconstruct the way she was but bits of her won't be the same. No number of graphs can fix that," he told Maverick, who had been persistently involved in her progress.

"Only in degrees. She will function normally but there will be times when her affliction will be exposed, hidden knowledge that only a survivor would know, footprints of the being that forced its way into her body, her soul."

Celeste lay in her bed, all manner of tubes protruding from her, and she was heavily bandaged.

Some manner of self must have resided inside surely but under a layer of darkness. Maud felt great emotion stir within. How could they help her? Make her whole as she once was? Maverick left and sparked another smoke.

He loved to get away from it all with some good old herbs. He owed Hariot a great debt. He had supplied the needed ointments to assist with Celeste's healing and also threw in the Casterka leaves he was currently smoking as a bonus.

On the bridge, Maverick turned around to see Stern loitering in the shadows...again. Maverick deliberately kept his back to him. "Do you think we can ever go back to the way things were?" said Stern finally.

Maverick turned to face him. A pause, and then, "No. The universe is in a flux. We cannot help the change," he said flatly. And as though that was all that need be said, the universe seemed to blink in response as the ship lurched into hyperspace.

Lolalia didn't know what happened. It was so fast. First, she was running from her homicidal sister and then.... the moons guided her, almost talked to her and journeyed her to what she had been searching the night skies for. She didn't know how she found it, how she had flown the ship through solar winds and micrometeorites, but she did and now she had jumped into a nightmare.

Once she was on board, there were blood puddles everywhere from the people she had slain. She didn't know what happened. She just knew these people were responsible for her mother's pain and they needed to pay with their blood. It was almost like she had blacked out during the incident.

Lolalia's blood soaked hands moved fast over the console, sifting through the manifest. She found her name. She waited there for a moment. Her finger touched the screen like it was an illusion and then reality snapped back like a rubber band. A bloody finger smeared the screen.

She had escaped the wrath of her delusional sister only to be brought here—to hell. "Mama," she muttered, running from cell to cell. Fat tears leaked from her eyes as she drove them into lost faces, scattered souls, but none were her mother. She kept going through until she found her strength paralyzed.

She ran the long winding corridors calling out "Mama!" And then she found the cell like hitting a solid brick wall. Darkness hit her in the face. "Mama, are you in there?" She feared the answer or the lack of one.

"No, go away! I know you're not real," came Lavinia's strangled voice. It was her. After all this time.

Lolalia's felt a surge of adrenalin and sheared the lock clean off with her bare hands, blood trickling across her skin. The pain didn't even register. She found what appeared to be a small mass huddled at the wall, gripping the ledge with her fingers that were bloody and raw.

She couldn't even acknowledge it was alive but eyes peeped through the mass of clumped hair. "Oh Mama," she exclaimed, sinking down on her knees. Lolalia went to embrace her but Lavinia retreated like she was a threat. "It's me, Mama. It's your daughter," she said through withheld sobs.

The gases were starting, an automated system. Lolalia could feel the effect as she began coughing. She wasted no time at all and swung her muttering mother over her shoulder powered by pure adrenaline. She weaved through the gas and made it to where she had started, to the ring of bodies. She and her mother collapsed in a heap, gasping for air.

She knelt beside her mother and then went to sabotage the pipe with a good kick. She then entered a new coordinate into the navigation system, hitting the unlock mechanisms by accident and freeing all the prisoners.

The prisoners cared not for her and her mother, who slumped down into two little mounds but made way for the escape pods. Spluttering as the gas dissipated, Lolalia was suddenly overcome with fatigue and fainted right next to her mother, hands intertwined as the Pits made its last trans-dimensional jump with its only two passengers.

57

No greater love is there than that of mother and daughter – Unknown Archives

Oma was Clan Leader of the Canssa Krelian Clan. Their ships were formed into stations that preferred to stay put instead of being vagrants. She tempted Lolalia back to consciousness with soft dabs of a wet towel. Lolalia's beautiful almond eyes fluttered open.

Lolalia awoke, flinging onto Oma like she was a life raft. "Oma! Thank god. Mama!" she said, acknowledging her old friend and suddenly searching for her mother.

Oma held her back gently. "She is fine," she said, motioning to the other side of the room where Lavinia lay peacefully, not the frightened woman she encountered before.

"Thank the Old Timer. You're lucky, child. You were tethered to life, so close to death; whether it was the lure of the Siren Moons on your side or your mother's bond, and it is without saying you are a miracle.

I must say you have grown into the woman your mother would be proud to see." Lolalia looked away, reminded of the pallid faces of the men she had murdered. One by one, they tormented her. That was nothing to be proud of, she was sure.

The Clan ships congregated and started to dismantle the asteroid's inner systems piece by piece, mainly carving out for the trans-dimensional drive. As far as anyone knew, there was nothing like it in the universe.

With this technology, the trans-dimensional drive could alter the Krelian's echelon in the universe. They may even exceed to becoming a super society. The thought was almost tantalizing. It took hours upon hours but they amassed the drive, the jewel of their efforts.

Oma was a porky woman with humble hips and a wiggle to her walk. She tended to the pot hanging over the fire. "You both seemed in a feverish dream. I remedied you with herbs and Tannika root. You should be feeling calmer," she said.

And indeed, there were herbs all around them, the essence burning with a smoldering flame.

"Tea will be on soon," she said and disappeared like she was just a droid seeing to their health before parting. "Taroks. They do trade but it comes with the heavy battering of philosophy."

Lavinia was roused by the tea. Her voice was hoarse and dry. "L-lolalia?" She turned her head and the sight of her grown daughter brought tears to a drought. She had longed for this day and that it was finally here it was hard to believe.

"Oh, sweet daughter!" Lavinia grappled open air before finding her daughter's open arms. It was like she was blind or weakened and no longer able to function properly. Those bastards! But they had gotten what they deserved—too much a leniency in fact.

Then their faces flashed in her mind. Lavinia retracted her arms. "I thought when they ripped you from me I would never again see you. But now I have a chance to be your mother again."

She was nothing but a skeleton, all emaciated and ragged. Her recovery would be long. But none of that mattered. Lolalia had found her before the end could claim her and she had the Siren Moons to thank for that—or whatever power funneled into her.

Whether she wanted to admit it or not, she was intertwined with the mistresses. But did that make her a tool of darkness? All those dead men, they were vile and deserved no less, but she had done that—frail, emotional Lolalia. Looked like Lavinia wasn't the only one stripped bare to instinctual primitiveness.

After a many battle, the last crusade is often the war of one's heart—Unknown Archives

Sean swam in and out of consciousness, his ship listlessly floating around space. He took in much-needed breaths. His injuries were healing but the biotic cells were taking their right time. He was surprised they still worked at all; years of abandonment on the ship had worn them down.

The echo of voices had subsided after a few hours. Whatever those things were, they were strong, potent energy. Sean was now truly alone. His thoughts passed one after another; thoughts of Celeste and why there was so much blood. Her blood. Thorn's voice had dissipated. He no longer heard him and it pissed him off.

He needed him, he needed his sole advice. The attack was brutal on both ship and in his mind and he was uncertain whether he would come out of it unscathed. He urged his body forward, exerting himself.

The ship was wrought in darkness as the Flashers died, so Sean had to stumble around before managing some more Flashers and laying them out like breadcrumbs. There was blood everywhere. All he saw was her blood. He tried hard not to weep—not now.

He was a strong man, not some mass of mediocre anguish, yet he was teetering close to the edge. He needed to be strong for her. He needed to have hope that he would see her again.

"Thorn, can you hear me?" he tried holding the Flasher in one hand and looking down at the console but it was inert, dead. Nothing but silence and it was deafening.

Before long, tears started to stream. Sean was covered in sweat and blood and now tears. He had held them back for as long as he could. When would fate take pity on him? When would something finally go right for a change?

The only thing that kept him from spacing himself was the thought of once again laying his eyes on her face. Of touching her again. But failing to keep her safe like he promised Shartoon weighed heavily on his mind. Shartoon would have loved to see him now, this mere human of insipidity.

It frustrated him to the point that he banged his fist on the console and bits of crap leapt into the air. The stars seemed to mock him, glaring their evil eyes. At one stage he adored the openness of space but now it was the one thing holding him against finding his love.

How he detested that distance, that mockery. She could be anywhere by now. She could be in pain. She could be held, prisoner. All these thoughts tumbled around in his head, making him almost insane. No, nauseous. He puked to the side.

The Coalesce Wave could be felt like a tremendous force for light years. Every hair on every being stood on end as a super charged wave flowed over everyone across planets and sweeping the universe and even reaching the tips of space. No one knew where this mystery wave came from but everyone felt the effects.

The Sprites writhed in pain everywhere as they were dissolved to minuscule particles. Flooding every spec of matter that had been ruined by the Sprites, the Coalesce Wave brushed them aside like the rubbish they were. People escaping near torture and death blinked in surprise as their attackers dissolved in an array of colour and illusion.

The Library was somewhere in the universe. And inside were the Patriots, the Librarians who watched over the Unknown Archives and who were responsible for this Coalesce Wave. A well of knowledge and now their Wave had swept over the universe. No one knew the truth: that they were the descendants of the once mighty race of the Ancient Ones. No one even knew they existed, but without them, the universe would be without its watchmakers, it's time-keepers who recorded every event

---

Soon the strewn stars turned to velvet purple Nebulas and blue steaks. The universe seemed to inhale as everything was frozen for a moment and then returned to its former glory. Though the universe appeared healed, people's lives lay in tatters. A lot would have to happen to right all the wrong. It wasn't as simple as clicking one's fingers. But something wasn't right; the universe had not been righted as it had seemed. True, the threat was diminished but not gone. Something else was amiss here.

The Choc-ra was buzzing with new energy. Jathmoora could feel it with a start as she awoke from her meditative state. Those who were attuned to the frequency of the undercurrent of space knew that something was coming but what they didn't know was that something was already here. She looked out the ship's port, arm cradled on her hip. Everything appeared peaceful, right. But something in her told that it was far from okay. Something had happened but it had started something else—the coming of something that awakened her from a deep meditative state.

"Something ill-bodes here."

What was strange was the Alteran Vessels had no pilots. Yes, they flew themselves. They acted with sole intelligence. And as soon as the Coalesce Wave swept the universe, the Alteran Vessels flew into action, called to duty.

Planets were murmuring. Stations were in a state of fit carrying for the sick and injured. The rumour spread, and hearsay of what the light was and where it had come from. Not worrying about what was to come, much relief had taken over people. Usually, humans, in general, could not see past what lay in front of them. It was their nature, their fault.

Others were more attuned to the under currents of space like Jathmoora and saw into the inner third eye. But to some extent, she wished to see no further than one foot in front of her. Her foresight made her nervous and scared shitless. The Choc-ra was usually so calm, placid, but what she experienced told her something fundamental had come undone like seams in a dress. To everyone's ignorance, she thought with the sting of jealousy.

In the corridor, no longer able to stay in the room and let things lie, Jathmoora bumped into Hariot deep in his inquisitive plant. She wondered briefly if he had forgiven her for before.

"You felt it, didn't you? The darkness. It's coming—no, it's here. We can't even comprehend stopping it. The Choc-ra, it's dimming away like the universe was given a jolt of electricity and now the heart doesn't pump to the normal rhythm."

Hariot gave Jathmoora a most puzzling stare and he trimmed his cactus, which gave a whirr. "Are you feeling okay, Jath?" he said, noticing the roundness of her eyes, opening like saucers.

"Maybe—or maybe not. Hariot, we have to prepare. This may very well be only the beginning."

Before Hariot had opened his mouth to say something, Jathmoora was gone, not worrying about his opinions for the moment; something of greater urgency had come up.

"The beginning of what?" he said rather to himself than anyone else and looked down at his cactus, who just murmured.

In the mess hall, Jathmoora turned so sharply that she knocked into Selene, who was helping Zias return to his fuller figure by supplying him with copious amounts of slushy nutrient paste. The food slid off the spoon and landed in a heap on the floor as Jathmoora pardoned herself, realizing the speed at which she was travelling.

"He has been in this state for 4 weeks now," stated Selene, trying to wipe the paste off his face but succeeding only in smearing it everywhere. Hariot had caught up to her. He cast his eyes away from the pale moon eyes of Zias and looked to Jathmoora, almost demanding an explanation.

Hariot tried to survey whether she was okay but received nothing. "There just isn't anyone home," suddenly said Selene, indicating the emptiness with the spoon.

Jathmoora seemed content to not worry about Zias's brief lapse of insanity. Like he would be fine with a cup of soup and pat on the back. She looked distracted like she needed to be somewhere else and everyone there was just keeping her.

Selene jumped five feet back when Zias blinked in acknowledgement and his hoarse voice croaked out, "It's coming." This seemed to also electrify Jathmoora.

This revelation amplified Jathmoora's anxiety to the point that she began to walk away secretively as everyone else focused their attentions on the now awake Zias. She knew this wasn't a good sign and the hairs on her skin stood up.

"What's coming?" said Selene, putting aside the bowl and spoon as a droplet oozed over its edge.

Selene looked back but Jath was gone. Her contemplation just kicked in as she realized Zias was awake. "What's coming?" she repeated.

"End."

And like he had just conveyed the most important message, he was out again, noncompliant.

After the vague declaration, everyone went back to their normal duties. When Selene returned to the bridge she saw Jath there, gazing out at the sea of stars. Hariot was back with Zias.

He had to forcibly part Zias's lips before inserting the spoon and then Zias gave a gluggy gulp while Hariot stimulated his throat to make him swallow. Selene was still worried about Jath. Why had she left when Zias had his temporary awakening? It unsettled her. Her thoughts were detached. A memory swam to the surface.

Hariot had come to his crew, a bulbous flower in his hand. "Look! Besewey Cradle. The rarest found in this sector and it was growing under a hover car if you believe that," he said with glee. Even in such a predicament as this, Hariot found the joy in unkempt and dark places most would have deemed unlivable.

He was so naïve back then but the world held wonder. Now though, the world held darkness and there was hardly a wonder like the Besewey Cradle to be found anywhere. He knew he had to look after Zias. He was trying to say something. And he knew it was important—just as important as a rare flower able to cure illness.

He returned to the pallid face of Zias and took the rest of the nutripaste and shepherded the stuff to his clamped mouth, teasing the lips apart with the edge of the spoon, paste smushing upward and stimulating him to swallow.

A bit later, Selene had crept up so quietly that Jathmoora started as she turned round to the creak of metal. "Oh, child! You gave me a fright."

"Speaking of frights. What's going on, aunty Jath?"

There was no point hiding it from her. She needed to confide in someone. Why not her?

"Selene…?"

And what are we but the product of our devising? What are we but the shape we have constructed through subconscious thought? — Unknown Archives

Jathmoora was in turmoil within her writhing mind. She nursed her head with her hands, overcome by bouts of memory that acted as headaches. Suddenly, she found herself on board a medical frigate. A fuzzy image that turned into Hariot placed his hand on her shoulder—a small act of solace, but she remembered her feelings of annoyance and even disdain.

"I am sorry. I overheard the doctors. They even tried electrical therapy but she doesn't want to come out of her world. This is beyond me. She has secured herself to an anchor somewhere embedded in her subconscious so she doesn't have to face the real world; she doesn't want to give up on her mission—that is all that matters to her. You have to admit, it is kind of brave."

Jathmoora had ground her teeth down. She was not going to swallow any of this. She was powerful and she could fix her daughter. Before long, she was wrestling out of Hariot's encompassing arms and heading for the side of the bed.

"I have to try. She can't be brain dead. She is alive. I can save her. Let me save her!"

But her hollow voice fell on deaf ears as they removed the machinery from her frugal body. Jathmoora fell into a heap and now welcomed Hariot's arms. Jathmoora remembered the metallic taste in her mouth like she had tasted blood. Then she awoke fully and noticed that her nose was bleeding.

She remembered that day when her daughter was taken from her, snatched like ripping away a vital organ. To this day, all blame left her broken, shattered. Yet she thought of her now in this time of unknowns. In this time of turmoil, she was selfish and thought of her flesh and blood that she had forsaken, just like Zias.

Her mission was all that mattered and she couldn't understand it—not until now. She had not changed, not one lick. But that wouldn't matter anymore if she had truly fragged things up here. The universe would open up its mouth and devour them all. Missions meant jack now. Her daughter, Salis, she wanted to be a pilot.

Who knew that tapping into the Choc-ra could have that effect while attempting hyperspace? No one could have foreseen the ramifications—none except the one who was closest to it. Jathmoora shook, overcome with the same feelings she felt that day. She was the third eye, yet her foresight could not prevent her daughter's demise.

What was the point of seeing the future if you were unable to alter the course? Another damned infallible question with no answer. She drew close to the Med Bay and assisted herself with her nose.

When the mysterious wave hit, it did something to Zias. It took a lag of two days but he had reawakened like a light switch had been flipped in his brain. Zias was fine. "Are you okay?" said Selene, trying to see if there were any problems. But he seemed perfectly lucid.

"I am fine."

"He's back, Jathmoora. Selene was there when it happened. She said he just clicked. It was like a miracle," said Hariot.

Selene smiled and ushered Zias forward. He was having trouble coordinating his motor functions but eventually worked one foot after another.

"When-when I was away, I was somewhere else. I saw the universe through different eyes. It was weird like I wasn't myself—or more I was myself, the true essence, a tendril of this substantial world. My decelerated state came about the moment I assumed captain of the ship Phantom like it had oppressed something in me. When you disconnected me, my brain went haywire and the lure of the moons...they chose me. But if you hadn't done what you did—tortured me—I wouldn't have come back. I wouldn't have been reborn."

Destiny again. Jathmoora had a bellyful. But she continued to let Zias talk. It seemed to do him good. She should have heeded her own advice but then she was always stubborn.

"We have torn a hole in the universe. The Choc-ra is not damaged but it is working overtime to repair it. We have a new mission. We have to learn more about the Choc-ra. We have to understand its true meaning. We have to push beyond the normal parameters of the mind."

Was this good news? Jathmoora hardly knew. What was he proposing? She was already on that path, but she had heard enough of destiny. Destiny was just another way of staying on a doomed path.

Meanwhile, the stations Alpha and now Omega had all fallen to the rampage and scourge of the Dark Matter Entities. The Coalesce Wave had rid the galaxy of them but like a plague, they continued on a set course. The barrage was hardly stopped, if not stemmed but hardly destroyed. They were coming.

The battle was huge, engrossing Hive Ships lunging forward into the newly awakened Alteran Class Vessels, unafraid to propel themselves on suicide runs. They had indeed grown desperate. The dark space was no longer dark but splattered with bursts of energy and live fire.

The two opposing sides were so engrossed in each other that they failed to notice the ethereal beings descending on their location. Not until it was too late and the vultures had feasted. It was a free-for-all. Raiders, Sprites and the ever-growing threat that was the undoing of the universe.

On board the Station Delta, the merchant waved his many hands in disarray. “Och! Ya miss’ dem a mom’n ago, leavn’ for some desolate plane’t,” he croaked to an officer of the law who bore down his malice. “P’ease leave mar limbs,” he pleaded as the officer went to boil his hand off in his own homemade soup. Everyone went silent, feeling the tremor like space itself had screamed; opened a chasm and just screamed. Space trembled. Something momentous had rocked the universe and everyone felt it.

Could it be that the universe was alive, that it had the breadth and thought and even age? Could it be the universe knew no limits, that it was never-ending, or did it have a life span? Was it soon to crumble? The universe was vast but no one has seen the edge. With each breath, it seemed to be dying. Maybe the universe wouldn’t live forever; maybe it was doomed just like its creations. Perhaps the Sprites were right. There was no room for matter because none of it mattered.

Delta station was ripped to shreds before a warning could be sounded. Bits of the station drifted through space, voices of the lost echoing into the stars. The Sprites were relentless; they could possess flesh and they could master metal. There wasn’t any place they could not reach.

But did they too have age, breath and mortality? Did they know time? Did they know death, or were they the ones who were unending? Maybe they were the species to end all species. Maybe they were right and all life was pointless when true gods reigned supreme.

No truer is the truth that we are all made of Trueskin, our cocoons discarded as we embrace our one and true form—Unknown Archives

Stella Rain 1.0

Stella Rain hastily dabbed under one eye. The funeral was short but grand. Jets flew overhead, marking the passing of a great leader colouring the sky orange and blue. But Stella knew what the public did not. She knew the true man that was now jettisoned up into the sky to be amongst the stars he for so long regarded with doubt.

All this was a cover to hail a hero that never existed. Stella thought it was more out of guilt that she shed those tears. Maybe she was wrought hard because of her job but more could be said about the man whose ashes would mix with space.

Stella withdrew a small handkerchief from her wrist cusp to better accommodate her feigned condolences. The casket shot up into space using a hyper-rail. Soon the evening was over and it started to pelt down with rain, a downer of already down spirits.

Stella hastily made her way to the chopper waiting for the entry. It was back to work for her. She wasn't all hard but she knew not to stop just for one man. She did feel for Harold but those feelings were dead like charcoal. However, some of her tears were genuine.

When she was younger, she knew what she wanted to do. Love came unexpectedly and it was a welcome change but reality came in hard and fast and the illusion dissolved fast. She was what she was. Not romantic. Not hopeful. She was a realist. She was a scientist, pure and simple.

And even as she stood there watching the casket shoot into space to be dissembled and ashes were strewn across the black, she understood one thing with absolute clarity: life was death; it was only life that we knew but death was still life's mystery. A tribute to our makings. Perhaps life wasn't so bleak, but maybe death wasn't either. Perhaps it was something to reach for, not hide from.

Stella Rain 2.0

She awoke with a deep breath, rasping and rattling like a strung piano. Memories had not congregated. She was lost. A Fawn. The liquid was viscous and she was cold—colder than anything he had felt before. She could not talk. She was…she was…young…

Jathmoora dreamed again in one of her meditative states. This time she was on Planet Risk, adjacent to the Planet Destry, whose volatile acid rains caused dead birds to fall and litter the ground as a great omen. On the outskirts, Jathmoora had laid the dirt along the edges of the laid-out stones. The grave stone belonged to that of her daughter, the one she left on this desolate planet and to her death.

She was feeling something deep inside arise, something foreign. She knelt hard on the ground, consumed by her worst fears: sorrow and regret, something she had staved off for the longest time until now. She guessed the longer time spent subduing it, the quicker it would come up to the surface.

Selene knelt beside her but she had not seen her for so long. This had to be a dream. Planet Risk wasn't like this and her daughter wasn't buried here. Her body was never released from the medical frigate.

She was in a dream but she didn't know the way out; knew not the identity of the exit. "I should have saved her. I should not have forsaken her," said Jathmoora between timed sobs echoing everywhere. The people around her were changing their faces. People she knew and even ones that made no sense.

"Maybe," she said to herself, "but she had a fruitful life. You heard her sons and daughters. She had a family, grew old, and lived a fulfilling life before the madness. Why would you blame yourself for her happiness?"

Jathmoora stood up sharply and everyone fell away into the dark. "Because I was not a part of her happiness when I had the chance. I melted away to better find my own resolve: the Choc-ra. She probably only remembered me as the witch who cast her into the wind," she said with more stifled sobs and more echoing.

Zias made a stifled cough to better address his presence. He was there. He was in her dream. She turned to him. He felt different. Solid. "What are you doing here? This happened before your time."

"If I may...we often forget that we are on the road to renewal; the once proud skins we were are not the butterfly of growth we become later in life. My point being, you were that person once, but are you really now?"

Everyone looked to him. Everyone cast their faces to him. Why had the Siren Moons saved him? Why was he the voice of reason and not the drooling cucumber? Had he felt the madness as her daughter had? Had he come back unlike her?

And then he melted, dissolved into nothingness. Then the world crumbled around her, everything fading away and only she was untouched, lost in dark space.

Jathmoora awoke with a start. She rubbed the sweat from her forehead. Nightmares. It was a constant reminder of her past. And the headaches, they were splitting. She had never left her daughter on that planet fully knowing what it would mean for her.

Her daughter lived and breathed and evidently died in space. Jathmoora had forsaken her for a life in mastering the Choc-ra, a force her daughter did not understand and never would until she attempted it once and paid dearly: with her life. And what did she have to show for it? She should not have forced the teachings onto her daughter. She should have kept her far away from it.

Jathmoora splashed water on her heated face. Coolness. She went to the bridge. Selene was up here. She was curious about things. She was still looking at the stars with young hope. Jathmoora had lost that. What was she now but an old crow?

The stars seemed to mirror her. Selene was unassuming like these stars. She loved to be tough on the outside but inside she was just like the rest of them, though she would never willingly admit it.

Jathmoora came to the front. "What is it, child?"

"I am not sure, Aunty Jath. I am not connected to the large power you are but even I feel it. The universe. It is calling or breaking, one of the two."

"And, how are you?"

"Scared, Aunty. Scared out of my wits."

When the ghosts of past revisit the present, will it affect the days of the future to come?
—Unknown Archives

The Altran Vessels were diminishing. The Hive Ships were also diminishing. Each cancelled the other out and that was exactly what the Sprites wanted. One by one, the ships were losing ground and the Sprites were gaining it. Explosions were happening everywhere. Brilliant spirals and star-like supernovas ignited the dark space.

It was almost a ballet of chaos, of destruction in leaps and bounds of laser hits and rupturing bulkheads. No one knew who was hitting who. Death was a visitor of the most frequent kind.

There was one ship that stood out from the rest. It moved differently like it did not fall in line with the others but more weaved out of the fire to a clear path. Cardvia cast her eyes at the chaos erupting around her.

She spoke in her native tongue, cursing at them as she saw the fall of the abominations she resented to call cousin. Though the Hive Ships were infested with Raiders, she shed no tear for them. She never knew the whereabouts of the Maker but she knew she had a lot of questions for him. She swung the ship low and fired on the oncoming wave of Sprites, but it was as useful as firing at smoke.

No amount of firepower could kill these things, yet they could control materialistic things. And what was worse was they were in the numbers, the truckloads. She hit the nearby console in frustration.

Cardvia could think of no other methods to destroy them. She had never encountered such malevolent creatures. She thought she was the worst of them. How wrong she was. Compared to these things, she was a puppy. But she would never allow herself forgiveness. She never deserved such leniency.

When all seemed lost, when the fight was left from her body, she realized something that made the hairs that did not exist on the back of her neck stand up: they originated from the Void. All this time she prayed, she willed herself not to go there, but in the end, it looked like Shakik had won. The Void came to them instead.

She flew the ship away and the other Altran Vessels did the same. The Hive Ships retreated like fleeing children. Everyone knew fighting for their food was no longer an adamant lifestyle with these creatures coming at them from all sides.

Now was a time to retaliate, to gather numbers and try again another day. There was no making a stand when numbers were so frayed.

Engaging hyperdrive, Cardvia made it out alright. But her fear gurgled underneath. If these things existed in the Void, what else would she find where no planets, no stars lit the path to safety? She prayed she would never have to find out and that she would continue to light a candle.

Celeste moved with agony but moved nevertheless. The ointment that Maud concocted a week ago healed her wounds nicely but her skin still felt raw. She tried to talk and then she saw Maud, who generously slathered more goo onto her scabby wounds. She recoiled but let him finish as the soothing effect was well worth the initial sting.

"You know you are doing great, Celeste. I was so pleased when you spoke your first words. Your vocal box is clearly on the mend, less scratchy now. The atrocity you had to sit through in silence, in stillness. I can't even imagine how that must have felt," said Maud.

Stern had played his part. Maverick had elected him—well, persuaded him to do a blood transfer as Celeste was badly in need of it. Ever since then Stern had held a grudge against Maverick. But then again, Stern always detested Maverick—even to his face. But thanks to his contribution, Celeste was on a rapid recovery.

"W-where is Sean?" said Celeste.

The others gaped at her as they joined Maud. Maud let the ooze drip off his finger and splat on the floor as he gawked at her. "Who is Sean?" He could tell that her mind had just wandered.

"I-I need to find him. I feel them inside still. I can't shake it!" she said, panic rising.

Maverick made himself known, clearly seeing what was happening. "Sean? We don't know, darling. We found you on the brink of death. You have been through a great deal. Why don't you—" He began trying to ease her back without touching her sores but she was starting to become irate.

Celeste was fast becoming hysterical. "Where is he? I have to get to him before they attack. They are everywhere, they are inside, and they are eternal, writhing!" she shouted.

And before she could continue her rant she collapsed into Maverick's awaiting arms. "I thought you said she was recovering," Maverick addressed Maud. The terseness in his voice was almost as if he blamed him.

"She was. I told you she would have some scarring. It will take time, Maverick," Maud said with a stern nod. Maverick placed her down, carefully maneuvering her head to the pillow.

Sean held his Decanter tightly like a safety blanket. The silence was almost unbearable. The lights flickered on and off as though the ship were struggling to maintain power, as though it were laboured breath. He was sure that the Decanter would become real friendly soon if some development did not take place. "Come on, Thorn. Give me a sign," he said.

But no voice could be heard. The ship had come to a full stop one hour ago and no longer drifting. He had failed to make the needed repairs. The ship was simply too big for him to do everything. Sean felt truly dead now.

Sean was paranoid that the creatures who had done this to them would come back for round two. Sean knew in the back of his mind that his Decanter was useless but still, he knew it would come in handy for something with that one shot—a shot that most people would never think of using.

Suddenly, the comms fritzed. Something was coming through the channels; faint but definitely something. Sean leapt to the console like he was bound to it with elastic. "Come in, yes, hello, is anyone there?" he called. His prior thoughts dissolved like water on sand.

Nothing but static. Sean thought for a second that his mind was playing tricks on him, that he had succumbed to some sort of space dementia. And then he heard it, clear as crystal. "T-this is Cardvia of the ship Lal-om. Who is this? Identify yourself or we will fire," a female voice said.

"No, no, no, no! Don't do that. I am friendly. My name is Sean Caleb. This is my ship, Thorn. Where are you? Can you come aboard?" he asked.

Silence and for a fretting moment, he thought the signal was lost. "Docking now." The sweet sound of the docking clamps set Sean on fire. For weeks now he had been dead, alive but merely existing. Now he was with another being.

At last, something happened, whether good or not was yet to be seen. He was about to bring a potential enemy on board, and right now he needed allies, not more friggin enemies. But another soul other than his own...it was sweet relief.

We do not know what we see; we see only what we know—Unknown Archives

When Sean left the door open he almost jumped out of his skin. It was different looking but the unmistakable teeth were most recognizable. He raised his weapon, taking stumbling steps backwards. "Who—I know what you are!" he stuttered.

Cardvia seemed unperturbed by the weapon he produced like he hadn't even drawn one. She seemed more intent on the ship around her. "No need for that. I am Vernom, not Raider, though unfortunately, we share some chromosomes thanks to Father," she said.

Sean was a little confused but more so he was thankful that she had not taken a bite out of him. She might be telling the truth but at least she was someone—another life form instead of the phantoms in his mind.

She sauntered forward, taking the weapon in one swift action. She took in the ship around her. Remembering his manners, Sean offered to show her. "Please, I will show you around," he said, grasping the gun back but keeping it firmly strapped to his hip.

It took only a few hours of contact. Thorn was slowly being revived by the help of Lol-om, a cousin of some sort—the details were a little fuzzy. He hadn't heard the full story because frankly, he was too tired.

He couldn't understand, it but they shared some profound connection. Sean didn't know all of the details, but somehow Lol-om was reaching Thorn in a way nothing could and reviving him slowly from the dark corner he had been forced into.

At first, Sean only heard low mumblings and then words formed. Before he knew it, he could actually hear Thorn—a dim whisper, but he was there. Sean sat in his pilot seat while Cardvia sat in the passenger seat. Sean frowned, realizing that she was in the seat Celeste usually sat in.

"So, you were attacked?" she said finally. Once the facade fell away, Sean could actually see her for a person and not some blood sucking alien. Though the constant revealing of those fangs did hitch his breath some.

Sean had finally put his Decanter away. He felt like trust was slowly building between the two of them. He needed her and he was sure that she needed him. Alive, hopefully.

"Yes, but it was nothing like I have seen. Then again, I have no memories of aliens thanks to some alien device that altered my memories. These creatures were in my mind and they were on the ship. They were like ghosts," he said. "I don't know if they can be killed."

Cardvia sat up. "That is where you are wrong, Sean. Everything that has a pulse must die. It is natural and it is the only way for the true cycle of the universe to carry on. No one is immortal."

Tinkering with his Decanter, opening the chamber and re-locking it, he was deep in contemplation. Cardvia swallowed hard realized the irony in that comment. Her own species was on the path to immortality but that went balls up thanks to her freakish family.

"My commendations on your nursing skills. I am sorry for before. I know you must have thought I was out of my mind—well, I guess I was." Celeste indeed looked calmer and sounder of mind.

"It was a friend of mine. Hariot. Perhaps you will meet him one day when all this madness has subsided. He was the one who supplied me with needed ointment he concocted on his ship by using exotic alien and sometimes ancient plants. And as for your outburst. It's natural considering all that you have been through."

After weeks with the crew, Celeste had healed immensely and now traversed the halls. Even her scars would soon disappear completely in time—perhaps even the ones in her mind. Already the inner turmoil had eased and she wasn't some schizophrenic spouting nonsense. She could actually produce sentences and string words together.

"You okay in there?" The voice wandered through the arch of the door and standing there was Maverick, chuffing on his smoked leaf. "You seem awfully quiet."

She turned around to face him. The sight of him smoking no longer deterred her. In fact, she had come to enjoy it. It made him the character he was and she couldn't picture him without it.

"I am fine." She smiled. "I guess I am still coming to terms with what is happening. The universe is breaking in two and we all might not be around to see it."

Maverick unfolded his arms he so characteristically crossed. "You know you are allowed to be scared. I am too. I never thought that it would lead to this. I knew there was some scary shit out there but now even the place where we live is no longer safe," he said.

"All I want to do is hold him in my arms again. He must be going out of his mind wondering what's happened to me."

"We will do our best to reunite you two. But for now, Celeste, you need to recover. You fought a great battle yourself. Let us face this one together."

Maverick had heard about the station in the Satanic System—a wayward station that had not been visited by the Sprites yet—but more importantly, he had heard that a certain Boric was there seeking passage.

He wasn't looking for new passengers but he felt this one was an exception. "Stern, buddy, you want to greet our new guest?"

Stern was used to being beckoned. Maverick was stamping his authority square on his chest. All he could do was obey but he would do it with gritted teeth.

Stern went to the air lock and his legs turned to jelly. "Selisca?" He was seeing a ghost.

The Boric approached closer. He stumbled a bit back.

"I am Naylin. Selisca was my bloodsister. I have heard great things about you, Stern. That you comforted my sister in her last hours." She forwarded her hand. Stern gulped and shakily accepted. It felt real, but…how...when…who?

Naylin's scales opened and the salmon skin gleamed underneath. "It's a pleasure to meet you."

Stern couldn't believe it. The air between them seemed to hum and contract with anticipation. "What is this?" he directed to Maverick, who had been secretly smiling behind Stern's back.

Maverick clapped a hand on Stern's shoulder as confirmation, pushing him forward a tad. "I tracked her down for you. She is who she says she is. I wanted to make amends for nearly killing you. The guilt over these weeks has been tumultuous.

Just look at it as a present. You can now make beautiful babies." And he clapped him once more on the shoulder, causing Stern to faulter forward once more.

With that, Stern shepherded Naylin to the guest quarters, allowing only a small distance between them. "She has a room but she can stay with you if you like!" shouted Maverick after them.

Stern was shocked. What had gotten into Maverick? A conscience, by the sounds of it—and a rusty sense of humour.

Naylin headed through the ship with her bags in hand, which was quickly taken by Stern.

"Were you twins? You look an awful lot like her." And that was putting it lightly. The immaculate detail was astounding, down to a single scale.

"Yes. We are twins of sorts—more complex though. The closest any are in this universe. I felt her leave when she died. It was as if a part of me had died too; the parting is often hard to even dangerous. But I think she was at peace when it happened. Because of you, because of the strength, you gave her."

Stern felt emotion tug at his chest. "I should have saved her. I should have tried harder."

Naylin placed a hand on his shoulder. He placed her bags down as they finally reached her room. "You did all that you could," she finally said, retracting her hand and taking to the room.

Stern knew he was slowly feeling better; his hole was slowly being filled. And this was all thanks to a man he wanted to be fifty light years away from. Perhaps this was another chance—a way to redeem himself for failing her.

Don't judge me for I am a complicated being with shades of grey, to many to ever be either black or white – Unknown Archives

Dr Stella Rain was deep in contemplation, her hands running through her usually kept hair now frazzled. She was stressed. She had gone through the research on her last project, the important one that involved the capture of a live alien and subjugation to extensive tests. She had given the order to perform those tests. She had signed her death warrant.

In the end, she had lost the subject. Dr Rain was still battling with that. She had let her hunger for knowledge consume her and it ended with the loss of a life—an alien life.

It seemed it didn't matter if you were alien or not; you weren't invincible and were susceptible to hurt.

She was a scientist—or was she? She now doubted herself. She usually didn't care about the small stuff like feelings. Still, she felt something. Why was she so cold and detached? She wanted to explore other alien life, yes, but not to the extent of losing her humanity.

She held onto her glass of gin. She was so used to working that living seemed a foreign concept.

The truth was loud and it deafened her. She could find herself in dangerous waters—waters that were a pool of feelings.

When Harold was alive, he had a way of calming her and now he was wandering the dark cold space comforting no one. She hated that she was like this, so cold and detached, but she was built like that and she found she was lacking the one thing her work could never give her: love and acceptance.

She could have had that with Harold but she stuffed it down like she always did with men. She couldn't help it. She saw them as inferior. And now he was gone, the one man who might have levelled her superiority complex and actually maybe loved her.

She swirled the hard liquor in her glass, taking measured sips. One way or another, she would find herself even if it meant she would have drowned herself in liquor first.

On a space station far, far away.

Stella Rain 2.0.

"Where am I? Who am I? This does not make any kind of sense. Help. Someone please…" But as 2.0 struggled to get out the tub of viscous fluid, a dark shadow fell over her. And then silence.

Lolalia eased her mother out of her bed as she was still shaky on her legs. "Honestly Lolalia, I'm fine. I have been taking it easy but if I lie in this bed a minute longer I will go mad." Lolalia's serious frown cracked into a light smile. Her mother was still as rambunctious as before—in mind, anyway. The Krelians had been hospitable, plying her mother with enough food to make up for all the years she was in that dark place.

Oma was a wonderful caterer for them. She provided Lolalia and her mother with all the Krelian festivity and tradition. The Pits were no more. The Krelians started dismantling the drive and reintegrating them into their own ships. And as for the Pits, it was drawn into the sun and vaporized with hopefully all the bad that came with it. Who knew; maybe one day this technology could give them the upper hand. For now, though, Oma was more concerned with helping her friends.

"Famous Jacor Stew?" said Lolalia over dinner.

Oma smiled. She was a large lady with round hips but her generosity was larger. "Of course." She chuckled.

From being terrorized on her own planet and then landing in hell itself, Lolalia was relieved that their journey ended with hot Jacor Stew.

The Skeleton Stations were in a frenzy, like blood stirring sharks. For the longest time, they had nothing to talk about except who was hotter in the Star Trek franchise: T'pol, an emotionally conflicted Vulcan, or Seven, a merely minted-human-former-Borg. And now they had to check out the Conductors in their hidden canisters. All this time, the Masters had not realized what their Stations were capable of. It was like they were sitting on gold or an explosion of uncertainty.

The DED was powering. The people had simmered and now rallied together. Thanks to the police, some form of civility was put in place. Some factions still fought but their words were not sharp and the unity of humanity was empowering. The engines thrummed to life and more would go into the rift following the Crusade.

The power of these ships was unbelievable and crowds of people cheered. One could guess how they would be in their own environment. Now that Earth was advised of the situation, many were watching as the ships prepared to take off. Many gathered like flocking seagulls. Before there was anarchy; now an overwhelming sense of union grasped the human race. The amount of support the Crusade was getting was unbelievable. Crusade.

That was what the band of ships was dubbed. Not a Fleet or intimidating form of force. A tool of profuse meaning, of potential peace. Bradshaw felt it was fitting, for they were going to venture into the unknown on a crusade to propel humanity into the future. No more would they be held back in the shadowed past. They set forth a mighty fist, an unbridled symbol that humanity was here and it was here to stay.

There are angels of mercy but there are angels of death, too—Unknown Archives

Kressangah had had enough. She ripped the curtain aside and her eyes met an affronting image. Gerof was alive but his eyes...they were burnt through. Dillis came at the rear. "I am sorry, dear. We got to him too late. The fire had done its wrath."

Kressangah sank to her knees and placed her hand on his. He was in a light sleep and was beckoned awake.

Kressangah stood there rigid, almost dead-like. She knew what she was looking at but to acknowledge it was a different matter. "So, he's...blind?"

Both looked down before Dillis placed his hand on her shoulder. Kressanagah wanted to shun him but she knew that this wasn't his fault. She was grateful for the next consoling words. "He is still the same Gerof."

Kressangah squeezed Gerof's hand tightly.

"K-Kressangah, is that…is that you?" His voice almost cracked. Kressangah couldn't hope to imagine the immense pain he was in. And the darkness; what was that doing to him? For the longest time he had seen so much, and now he would never see those things again.

She was there. She placed a tender hand on his forehead, a gesture of condolence in his race's culture. He grappled with it like he was seeing a light in the darkness and a smile appeared.

A towel had been placed over his eyes. Kressangah couldn't help it. The tears began to flow.

"My child, do not cry. I do not regret a single thing since leaving the Order. This is not your fault in any way. Come. Come tell me about this Kroden fellow. He seems like a keeper."

He was unaware of Kroden's presence or how he had turned red. Even in his most dire state, Gerof managed to speak spiritedly.

"Well, he is a story to tell," she said finally after working back the gagging that came with crying.

She sat by him for hours reciting the whole love saga. For the first time since being in this situation, Kressangah realized she had not lost her friend and things could have gone a lot worse. And despite his blindness, he saw more clearly than any other with sight.

The Hive Ships continued to descend their Detachment Palaces though it was to an armada of Sprites. Anarchy was exploding everywhere in the galaxy. The seams of the universe were coming apart. The vultures would come soon and The Dark Matter Entities would finish what the Raiders could not.

The Dark Matter Entities had reached Planet Isis. In the apartment, it was anarchy too as the beings swiped in and out of the walls. Everyone ran for cover but there was no cover to be found. No matter where you went they would find you.

Cleo moved in and out of consciousness. Her mind went back to when they were on Isis.

"We are leaving." Boris was not one for long winded sentences. He was blunt and to the point. They managed to get to the ship but not before encountering the ethereal beings. Boris tried swatting the things like they were mere bugs, but this did not help when the beings encompassed Cleo and merged with her body.

Boris could not believe was he was seeing. Cleo seemed to be fighting back with every fiber of her being. And then it passed through her like she was merely in the way and she was her hysterical self again. She didn't care about herself, only the child she carried inside. Boris clapped her across the face to silence her.

Boris wasted no time and shoved her inside his ship as the apartment fell apart around them. He didn't care that her feelings were hurt or that there was blood that dripping out the corner of her mouth. He was annoyed; annoyed that these damnable things had found them again like they were permanently attached.

And then Cleo's eyes opened wide. The scream she produced was phenomenal.

And then when the long day has ended, will we meet the new day with open arms or will we hide in the cover of darkness?— Unknown Archives

In the Library... (Location Unknown)

The aliens scuttled about, their nimble fingers encapsulating files in crystals and storing them in the layers of archives that towered so high. They spoke in pitched squeaks and garbled undertones. Their language was almost musical.

A Librarian, as they were called, looked the strangest of any aliens yet to be categorized up in the shelves above. They were short in stature, about five feet and green with small eyes that didn't even seem to be open, long nimble fingers, four on each hand, and small compact bodies.

They were the descendants of the Ancient Ones, the Alteran Class Vessels—or by their better name, the esteemed Librarians: the time keepers of the universe.

☟♐□◆□◆◆ ◆♎□◆ ♋□◆ ♐♌♌◆♋

"We must keep this secret. We initialized the beam. The threat should have been eliminated."

■♐□◆ ♋■◆■■ □◆♋●❍■♐♏

"Secret? That is all we do around here. Keep secrets. Maybe we should disclose our position to some—"

♈♎□◆♈♎□❖♐□■□◆ ✏✏✏✏✏✏✏✏

"You suggest hypocrisy! You suggest betrayal. We can never disclose any such thing. We will learn why the beam didn't work but until then we continue our jobs. Understood, Du-du?"

The lean Librarian inclined his head in submission and didn't pursue the matter, returning to his crystals.

Now it was war. The Generation War seemed long forgotten as a new eternal war erupted into fire across the galaxy. The Librarians were a secret race but they were not people to show themselves, to expose their identity or meet other cultures.

What they did was far too important to indulge in such frivolous pursuits. Du'du, on the other hand, wished for something more than this, more than placid existence. He wanted to live; he wanted a life of his own not bound by duty. He wanted flight but with the universe breaking in half he doubted he would get to even do that.

Du'du was not one of the leaders. He wanted to be known to the universe, let their accomplishments be known, let the Unknown Archives be spilt onto this universe, but his counterparts didn't feel that way and wished only to be secret, elusive, a mystery.

But as one of the quotes up in those high reaching towers stated, "all mysteries are eventually to be solved". The necessary aim for their race was what his counterparts stated. That they were platonic and not to feel emotions but to be like a drone, a mere functioning robot. They were time keepers—nothing more, nothing less.

To feel the sensations of life, as Du'du put it, would start something no wave could stop.

That wave should have fixed the universe but it didn't. What did they do wrong? What were they missing in their equation? And worse, what did it spell for the rest of the universe?

Rifts were popping up all over the universe. The Kale galaxy was soon dissolved but other galaxies were in mid-process or just beginning while others were nothing but specs of dust, a washed-out imprint of what was billions of stars—a home. Nothingness yowled and everyone was running. It seemed a feat in itself to save the universe—if anyone had any chance at all. The only ones having a good time, if they felt such things as elation were the Sprites wreaking havoc across the cosmos.

Celeste smiled as she tried not to cringe in pain. The wounds were taking longer to heal than any ordinary wound. The Sprites were corrosive. She was lucky to even be alive. Maud applied the ointment smoothly across her arm. "You smiled. You haven't done that in a while. That is something."

Celeste smiled again and saw the joy light up in his eyes. '" Yes, funny enough, I can. I never thanked you for your dedication. You nursed me to health; you were by my side when I was at my darkest."

Maud inclined his enclave head. "Many thank yous. I am a monk; my dedication, as you put it, is to life. I couldn't have said no; it would have killed me in ways you could not conceive. Tell me, my child, this Sean, is he your partner?"

Celeste took back her arm; Maud was finished now. She looked far away. "He is...everything. I met him on his home planet. I just can't get enough of him, his soul, his traits, his mind—every living morsel of him I want to absorb until he has meshed with me."

"That is what the Sprites did to you, only they were more violent about it. And though you love him with every fibre of your being, you wanted to kill yourself?"

Celeste knew what he was talking about: The Flasher Liquid. "Ingesting Killer Honey was the only way I could be free of torment. I wish I had thought of something else but I had to die. The pain, the onslaught they committed on my mind was unbearable. I knew I was being selfish leaving him alone in this universe but I was not strong. Not strong at all."

Maud took her by the shoulders and directed her faltering eyes to his. "You are strong. You may have had a moment of weakness but in its own right, it was a wise decision. You saved yourself even though you tried to end your life. A tipsy turvy account of events."

Later, Stern met up with Celeste. She had to admit that having someone on the ship of her kind was comforting. "Admiring the view?" he said from behind her.

Celeste twirled around, the backdrop of space highlighting her features further. "Beautiful yet tumultuous. And yet it wants to end us. A swirl of the storm that seems to have grown teeth. Stern, I did not thank you for your donation."

"You mean saving your life?" In this light he kind of looked heavenly.

She laughed. "Well, essentially. I know you were reluctant."

Stern suddenly looked uneasy. "Well don't take it the wrong way, but I wouldn't have. Maverick forced Maud to do the transfusion."

"Anyhow, you have my gratitude."

Mayes laid long ways on the couch. She seemed like she was sleeping. She had her eyes closed and sadly, they would never open again. Ginger lay on her chest, determined not to move as though to warm her heart to life. But she was gone. She probably didn't feel anything; a painless death, her tea toppled over.

The paramedics arrived when neighbours claimed they hadn't seen her in days.

"She had moisture on the lungs. Probably some form of pneumonia over a long period. She probably died with no pain, like going to sleep."

Seemed a small comfort. It simply was a ship moored, a dying light in the distance. How quickly lights go out in the shroud of darkness.

The cat meowed and brushed up against the paramedic's leg.

Cardvia doubled over like she had been socked in the guts. Sean rushed to her side. He was amazed at how concerned he was for her. "Hey there. You okay, Cardvia?"

She looked up into his face and managed a smile. "No, but thanks. I haven't had anything to eat for a long time. Guess it's catching up with me."

Sean couldn't understand. Why didn't she just go to the galley and help herself? Then, realization dawned and he felt like an idiot for not realizing earlier. "You need blood."

She smiled but it was weak. "Yes, but I can't. I don't want to."

He couldn't figure out why she was so adamant in punishing herself. Then he realized what she was and how she drank blood. He eased her up and cupped her chin. "Hey, there are other ways. We will dock with a station and get you some blood. Whatever you think you did and whatever punishment you think you deserve, it's not worth your life."

She didn't know why but this human spouted a lot of sense. Though she wouldn't allow herself to fully be forgiven, she knew starvation was not the way—not after the ordeal caused by Shakik. An image of him flashed before her eyes. "Thank you, Sean."

What light glows, the darkness takes; what life breathes, death suffocates, and what hope beats, dismay rules. When is life going to ever tip the scales in favour of good?
—Unknown Archives

The void was exactly that. No stars peered into its sky, no comfort was sought among its inanimate face. Sean was a ball huddled in the corner, the raging madness inside spilling into his waking hours as he rocked back and forth wandering, waiting, not hoping but spiraling. His fists were clenched, his rage palatable as spit flew from his mouth.

He seemed possessed by a demon or worse: A Sprite. But the truth was darker—far darker than the concentrated depths outside that threatened to crush. No mind was meant to sustain in the darkness, no mind was meant to survive. Sean's mind had been cracked in half like an eggshell and there was no putting the pieces back together, not as long as they stayed in the Void.

In the darkness, Cardvia prevailed, piloting the broken-minded ship as best she could. Under the duress of the Void, the much-beloved ship had succumbed to its power as well.

This only allowed manual control as Thorn slumbered. She got up and stretched, feeling the pang of hunger. She wandered the passages on her way to the galley. Sean was somewhere but he was nowhere. She knew he would be scared, frightened of the unknown, but she couldn't even converse with him these days.

It was just dribbling and outbursts. She turned left and entered the galley with relief. Chowing down on a blood bag, she looked to her right and saw blood. This was not good as she could smell it. It was Sean's. She followed the droplets to the cargo bay where Sean was huddled and a bloodied hand hovered near the release. She made way with her blood bag and attempted to advance, but each time she stepped forward he inched his hand closer to the release.

What could she say in this instance to tempt him from the edge?

His slippery bloodied hand was because he had tried to cut his wrists to no avail. Cardvia now crouched down and placed her hand on his face. Tortured eyes stared back. He was there underneath, trying to push through. "She wouldn't have wanted this. Celeste."

With the mere mention of her name, a flash passed through his eyes—a gleam that promised his return. He convulsed in fits of sobbing. She pushed her hand over his eyes so he closed them. "Picture her. The way she was. Her smell. Her eyes. Her wings. She is real. She may still be real, alive. But if you do this, that picture will fade and she will never see you again. You will never see her again. Take my hand, Sean and we can stop this right now. We can bring her back to life. Are you picturing her?" she said, realizing that his eyes were still closed.

Sean trembled, his arms loose like Jell-O, and his head bobbled as if held by only one tendon. Cardvia approached dutifully, her steps quiet and gentle. She reached out and touched Sean on the hand. He trembled but stilled when she made contact.

"She is gone, Cardvia. Gone out of my life and to who knows where? We have to get out of here. This place. We have to get out." Fat tears oozed from his eyes. With a clatter, he dropped the knife. A chilling relief rippled through Cardvia's body. He reached up to her and she reached down, clasping his hands.

The gulf of darkness ended as scattered stars started to light the horizon like candles in the night. "We are through." The elation in Sean's' voice was undeniable.

This region of space was unbelievable. No eyes had seen this for aeons. In the middle, like a gleaming gem in a clear river: The Old Timer. Before the voices of the dark threatened him to the maw of oblivion but now as he stepped across he knew it was all worthwhile. "Bless the Old Timer!" remarked Cardvia. Sean smiled.

"Are you okay," he asked as they settled Thorn around The Old Timer, biding their time.

"I am," she said, straightening up. "Thanks for your concern, Sean. I only just thought of something. The rifts were here long ago. This was not a good sign for my people, who were in this circumstance many eons ago. Three hundred thousand years ago we were abundant, a thriving race. I may be one now but there is a reason for that. Rifts appeared and we thought 'this is good. A new way to travel.' We never paused to analyze the situation. We did not think to ask the question of why it was there; we simply used them. Rifts are not natural. They are man-made. Long ago, the universe was rife with pre-humans. Basically, the universe was a free place and these pre-humans seeded planets far and wide and Earth was the last one. An epidemic erupted and millions upon millions of pre-humans died, leaving only a handful to send ships to seed Earth—the last remaining human world. Our race followed soon after the humans, but where you survived and to a point thrived, I became one. Sad, I know, but some believe we are weeds just like the pre-humans were. In their delusional quest, they sought to travel faster than light and disrupted the flow of the universe. We simply used what they left behind."

A light bulb flashed in Sean's mind. It was all making a warped kind of sense. "Pre-humans did this. They are the reason the universe is rumbling," he said.

"Yes," she said. "The Sprites were just opportunistic. They used these gateways to their advantage. And the Raiders are a sick result of what happens when weeds aren't eradicated but rather upgraded."

Sean saw it all so clearly; saw past the mirage. She was talking about herself. "Cardvia, you wouldn't be referring to yourself in that little statement, would you?"

A giggle erupted from Cardvia like a bubble. "No. But I don't believe I am innocent. I have done things, Sean. Things that would have stopped you from letting me onboard."

"You are not a weed. Humans are bad in many ways, but I do not believe we are so bad that we should be eradicated. It was a sadness what happened to your people, Cardvia," he said. "I thought the first time I saw you that you were a bloodsucker, I admit it, but then I saw you and realized my preconceptions were totally wrong. Some people aren't as lucky as to see past that pre-notion," he said.

By now Cardvia was tearing up. He wished he had tissues to give her. Before Sean was unbelieving of this character, but now he'd rather not store faith in anyone less capable. She had been through lots—more than he could ever imagine as the two sat there discussing things, chatting to the ends of eternity it seemed. He could tell he had just made a trusted friend and it couldn't have come at a better time. He just wasn't sure of her true intentions because sometimes the first impression was the right one, but for, now he, would rely on faith, for that was all he had.

Thorn was at full strength now. Thanks to the diligent assistance of La-lom, Thorn was now fully functional. Sean shook when Thorn's presence became known. It was unbelievable, like he had been working with only half audio.

Thorn was coming through loud and clear, but something was different. He could also hear another voice. La-lom's. He didn't think this was normal until Cardvia explained that La-lom's connection with Thorn had bled through to Sean. He didn't mind, but it was a little crowded in there.

"Thorn, pal, what has been happening?" he asked.

It looked strange, Sean talking to nothing but the wall and then acknowledging seemingly no one. "What is it?" asked Cardvia, noticing his change in facial expression.

"He says that the Alteran Class Vessels have all rallied together. He says because he was out of commission he missed the call. A signal has been dispatched, some hidden command that tells them of a mission. The Alteran Vessels are the warriors. They are the army that can help us gain what we have lost. This war may still be won by us. We may have a chance now." His enthusiasm was catchy but not altogether convincing.

"But they are few. La-lom is only one," Cardvia said.

"Like you," Sean stated. "But I imagine that like the Raiders who are from you and many she can be duplicated.'

"Cloning? You think that La-lom was artificially created?" Cardvia asked. This was astonishing news.

Sean continued. "Based only on what Thorn has shared with me, and La-lom agrees. She has no past memory of her people. She has gaps in her mind. She says she wants to thank you for helping her. If you had not saved her from that greasy shipyard scraper she would have been scraped," he said.

For the first time, Cardvia allowed a smile. It seemed to take all her energy. She looked bizarre smiling. It was nice to know that she was able to convey feelings of joy instead of just seething behind clenched teeth.

"He says they are ready, that they have waited for this moment since their last encounter thousands of years ago when he was first made," he said.

"I knew something like this had happened to them," she said. "They would not tell me, but Thorn is more trusting of you. La-lom told me nothing. She would not bond with me. I initially took offense but now I see it was for a reason. She couldn't. She wasn't compatible with me. Oh, La-lom. If only you could I knew you would."

"Looks like we have another player on the board. The Maker," said Sean.

"The Maker is the one who has done all this splicing and dicing. He is the reason La-lom exists and those horrible replications muddy the galaxy with their vileness. Curse them! Sorry. Sometimes I get carried away thinking about them, but at least La-lom is nothing like them. Let us march together, let us take a stand."

Five days earlier aboard the ship Thorn....

The ship Thorn led the front followed closely by La-lom. Cardvia piloted La-lom and Thorn was piloted by Sean. The other Alteran Class Vessels seemed to obey easily, assuming Thorn the leader. Sean wasn't sure about them yet. He only knew Thorn and these ships were like strangers—an anomaly. He would have to measure their trust another day. He didn't know their history but he knew they were essential, their only army no matter how minuscule.

Cardvia pointed out a vast patch of stars that started to stem and thin out. "See there?" she said. "That is where they come from. Last time we managed to force them back there, but they regrouped and came back even stronger."

"Voids?" The high octave alerted Cardvia that this was no new news to him. "Yes, I have heard of them. Not a nice place," he said.

Cardvia turned red. "Not a nice place! That is saying it nicely. If you really want to know, they are spaces where no stars or planets exist. I have been banned to go there. It makes me shudder to think of it. Imagine a place with no light, no stars to guide you, consumed by it."

Sean swallowed hard. He knew only too well of the darkness she spoke of. He experienced it after all—the attack where no light shone. "Unbelievable. Maybe we can drive them back there but we need more numbers, Cardvia," he said. "I think we will have to pay this Maker a visit."

There was no response. "Why so quiet, Cardvia?" he asked.

Cardvia had to tell him. Better to break the illusion now. "The station has never been found, Sean. Some say that it is because he uses some sort of temporal cloak shielding him from those in search and from time and space," she explained.

"But it may be possible?" Sean asked.

"Are you kidding?" she exclaimed. "The Voids are avoided for a reason, Sean."

"Hey, don't bite my head off," he said. Sean and Cardvia realized the humour in that later. "Why so snarky?"

"Because in order to get there we have to travel through there," said Cardvia. "And well…"

"Yes?"

"It is said the Old Timer is situated at the edge of nothing, where stars end and darkness starts."

Sean realized in that moment: he had to do this. Celeste's mission was to go to the Old Timer. He didn't care. He was onboard. Besides, how hard could it be?

"You have never had friends? That is sad. Well as your first friend, I am here to tell you that it is all right to fear something you know nothing about."

Cardvia blinked up at him and smiled, exposing her sharpened teeth. "Are you hungry?"

Sean almost bit back his lip and gulped. "Why?" He exaggerated the word with sharp caution.

Cardvia saw the shock on his face and couldn't help but laugh. "I didn't mean…I meant to say would you like to join me in the mess hall. Some food sounds nice about now," she said, nodding towards the stellar view.

"In the middle of a war? Shouldn't we be commanding or something?"

"These are Altran Class Vessels. If they need our help they will ask for it."

What redemption? There is no redemption for those who have committed atrocities. But isn't forgiveness a human trait? An amiable quality?—Unknown Archives

The universe, as Jathmoora explained it, was as intricate and detailed as the galaxies it housed and as personal and small as one's mind. She was always so connected to the universe. But as the universe shook, so did she and her mind didn't feel all that sound.

The war had crept upon them and throttled them at the throat. Jathmoora was honing all her energies now. She needed to be at her best if she was going to have a go at this. She had never fought such things before. She had seen through a lot, her daughter in particular, but something like this? It was unfathomable to think that such things could exist, yet they did, yet they came and came in numbers so unperceivable.

Sean was flung to the other side, his custard or whatever splattering across the floor. "Thorn, what is it?"

The Altran Class Vessels were dispersing, thinning out too much. The Sprites were winning and they were not relenting.

Cardvia rushed to her feet and helped Sean up. "We have to leave. We haven't got long."

Sean felt a pang of annoyance. Turn and run? After traversing the gulf, where no stars gleamed?

After fighting tooth and nail to get here? Turn away when they hadn't even reached their destination?

Sean couldn't help it. He balled his fists and went straight to Cardvia. "What's going on?"

"This is it, Sean. This is the epic journey's end. I feel it, do you not? The universe is getting ready to swallow."

Both rushed to the bridge. It was to mayhem. The Altran Vessels were either on fire, combustive, souls crying out, or running for dear life. Sean's mouth dropped down. There was not a hope in hell they were going to survive this. Not a—

There was static on the line. "Thorn, what is it?" And then the view got a whole lot nicer. Sean had never seen such a sight—at least not since the beautiful Old Timer, which was only a few hours ago.

"What? Who is that?" added Cardvia disparagingly, as though she was miffed about discontinuing her rant.

The static cleared and the voice boomed through the bulk of the ship and seeped through Sean's skin. "Hello, son. Thought you could do with a hand."

"Bless the Old Timer!" was all he could retort—that and other obscenities. "Father?"

Mitchell Caleb had a ship unlike any of them had seen. It had intricate detailing on the outer hull and the source of energy seemed to glow ever iridescent like it was alive. "Dad, can you hear me?"

Nothing. For a split second, Sean thought the worst: he had lost his father for the second time. And then Mitchell's voice filled him with relief. "I am still here, son. Let's get through this and then we can talk."

As he spoke, a jutting laser hit the port side of Sean's ship. Sean felt it like a sizzling sharp pain in his head. As his bond grew longer, the bond also grew deeper. Sean could feel everything Thorn felt. But still, there was something he was not telling him. A secret embedded deep in his conscience.

The Sprites that operated the vessels suddenly left. It was like they had heard someone call them and they went to them immediately. In their wake, they left debris of both Altran Vessels and ships the Sprites had taken over.

When the door opened, the steam rushing from the gap of the docking passage, Sean did all he could to not gallop right up to his father and punch him in the face. He was thankful he came to the rescue but there was way too much water under the bridge. Sean went for a traditional handshake instead.

Mitchell looked rough. It was easy to see the resemblance. He hadn't shaved for a good month though, a layer of growth evident. He winked his slightly scarred eye. Sean could see he had seen more than his fair share while being dead. He had to ask him about that sometime. Mitchell paused then grabbed his son and hugged him so hard that a crack could be heard. "Son, it's been too long. Let me look at you." Mitchell was overtaken by him but Sean didn't protest this overconfident coddling. "My, you have grown into a fine gentleman. But alas, we have come to an apex in our paralleling destinies." Suddenly his bubbliness fizzled and he was serious.

Sean couldn't believe it. He was in shock. His father wasn't dead because he had to fake his death. He had to take on a secret mission that meant he had to go to the ends of the universe.

He had to abandon his family. Sean fumed. He could feel the heat rise to his eyeballs. He almost wished he were dead.

"You can't yank the chain. You can't say you're gone and then return twenty years later with promises and plans. It just doesn't work that way."

"Sean, please, sit down." But by this time Sean was walking back and forth solidly, tapping his Decanter.

Cardvia appeared quickly. "I am sorry to interrupt."

Mitchell looked aghast. He only heard her voice on the comm. She was magnificent. Sean spun on his heel, his eyes hot like lasers. "Yes, Cardvia?" he spat. He regretted his tone the moment he spoke.

He took a moment to compose himself, realizing he shouldn't have taken this out on Cardvia. "The Altrans have something to say to all of us."

"What do you mean—" But before Sean could finish, an ethereal, deep and wise voice echoed over them, through them, piercing their very fabric of being. It took a while for Sean to realize he wasn't the only one hearing this.

"We are one. We are many. We are Altran by some, we are the Librarians by others. And once we were flesh, ancient. We died and only reside here. We tell you know the truth of that which was. That which we kept buried. Long ago, the galaxies were tighter clusters, super galaxies. Now their strength fades, their cohesion dissipates. Rifts threaten to tear the universe apart. The only thing we fear worse is that which annihilated us. The ghosts that move through dark, that only care to consume and grow. We are all but gone. As a last resort, I ordered my people to infuse their neurons to machine. Many died but we intertwine with metal. We are machine and memories now—a distant echo. We were mighty then. Had discovered immortality. Then stolen. The Raiders took from us what we left behind. Parasites. But they met a most unsightly end when we initialized the Wave of Redemption. Now they are threatened too; now they run. We are forwarded toward death but before we see demise for a second time, we decided to vote as one and let you hear our voice and decide for yourselves your fate."

68

And until we realize we are safe, we always run for cover, frightened even of our own shadow—Unknown Archives

Thoughts entered Cleo's mind as she succumbed to sleep once again.

Cleo couldn't help it. She gave birth during hyperspace. The child seemed to use the gravity of the shift, and out it came. The cry pierced the silence in the ship. Boris put the ship on auto. He grasped the baby, practically ripped her from her mother's arms.

He didn't even register that Cleo was there. He let the baby cry. He inspected it like it was a new tool. Cleo fought to speak. She reached out to her child yet Boris kept her at a distance. It tore her inside.

Finally, Boris clasped the binders to Cleo without flinching, without a second thought. He held the baby from her just enough for her to grasp little bits of blanket. "I thought that you were doomed after conceiving but you have proven useful. I am taking what is mine. You were a convenience. You were an incubator for my progeny. I wanted to snuff this life I hold now but she may be of use in the future."

Cleo tensed against the binders, unflinching to the pain. She was spitting and raging but unable to produce words. The ship trembled all around her. The possession would happen soon. Boris ran for an escape pod with his child tightly grasped underarm who continued to cry. And he had forsaken his lover to a most gruesome death, no thoughts of pity, no thoughts of remorse. Then he halted and found himself spinning on his heel.

"Aunty Jath? Is there a reason why we aren't doing anything? Shouldn't we be preparing, donning our armor or something?" Always the gung-ho warrior. She had spunk but she was short-sighted. "Child, it's hard to explain. I can feel the universe and it is trembling. We haven't been good house guests. I think I can contribute but it would mean leading us into battle, and I don't want to do that. I don't want to lead us to certain death."

"What if it works?"

"Then we will be saved."

"Well?" Jathmoora swallowed a smile. She knew her too well. Selene was working her towards a meeting with Maud. Separate, they were menial bodies but together they were a tidal force. Together they were a powerful element.

"C'mon, Aunty Jath. You know you miss him. If the universe is about to go kablooey, don't you think you should risk seeing him again, even if old feelings should…I don't know, mysteriously awaken?"

She had a point. The child did have some wisdom. Jathmoora realized something at that moment. A procedure that might help them, shift their status on the board. "All right. I will invite him but don't be surprised if he doesn't come."

Selene did all she could to conceal her rapid smile.

The battles were fierce. The Sprites moved through metal and flesh with equal ease. Possession was rampant. No one could hope to outrun these things. And yet there was hope, ever so minuscule. Now was the time to rally together. Petty wars like the Generation War no longer mattered, the reasons for its initial start long forgotten in the winds of time.

Taroks, on neutral ground, met with an open hand the Gaul, who reluctantly accepted peace and neutrality. Now the fight for the universe began.

Kressangah was readying for battle. "What are you doing?" came the brazen voice of Kroden.

"What I am meant to do. I am preparing to hit these shitheads in the arse, assuming they have one."

Kroden twitched like he was amused but not quite stimulated enough to laugh. "Look, I know more than anyone what war can do but this is different—this is anatomical. We are facing the battle of our lives and this attitude just isn't going to cut it this time."

Kressangah swivelled round to face him. He noticed her top that was wrapped around her nicely, exposing her belly. "I know that we are not ready but I heard about the Alliance and I need to be there," she said.

"We had hoped for something like this but now that it is here I am a little reluctant to regain my rank."

Gerof was quiet and everyone jumped when he chose to spoke. "Sweet Kressangah. We are little grains but perhaps certain sown seeds might allow a forest of hope to erupt. I know you want to change things, make a difference. And in doing this you may achieve the elusive Serenity your kind forever pursues."

Kroden spoke out. "I won't lose you again."

Kressangah sheathed her last blade. She had them all affixed to areas around her body. "So, what do you suggest? We simply stay in the corner and hope the Sprites don't attack, wait while the universe dissolves? I know what they are capable of. We got off lucky for some unknown reason. But others know their wrath—their full wrath—and if there is an off chance, however slim, that I can contribute, I mean to."

Kroden grabbed his armour and donned it. "Well if you can be foolish than so can I."

Mitchell was on the bridge, his hands clasped behind his back, the space mirroring in his eyes. Sean crept in. "Beautiful, isn't it?" said Mitchell, sensing his presence. There was a great deal of emotion in his voice. For the first time, Sean felt it, the niggling feelings of regret and despondent hope.

Sean had not let his father explain. Perhaps now was time to do that, to actually listen for once, but his father did not go on. "It is, Father. Where were you?" The question came out faster than Sean could hold onto it.

Mitchell looked away. "You wouldn't believe me if I told you, and that is if I could tell you. See, the Parliament sent me on a very important mission. I have been to the ends of the universe. I hoped to find answers there to the nagging questions here. Just know there is hope for us but time is not on our side. That is all I can say. The rest I'm afraid is...confidential."

Sean felt the tightening of his throat. That word: that abomination. Confidential. It meant a whole lot of bullshit for not saying the truth. He couldn't have hoped for anything different. Mitchell was here at least. Perhaps he might forget duty, but Sean wasn't holding his breath on that one; he would rather turn blue.

"I see you got my present."

Sean realized he was touching his Decanter without knowing it and Mitchell eyed it with a sheer sentiment. He didn't know his father recognized that emotion. "You said that it was for the battle. Is this what you meant? Are we embroiled in the lasting battle of our days?"

"Not so soon, but yes son, this is the battle, the precipice."

Once the time comes to rule, the time for servitude is due—Unknown Archives

The docking doors opened and the clamp docks locked. As Muad approached Jathmoora felt a pang in her belly like someone was squeezing her intestines. Jathmoora felt so hot and under pressure to act nice when all she wanted to do was scratch his eyes out.

"Tell me again. I have to do this?" she remarked to Selene whilst her eyes stayed glued to Maud. Jathmoora couldn't help the child-like quality to her voice; he had always made her feel nervous, quivering within.

Selene smiled happy to see Maud once again, but also in the corner of her eye noticing Jathmoora's unease. "Yes, you have to. Besides, he may have forgotten what you did."

"Thanks, that makes me feel a lot better."

As soon as Maud was close it was clear he had not forgotten; the disdain was written all over his face. "Selene. So good to see you're still alive."

What was that remark supposed to mean? It sounded so stately like he was trying to declare something. And what did he mean 'still alive'? Like she would be any safer travelling with him. She has seen the scratches, the ones that could not be seen. She had been through the tumbler with him, hoping from planet to planet, monastery to monastery. But as soon as he was close enough her feigned demeanor kicked in and she was all manner of politeness.

"So wonderful to see you again, Maud." She even ventured to place a hand on his shoulder, a brief contact but the comfortableness was there.

Maud inclined his head as a mark of respect. "So, what do you hope to achieve with me around?"

"I was hoping for something that you might consider radical."

"And what is that?" He could already hear the gears in her mind working. He had dreaded this. He knew this day would come when he would be required to do something he hated completely.

"It is joining our minds and hoping our minds are compatible enough to create an energy field funneled by the Choc-ra. We may be able to force matter, re-shape it."

Sounded impressive and dangerous and so like Jathmoora.

In the Library (location unknown)

Du'du had combed the archives making sure they were perfectly placed. He was somewhat of a perfectionist. Every known poet, philosopher, and idealist in the universe had been recorded and archived and placed in the spiraling shelves of towering pillars. The crystals were living memories. When the planets were dust, at least at the birth of a new universe, their voices would be heard and echo across the scattered galaxies.

⧫⧫🕯⧫🕯⧫📪 ⍓□◆ ❍◆⬧⧫ ❒♏♋♍⧫♓❖♏ ⧫♒♏ ♌♏♋❍✍ ❄♒♏ ♑♋●♋⌧♓♏⬧ ♋❒♏ ■□⧫ ♍□♒♏⬧♓❖♏✍ ❄♒♏⍓ ♎❒♓♐⧫ ⬧⧫ ♓●●✍

"St'du, you must reactive the beam. The galaxies cohesiveness is not holding. They drift still," advised Du'du with urgency. That was bold of him. He was usually so quiet and reserved but this matter was not made for the shy; this matter demanded boldness.

🕯✋◆♎◆📪 ♎□ ⍓□◆ ♐□❒♑♏⧫ ⧫♒♋⧫ ⬧♏ ♋❒♏ □♌⬧♏❒❖ ♏❒⬧✍ ⬥♏ ♎□ ⬧♒♋⧫ ⬧♏ ❍◆⬧⧫ ⧫□ &♏♏◻ ⧫♒♏ ❒♏♍□❒♎⬧ □ "We could not have hoped for the laser to work. We used the Light Conductors last time, and they are gone. This Wave was meant to correct the universe. We are a fractured race. We need our compatriots. We need our ancestors' knowledge and wisdom."

🕯✋◆♎◆📪 ♎□ ⍓□◆ ♐□❒♑♏⧫ ⧫♒♋⧫ ⬧♏ ♋❒♏ □♌⬧♏❒❖ ♏❒⬧✍ ⬥♏ ♎□ ⬧♒♋⧫ ⬧♏ ❍◆⬧⧫ ⧫□ &♏♏◻ ⧫♒♏ ❒♏♍□❒♎⬧ □

"But they were said to have died long ago. Why would we need their help? Du'du, do you forget that we are observers? We do what we must to keep the records of every life that is born into this universe intact. We are the time keepers. And as the Old Timer as my witness, we will save this universe. But you must understand, if we interfere too much then questions will arise about where it came from, who sent it, and eventually we, will end up being sought out. We do not interact with others."

The Librarians were isolated from any other species. They chose this hermit style life for the sake of preserving the universe. Sometimes secrets are best-kept secret. St'du believed that. Du'du on the hand felt like their exposure would greatly benefit their race. But what was he but one? And the voices of the many would triumph over the voice of one. At least in this instance. Until another solution presented itself.

"Father, please tell me what you have planned." Sean could not help it. As he stared into the steely grey of his father's eyes, he knew that he was asking for a lot. He was holding things back and he had a bellyful of secrets. Did his father not deserve to look out for his family just this once? Couldn't he just say to hell with duty? Couldn't he just be a decent man, a father? Sean felt like Mitchell had left them once and now would be a time to stay. He knew the hidden truth, the one that stated Mitchell was there for the mission and nothing else. He knew that he needed to let him go—again—to save the universe. But to do it was another thing; a harder task.

"Son, you are doing so well. You will be triumphant in all that you do. You have yet to scrap your potential." Sean noted the brazen pride in his now warbling voice.

"But why can't you forfeit your duties this once and stay with me in this fight?" Sean could not help the desperation escaping in his voice.

"Think of me as the backup unit. I will be there when you need me, waiting in the shadows. Just know what I am doing will be in the benefit of saving the entire universe. And you will be proud to call me father—this once anyway."

Sean hmphed not to be rude but to simply say do what you want, just don't expect me to care about it. He made the mission sound so valiant, but Sean didn't feel valiant. He felt inept. He felt like he had failed and no amount of plying would change that fact. He wallowed in his father's failures.

Sean watched the strange ship disappearing before the view screen and along with it, the one chance he had to make amends. Well, at least he had a chance to say goodbye this time. Sean pressed his hand against the glass as though to reach out to him in comfort. But there was no comfort, just the stars mocking him and the breath on the window.

Cardvia looked Sean up and down, scrutinizing him a fraction. "Perhaps he is right, Sean. This way no matter how the battle to come turns out, you will be reunited with your father, be a family again."

"It will take more than him returning to become a family again. Now we are fragmented. This universe is in dire shit. And what's worse, I only care about my petty feelings."

Looking through the eye of the needle we see only a small piece of the picture—what lies beyond it is far bigger—Unknown Archives

The Boric had padded hands and long, almost claw-like nails, which gave her the misconstrued appearance of an overgrown rodent. Stern had not taken his eyes off of Naylin. She was exactly like her sister, even down to her mannerisms. He studied her. Every inch from tip to toe. She was... perfection.

"I hoped to somehow repay you for your services."

Now Stern felt worse. Repay? He had not saved her sister; she was gone and now Naylin wanted to owe him something. No. He had to stop this. "Please, Naylin. I know that you somehow think that I am to thank for her ease, but she shouldn't have died. That was a failure on my part, not an accomplishment."

Naylin looked frustrated. "You take no credit! You did your part. Don't you see? Well, you wouldn't. You have no knowledge of our species interlinking. You see, when we die we lock onto the last compelling and emotionally charged image and sound of our bloodline. Because you were with her in her more emulated hours, she had something else to lock onto, something to anchor her to peace."

Stern chose to gracefully accept this rather than refute her explanation. He did not like upsetting her. "Thank you. I had hoped to do more but by the sounds of it, I did all I could. I see that now," he finally came to say.

Naylin looked around inquisitively, her scales closed for the moment. "Your ship is impressive."

Stern gave a giggle. She failed to see the humour until he replied with, "This is not my vessel. Maverick, the big bald man you met first? This is his ship. I am his…servant." He suddenly looked away, ashamed.

"You are a slave?" she asked, looking a little on edge. She started to pace. Suddenly Stern felt like he had offended her and went to interject when she said, "I had no idea. Our races aren't prayed on, but occasionally one or two do get taken." Stern realized her pain evident on her face and allowed her to go on. "We avoided enslavement for many years and then when we were taken a great rebuttal happened on our planet and we were spared. To think of it sends a cold icicle through my chest. Borics are appealing to the males, and sometimes we are punished for it."

"Like Selisca was." He couldn't help the sadness in his voice.

"Yes."

Sean wasn't sure how they were going to fair. But somehow, whether instinctual or intuitional, he knew they were going to be all right. He eventually went to show Cardvia the scriptures and plaxes in the abandoned rooms. He had held out on it before, but now he felt like she had shown him enough that he could trust her.

With his father's departure, Sean had an overwhelming urge to go through all the stuff in the rooms. He unlocked rooms that Thorn denied him by threatening to disconnect from him. He thought it funny that he took him seriously. He didn't know how to do that.

She was intrigued by them. "And you say they were left here from when your father piloted the ship?"

Sean felt a twinge at the mere mention of his father. He was probably thousands of lights years away by now with that exotic engine of his that he regrettably did not get to inspect. "Yes, or more so they were left here by whoever piloted before. I don't think he left them here on purpose. I think that there might be something here."

Cardvia pondered and held the plax flat on her palm. "I believe that these are from old galaxies, ones now dissolved and but a swirl of dust and gas."

"Then perhaps therein lies our answer. In the mass of ashes."

Celeste let the natural oils coat her feathers, using her scowler to spread them throughout her body. Every Angel had one. It was a sonic electronic device that emitted faint particles. It was needed to keep Celestial Beings pristinely well preserved. Appearance was everything to a Celestial Being, particularly to the females and incidentally the males like primped peacocks.

There came a knock at her door.

"Enter." She tucked the scowler away. It was personal to Sedukar, like having your daily appliances displayed in the open. "Maverick, how can I be of assistance?" she asked walking around and shedding the uncomfortable vibe but as she was about to find out, it was going to get a lot more uncomfortable given the smell of booze.

Maverick was smoking his special leaves. This one emitted a blue smoke. He had his arms cross ways leaned against the arch of the door, preventing it from automatically closing. "Celeste, lovely. We were wondering when you were going to join us in the galley. We have prepared some tantalizing dishes. None as exquisite a dish as you, but..."

On closer approach—after he finally allowed the strained door to close—she could smell his breath. He had been drinking—a lot by the looks of it. He tried to approach her with an open hand seemingly to graze her face but she moved away to swat him and in his drunkenness, he stumbled forward into her cabinet.

Clearly, the strain of remembering what had happened to his galaxy finally had bubbled to the surface in a surge.

"That wasn't very nice." Maverick tried to grab her again and this time she screamed.

"Maverick, you are drunk and I know for a fact that this is not who you are!" By this time Celeste was backing away, looking around warily for any kind of exit but he had blocked them.

"You know how hard it's been to be around you. Knowing that you are untouchable. I thought I could contain myself but I must taste. It has been a very long time."

A bed was all that stood between the two. A weird invitation. Celeste was bound to Sean. She could not be with anyone else now that she had melded with him. It was against her beliefs. Once a Celestial Being mated she was tied to that male for life and any indiscretions meant eternal failing in front of the Old Timer. It meant shame.

"I know that you are hurting and afraid, but Maverick I am not the answer."

When Celeste moved left, so did Maverick, intoxicated and emotional.

Suddenly Maverick lunged forward with unrelenting passion only to be greeted by the brunt force of Celeste's white wing.

He was out before he hit the floor with a satisfying crack.

Upon the first viewing, we often forget the circumstances to that which we see
—Unknown Archives

Eric was so close—close to madness that is. He couldn't remember his family so he made Charlie his family; made him recite what they looked like, what they wore. Charlie was an AI constructed using Eric's brain, but his personality evolved independently. This gave a contrast in personalities and a new perspective though not always wanted. Eric had lost his family early in his life but he had not murdered them. He had suffered a black out and so was not culpable for their deaths.

Now at his lab table, he took the strand of hair in the pincer of his fingers. DNA. His love, his passion, his ultimate downfall. He glanced through his magnifying glass, his eye three times bigger, giving him the lopsided appearance of an ogre. He felt like he could do this, the zinging feeling goading him to continue on this path. The DNA he took from Robert could very well allow him a second chance at rectifying his past mistake.

"Charlie, my friend. Do you believe we can bring back the dead?" This was more a rhetorical question. He did not hope for an answer, yet he got one nevertheless.

"A conundrum, master. For how can we come back from non-existence? I know where this is headed, master and you must not. She died. She will never again come back. I appreciate your insight as a scientist but you must know when to draw the line."

Charlie just sighed this time instead of replying to his inane silence. Charlie knew him too well to know when he was developing ideas, and forlorn ones at that. The cut off sentences usually foretold it. Then again, Charlie's programming had a lot of Eric's personality traits. But once he was activated he had formed his own personality, humor and memories. He also unfortunately inherited opinions. Sometimes Eric wished he had averted that part of his programming.

Stella Rain 1.0 lay in her blood, her shoes to one side and her glasses broken. She groaned and tried to move but her body felt broken. She gasped, taking in needed air but tasting the death on it and chocking. She could hardly see without her glasses, but she could ascertain enough to know that something was terribly, terribly wrong.

Dr Stella Rain eased herself to her shaky legs. She stepped on what remained of her specs. She saw them—her men—all dead. Not just dead, but eviscerated. Consoles sparked. Alarms whirred. She couldn't remember anything except her name: Stella Rain. Everything else was gone, wiped from her brain like wiping a program from a computer. She stumbled around more, her vision hazy. "My n-name is Stella Rain. B-but who am I? Where is everyone? What happened?"

Amongst the dead crew Stella did not see Bradshaw among them.

The Raiders were retreating, taking the Detachment Palaces and reconnecting with the Hive ships, leaving with their tales firmly placed between their legs.

The Sprites were taking over the galaxy piece by piece and the Raiders had no chance in this system or any neighboring one. The Raiders were not easily scared but this was a new type of fear. They needed to venture far, far away into the most sacred of spaces.

The Sprites were malicious beyond the Raiders own velocity and they could not hope to parallel their power. The blood suckers—mere masses, piles of flesh like the rest of the universe—would surely perish. So, with that in mind, the Raiders had one and forlorn choice: retreat to the sacred place and slumber until a time was due for their return.

Before the Raiders let blood run like wine but the massiveness of these beings' goal outdid any hope of reigning supreme for this time, so they would wait until the right fruitful time came along.

Not only was the entire galaxy overturned and in chaos, but everywhere the universe was breaking at the seams: Raiders with everything to lose, Sprites with such tenacity, and the galaxy seeming to turn on itself. The universe was not a kind place to be in at the moment.

The shot-up ship landed and upturned dirt in the grassy fields of Jelec. The fine weather made it look like nothing was wrong, but in the villages, there was a new nightmare. The fire erupted, towering high like skyscrapers.

"Mother, how can we? Our planet. It is in ruin."

"Yes, but not gone. Come, Lolalia, do you not feel it? The call. It has been calling you since your birth. Your mark holds more than our culture. It holds power over the skies."

"The moons. How did you know about that?"

"Your birth was tumultuous, to say the least."

"You have to tell me about that someday."

"Perhaps, but for now, child, know that your time has come. You have an internal compass swayed by the power of the Siren Moons. And your mark, your prosper tattoo is the anchor you need to finally rid this planet of scum and take your place on the throne of your grandfather. Do what he could not: rule."

Her sisters were dead. All dead. "What happened, Mama?" said Lolalia, her mouth wide open at the viciousness of the attack as they each stepped into the throne-room puddled with blood.

Lavinia looked away, realizing the situation to its full opening gash. "Vivian. She succumbed to years of abuse by that madman. But this…something has come to our planet."

All of her sisters were gone. All that remained was the throne.

Lolalia closed in on the throne, outstretching her hand to the gold of the heavy laden arms. "You think that I can rule, Mama? After what I have done? Am I not like my dead sister here? Am I not worse?"

Lavinia encroached with an open hand and laid it softly on her daughter's shoulder. "Like the Siren Moons, whose ferocity is well known and deep, you also have a magnetic beauty. You will rule well because I know you will."

And so Lolalia sat in the throne stained with her sisters' blood and tainted by the ruling days of her grandfather whose passing she never mourned. Today was a new day; today she was a mighty storm to behold while her people and planet lay in tatters.

And when we are propelled by desperation, does not the insane notion sound more logical than doing what is right?—Unknown Archives

Sean was a wreck. He hadn't shaved in days; his clothes had smelled better and he would not eat. He was inconsolable. Cardvia did her best to aid him but he little cared for company nowadays. Sean was in his pilot seat, twirling his decanter. He often thought of suicide.

Twirling and twirling. The Decanter looked awful friendly, but something stopped him from actually falling off the edge. Something that he never knew was in him: faith. His Aunt had always been there, like a light leading him away from darkness. She would save him in this time of need and utter hopelessness. She was a heroine and he admired her efforts. He had to be strong just like she was. He held onto the hope that he would see her once again.

Cardvia passed Sean in the corridor. "What are you doing?"

Sean smiled, turning back as he continued walking. "Having a shower."

Cardvia smiled; well it was about time she secretly thought. At last he was coming out of his hole. She thought he was going to be consumed by his self-pity. She was all about self-loathing. She knew what it was like to truly feel like you were an utter failure with no future of ever coming out of it. But nowadays she realized that kind of intense loathing was exhausting and had no point. She realized when she was faced at Devastators Edge with death she did not seek it out like she wanted or thought she would. She felt scared and wanted more than anything to live.

Sean let the sonic rays pass over him. Blissful. There was no water on his ship, just good old fashioned sonic rays. It did the job alright but wasn't as pleasing as water. Sean dreamed of having an actual shower one day, of letting cold clean water cool his skin.

Jathmoora and Maud combined their forces. "I am trying to hold on. You need to push through, Maud!"

The two were on the bridge trying to stop the onslaught of infested ships closing in on their position. They kept their hands up like pushing up an invisible wall. Nothing seemed to be happening until…

Maud looked at Jathmoora and with his glance, he surged his last strength and both created a force field that crushed the ship like a tin being crushed by a giant hand. Then it was a domino effect and the rest of the line of ships each collapsed and were destroyed.

The episode was enduring. Maud collapsed. Jathmoora rushed to his aid just in time as his head was about to meet the floor grate. His vision was blurring but he grasped for her comforting arms. "Maud, look at me." She could see his eyes wavering. "We have done it. Please answer!" she said through tired sobs.

Maud was still and not moving and then his eyes fluttered open. "I felt it, Jathmoora. The undercurrent that runs through space. We have tapped the vein. We have altered fate," he rasped before his eyes shut.

Jathmoora held him tightly, his head nestled into her lap like if she let go he would be gone. The onslaught continued outside and the enemy ships combusted from the inside out. But the sorrow inside Jathmoora's body was far more chaotic. Maud was in a critical state as the others helped to bring him to the Med Bay. Jathmoora was at his side worrying. She would not let him die—not by the dying light of the Old Timer.

She would not allow him to leave her a second time. Once she knew that she could not let him die her decision was simple: she would transfer some of her life force over to Maud and save his life, even if it meant depleting her own."You can't do this," muttered Maud through gritted teeth. She didn't tell him what she was planning but unfortunately his state had not deteriorated his perception. He knew her too well. He saw through the veil of you're-going-to-be-okay-and-I-will-take-care-of-it.

Hariot had made a sedative with some of his plants. Maud had little choice when he was rendered unconscious. "You sure about this?" asked Hariot.

"Yes." Jathmoora got ready, placing herself in position. "This is the way; the Choc-ra will strengthen me. He can't die—not on my watch. Hariot, you go to the bridge and make sure that Selene is honing her target practice. We diminished most of the enemy forces; she can pick off the rest."

Hariot didn't want to leave but Jathmoora was insistent. He blinked sideways, the membrane moving across his retina.

Entering a deep meditative state, Jathmoora placed two hands on Maud. She closed her eyes and began to drift away. She networked the pathways in Maud's mind and began to fix the damage. All the while she was assisted by the Choc-ra like an ebbing wave that kept her buoyant.

Before long there was gasp. Jathmoora opened her eyes. Maud was awake and he was, to her assessment, one hundred percent well. "You didn't…" he began.

Jathmoora just smiled before collapsing to the ground, dead.

The Old Timer sat in view. Sean watched and watched and watched, almost developing a shadow of stubble on his face. He wasn't sure what it was. A glint? An instinctual nudge? Fate? But he got up and told Thorn as clearly and directly as he had ever commanded. "Thorn, go around the Old Timer. Now." There was no arguing. There was no debating. Sean looked on, not once blinking, his eyes on the verge of watering.

Maverick locked himself in the ship's docking bay. He had taken them to the Old Timer as a gift to Celeste, but he would not dare go out there, nursing his broken arm in a sling. He had shamed his crew and he could not look them in the eye nor look himself in the mirror.

And at last, at the very end, we realize we have come this far only to realize again that we have much left to conquer—Unknown Archives

The Wave Of Redemption was well known but what of its makers? The Librarians were notorious for being secretive. Most never knew their existence and others just warned to stay clear of them. They had a great array of technologies. The Light Conductors were able to generate a massive amount of energy resonating in a large cumulative wave.

The Wave of Redemption was the most renowned event to happen in the Kale Galaxy. The most recent Wave seemed similar but it did not do what it was supposed to do. In fact, no one was affected by it, yet there was cause for concern. Who was initiating these random bursts? And what was the purpose of them?

The Librarians were solely responsible for their technology but when they faced the Sprites aeons ago, they lost their artefacts to humans.

Du'du could not understand the slackness of St'du. Did he think that the universe would mend itself? Did he think that they were safe from the impending doom? St'du would not seek out other races solely out of fear. He did not want to think about explaining the fact that they were time keepers. But merging was inevitable. The universe's future lay in their hands while others squabbled about trying to make sense of everything.

Sean lay in the pool of his own blood and Cardvia's when he heard a voice. He thought he was hallucinating. "Celeste?"

Sean could feel his head splitting in two. He remembered the minutes before he succumbed to unconsciousness. Thorn was surrounded. The other Altran ships were fighting their own battle and the Sprites were ruthless. One swipe after another, and not just ship but mind, body and flesh.

Sean was sure he was sharing two consciousnesses at one time before being ripped from his body and yet the Sprites had not killed him. Sean, panting, grasped for the edge of the console. The ship was dark and Cardvia was alive. He tried to talk but his mouth was full of blood. He spat it out to the side. "Cardvia, what happened?"

"We were attacked by all sides. The Altrans have taken great causalities. They had decided that they must retreat. We are not an army, Sean. The Sprites are increasing numbers every single day. We are merely holding on to a single thread."

Sean eased himself up with the aid of Cardvia. "So, what about the Old Timer? Are we on the other side? Is there…"

"Sean?" But he had seen. He knew. His insides erupted in fire and he felt like he was walking on air.

"Thorn, open communications."

"Celeste?" It was one word resonating through space.

Nothing. Then…

"Sean?"

Sean's eyes sprung with water. She was alive. That was her voice! He couldn't believe it. "Thorn, dock with that ship immediately."

The ship locked into place and the shushing of steam erupted. Sean stood at one end, Celeste on the other. And like pulling magnets, they ran to each other and clashed in an array of arms and kisses and tight embraces. "Thank the Old Timer," was all Sean could say.

The Siren Moons loomed overhead, a ring of destroyed ships a halo around its bust. The magnetic ethereal wisps languished in space like tendrils wanting to wrap around something. A convoy of ships passed the Moons and the Sprites did not see their demise coming. It was somewhat of an unknown factor. To them they were invincible, but it looked like they were mortal just like everything else in the universe. The ships fell into a chaotic descent. The Sprites tried to leave but the magnetic pull sucked them down and dissipated their disembodied bodies on the ragged edges of the sharply toothed mountains.

Du'du managed to catch up to St'du, who was avoiding him like the plague. "St'du, the wave you coalesced...it worked." There was a fraction of doubt in his voice. He only realized cause of the face m a failure."

She shook her head. "No, Sean. You kept me afloat. I gave up the moment those things possessed me. I thought there was no hope. I didn't want to die but it was the only way."

Sean hugged her, stifling her sobs. "It must have been unbearable. The pain you went through. Celeste, I am in awe of you. Your strength, your mentality, you have fallen but soar now high in the clouds. You are my angel."

The membranous sac tumbled through space, an unborn child visible through the viscous fluid it contained. It was a far outcry against the harshness of cold space. The unnamed station was waning in the distance.

"What have you done, Charlie?" shouted Eric. He was becoming hysterical, waving his hands about.

"You did away with the law. I have watched you many years now, splicing, integrating. But this—this cannot be. Your wife is gone. I am your only family now. So, I jettisoned your project out into space. Whether she lives is now in the laws of the universe."

Crazed with unquenchable rage, Eric tore the vital organs that functioned to keep Charlie alive. Now he truly was alone without his one and only companion.

The end looms ever nearer like an ensnaring net no one could hope to evade
– Unknown Archives

All the Raiders had disappeared. They entered deeply frozen sleep in cryotubes. They waited in a dark corner of the universe, precisely the Unknowns until they were reawakened once again. When and if the universe survived, they would be that thing to be feared. For what was natural? These things were hardly that. But neither were beings intent on wiping the board clean.

After travelling so far, Robert never thought to regain consciousness in this universe. He knew what he did was reckless but every day without Cheyenne was a day he wished not to have anyway.

Robert breathed in much-needed air. Eric handed him a cup of something. Robert looked at him with a scathing stare. The last thing he remembered was his head meeting with a large spanner of some kind. Eric produced the glass of Haldo Gin. Robert took it rashly and downed the lot. Unaccustomed to its potency, he gagged before the heat soothed his insides. "Why did you attack me?"

"I had to have it. My dear wife. Her genetics, her immaculate detail might be lost, but when you brought that specimen I had to try. I had to get her back."

"Specimen." Robert looked at his hand where the specimen had fused to his skin. "You took it! Where is she? Where?"

Robert could feel insane rage creep up. And the man responsible was an old man he couldn't lay a finger on. But in his rage, he saw the incubator tubes full of Eric's mad creations. He swung a chair at them and destroyed them all.

"No, not my creations! Please!"

But Robert was inconsolable. He continued as half- formed Raider bodies collapsed onto the glass strewn floor dead and a grotesque sight.

The membranous sac tumbled through space. It was like it could foresee the threats around it and ahead of it and somehow avert them. Who knew what DNA cocktail Eric had mustered before the sac's untimely jettison? Was it half Cheyenne and his wife? What was she? And more to the point, where was she headed?

The oblong shaped sac tumbled through space, passing suns and moons and avoiding even asteroids. It seemed to be honed into something not even Eric would have conceived. What had he created? Was it good? Was it bad? Was in containable?

There was an honourable funeral. Mayes's ashes were jettisoned and strewn across space. Now she was a lost voice. Who knew where her particles would take her. There was rumours and heresy that when the passing happened the ashes were free to roam the galaxies. Could perhaps her remains be found by an advanced alien race and reintegrated into a new body?

Celeste and Sean were bunked in his room for days. Cardvia was a little peeved but overall esteemed that Sean was once again happy. Actually, this was an emotion she had never seen him wear and he looked good in it.

Celeste was in the crook of his arm. "I thought I would never see you again."

He took her face in his. "I gave up, Celeste. So many times, I just surrendered myself to the dark. I -"

Celeste shushed him with a quickly placed finger.

Both smiled into each others eyes completely and utterly alone in this vast universe.

Space was screeching for survival. Space was a void and the stars its children. Who knew the future ahead, who knew what darkness lay in wait, who knew if tomorrow would ever come? But this much was known: the universe was in the grips of an eternal Dusk...

THE END

Printed in the United States
By Bookmasters